# LA CONFRONTATION

# LA CONFRONTATION


A SPENCER MARLOWE ADVENTURE
ONE MAN, TWO CENTURIES


Kelvin White

This book is dedicated to my wife Jenny. Her advice and
suggestions were, as always invaluable.

# CONTENTS

# THE JOURNEY

Spencer,
Travel-weary,
Caught in darkest crime world.
Trepidation; must survive this,
Stay strong.

~Jennifer White

# CHAPTER ONE

# THE LADY FROM TEXAS

The heat of the sun scorched the man's body, penetrating, it seemed, to his very soul. Sweat bathed his brow, trickling down his parched cheeks then mixing with the arid dust that coated his face before evaporating.

This wasn't where he was supposed to be. How had he gotten here?

*Oh my God, this has to be just about as hot as it could get without the world going up in flames. So, is this how I'm going to die?* He leant against a wooden pole supporting a sign, emblazoned with the words "Pione…oon Good Springs Nevada thirty miles." Riddled with bullet holes, the sign left its complete message up to weary traveller's imagination.

The man removed his Stetson, wiping his brow with a bandana that'd been wrapped around his neck.

*I reckon that sign is meant to say 'Pioneer Saloon'* he found himself trying to laugh as he deciphered the wording, but his throat was dry, nothing but a hoarse wheezing sound sputtered from his chapped lips.

*I could sure use a drink of water, and…Something to eat, when did I last eat?* He glanced at his wrist. My watch, what on earth happened to my watch?

Grappling with his memory, unease bubbled up inside him. *Nevada? And the watch?*

Momentarily forgetting his hunger and thirst, he tried to remember. *The watch damnit, it was valuable, it was a gift, who from? Can't quite…think…think.*

A faint sliver of memory flashed in an out of his mind. Elusive. When he tried to focus the memory would run and hide like a child, yelling 'you can't see me, you can't see me.' A moment of triumph. He could see the watch. He could remember the man. The old man saying, 'Happy birthday, son.'

He could see it now, gold and steel, the words on the bezel 'Rolex'.

Rubbing sweaty hands against grimy jeans, then rummaging through a pocket, he discovered a ten dollar note. *That should buy me a cold drink, something to eat surely.* Delving further into the pocket he grasped a small metallic object. He pulled it out, examining it, silver, embossed, what is it? *Well, it's old.* He held it up. It glinted in the morning sun. *I remember this. I've seen it before. I think it may be important.* The man tried to remember. *What is it? I just know it's significant, but why?*

In the distance a cloud of dust sprang up from the road, the only sign of life or movement in the forbidding desert.

As the swirling dust drew nearer, he could begin to make out an automobile wavering through the liquid heat mirage. *Thank God.*

The candy red Chevrolet Impala convertible jerked to a stop beside him, throwing up a splash of dust like water from a roadside puddle. He observed an attractive lady, her titian hair largely hidden by a black and silver scarf, her face partially concealed by the biggest pair of sunglasses the man had ever seen.

In a slow drawl, the lady spoke in that soft Southern accent that sounded like an invitation even when it wasn't.

'I'll just bet y'all are fixen to head to the Pioneer?'

The man beamed. 'You're a lifesaver.'

'Priscilla. My friends call me Prissy.' The lady held out a hand.

The man smiled, shaking the proffered hand. 'Hi my name's…'

'Yeah honey, your name is?'

*Oh my God* 'I don't know.'

## CHAPTER TWO
# REALISATION

He momentarily forgot the heat, the sweat, the desert his throat was turning into. Instead, he stared inward and tried to remember who he was. Tumbleweeds and dust devils, scattering as if they possessed a demonic life force making them run as the Chevrolet passed by. Cactus and impressive granite formations loomed in the distance. 'What do you mean, you don't know? I figured your automobile must have broken down. I mean, you're miles from anywhere? You don't have any luggage? You sure as hell don't sound American? Are you English or what?' she said sharply.

He continued to gaze around at the desert surroundings. An unending vista of cracked land and crumbling rock.

Snatches of images were beginning to swim up out of the heat haze. The Qantas A380 aircraft, the smiling hostess handing him a menu. An airport, with a multitude of signs, and the relentless hustle and bustle of people on the move. What did the signs say? "LA International Airport." *Customs, going through customs, a mild argument with an official. Resolved…all resolved…welcome to the USA. Michiyo, oh no…where's Michiyo? A moment of panic. Where's Michiyo?*

'I'm from Australia. Perth. Western Australia.'

'Waal, welcome tall handsome Australian from, where did you say?' Again, the broad Texan drawl snapped him to the present.

'Perth. Western Australia.'

'Uh ha, now…all we need is a name.'

The man felt the outline of a hard metal object sticking into his leg. Thrusting his hand into his pocket he pushed the trinket into a more comfortable position. Touching the metal this time felt like a shock, a live current coursing through his body, a current, switching on the previously darkened recesses of his mind.

*Oh. Thank God, the cornicello.* The silver talisman given to Spencer by Bert Weadley now sat reassuringly in his hand. Spencer breathed a sigh of relief. Recall was now complete. Frightening but complete. The cornicello given to Spencer by a grateful Bert when Spencer had been cast back in time to wartime Australia 1942.

'My name's Spencer Marlowe. I think I must have had some type of amnesia. I'm from Australia and I know I've recently flown into LAX.'

'What's an LAX?'

'You know, LA international airport. Just about the biggest airport in the US.'

Priscilla looked at him curiously. 'Ok…if you say so. Sorry if I seem a little suspicious. But you know with all this stuff going on in Cuba, we've all been warned about commie spies. And you must admit your circumstances are a little odd.'

'Cuba, what's up with Cuba? I haven't heard.'

'You gotta be kidding me. Bay of Pigs. Kennedy. Castro. C'mon, even in outback Australia you must've heard about this stuff?'

Spencer gazed at the young lady as the full horror of the situation hit him like a thousand-pound weight. He'd been there before. He knew what was happening. 'What year's this?'

'Pal you're starting to scare me. It's June 1961.'

The colour drained from Spencer's face. He knew exactly what had happened. He shook his head, gazing around. The Chevrolet was clearly near new, big and bold with its pedestrian slicer fins. The lady looked like an extra in an Annette Funicello and Frankie Avalon beach party movie…from the sixties.

Memories flooded back, cascading through his mind, jostling to find a place as image upon image thrust themselves forward.

Spencer, Michiyo and their beautiful five-year-old daughter Trilby had flown into LAX on holiday.

It had been over five years since Spencer had found himself cast back in time. Long enough that he was beginning to think it might not happen again.

The last time, he and FBI agent Savannah Steele had been instrumental in dealing a mortal blow to the Romano crime family in New York. Dale Fletcher the boyishly enthusiastic FBI chief had labelled the operation the 'Manhattan Sting.'

As the years passed and Spencer's vivid and disturbing dreams vanished, both he and his wife Michiyo hadn't spoken of his time travel episodes. Try as she might Michiyo had never been able to completely grasp the enormity of Spencer's journeys into the past.

Spencer would go to bed as usual, be transported to another time and be involved in life threatening situations, then when least expected he would wake up next to Michiyo, having been gone sometimes for years. But in real time he'd never been away. He would awake and pour out his hair-raising tale to a confused and scared Michiyo, who tried to believe and accept what Spencer had to say. But in the end, she could only compartmentalise it, effectively put it into the too hard basket.

Spencer had some business in LA. He was now a senior partner in the Perth firm Dynamic Marketing. When the business was complete Spencer Michiyo and Trilby were going to do LA. Disneyland, Universal Studios, the Farmers Market and Hollywood Boulevard, they were going to do it all.

CHAPTER THREE

# THE HAPPY HOOKER

*You can only play the cards you've been dealt.*

'So, Priscilla, thanks again for picking me up. What do you do for a tortilla'?

Priscilla blushed…hesitating. 'I work at the Big Four Ranch.'

'Really…what would that be…cows?'

'Well, I know Dolores has put on a few pounds. But calling her a cow is a little unkind.' Priscilla emitted a rather unladylike guffaw.

*What on earth's so funny. If not cows then what? And who the hell is Dolores?* Spencer was completely mystified.

'Look I'm sorry, but I don't have a clue. What are you talking about?'

Priscilla giggled this time, a little more refined and ladylike. 'Spencer, 'The Big Four' is a cat house. A brothel.'

'Oh…really…ok.' Now Spencer was a little embarrassed. What to say? Do you enjoy your job? What exactly does it entail? Hang on…I guess we know what the answer is. 'Well, I guess it pays well.' *My God what a lame response.*

'Don't be embarrassed. I'm not. Yeah, honey it pays well. Tell you the truth, I quite enjoy it.' Priscilla chuckled.

Spencer sat morosely in the Chevrolet. *What now? I know no one. I appear to have the princely sum of ten dollars.*

'Do you have any cash, honey?'

'Well, I seem to have ten dollars. I'm more than happy to buy you a beer and lunch, if a ten will do it. I can't tell you how grateful I am you picked me up.'

'I guess the hooker with a heart of gold is a bit of a cliché, but shucks honey, call me a fool, but I believe your story. Lunch and a beer are on me, ok?'

Spencer and Prissy spent the time discussing the current Cuban crisis with the world seemingly lurching towards Armageddon.

Spencer was supremely grateful he'd been rescued by this amiable lady; at the same time, he was trying to quell a feeling of dread. He'd convinced himself these unexpected journeys to the past had finished. He thought as he had before: *Why me? What have I done to deserve this?* He felt himself being sucked into a morass of self-pity. Just as before, the overwhelming emotion was loneliness. Knowing he was on his own. There was no one to help. No one to confide in.

He feared that he might be here forever. He might never see his wife again, his beautiful baby daughter. What if he didn't survive? What if it was all a giant cosmic joke and the pranksters decided to finish him off when the gag failed to amuse the puppeteer pulling the strings. He closed his eyes and took a deep breath and repeated his mantra *You can only play with the cards you've been dealt.*

Prissy grinned. 'And look, there's the Pioneer. I can taste that cold Bud already.'

The Chevy sighed up to the front doors of the saloon. Two solid wooden portals battered and scarred, supported an oaken beam with the words, "Pioneer Saloon Good Springs

Nevada." The two hefty chunks of tree had surely been hewn out of the oak by hand, with a chisel, Spencer guessed.

Spencer stared, agog at the Pioneer Saloon. *Oh, wow this looks like the Wild West.*

A horse tied to a hitching rail, his snout buried in a concrete water trough, raised his head briefly to examine the new arrivals. Two Harley Davidson motorcycles, one a chopper with extended raked forks and a Confederate Flag design on its petrol tank, the other a pan head with the Hells Angels insignia on its rear guard. The motor bikes owners were unlikely to be pillars of society. *Be prepared, they could be trouble.*

'Is this place safe, Priss? I mean Hells Angels and all that?' Spencer pointed at the Harley's.

Priscilla laughed. 'Good lordy no. Nothing to worry about, sweet pea. Those two are pussycats. Customers, actually.' She gave him a wink.

Spencer half expected to see Peter Fonda and Dennis Hopper appear, dressed in their hippy bikie gear.

A collection of dusty pickup trucks, working men's vehicles, battered and baking in the heat, made the parking lot look like a junkyard. Dusty, weather-beaten, and worked hard like the men who drove them.

This looks as rough and ready as a Wild West saloon that Doc Holliday or Wyatt Earp frequented.

Spencer quickly decided the Pioneer Saloon was Western character at its best. Rough? Certainly. But with lashings of raucous charm.

Inside, a group of rowdy oil field roughnecks were talking shop. A couple of cowboys wearing leather chaps and chunky boots with silver spurs, were engaged in a lively debate about football. The two Hells Angels sat quietly in a booth, each nursing a beer. Big solid tattooed men, big arms, big legs, big chests. They smiled and waved at Priscilla.

*Looks are deceiving. Not a problem here.*

Spencer and Priscilla moseyed up to the bar. *I'm sure mosey is the appropriate description,* Spencer thought.

The full-length mirror behind the bar was framed in burnished walnut. On the shelf in front of it, every possible brand of Kentucky Bourbon. A Confederate flag with a host of signatures on it occupied pride of place on one wall. A black and white photo of the Reno Silver Sox baseball team sat amidst the clutter.

*I guess a glass of Margaret River Chardonnay and some fresh Barramundi would be out of the question.*

Orders were being yelled to the short order cook in the kitchen behind. The tantalising smells of meat and fries washed across the room in waves. Big chunks of Texas Cows were being broiled on cast iron skillets, then thrown unceremoniously onto chipped enamel plates. A mountain of French Fries accompanied the beef. Spencer's mouth was watering at the sight and the enticing fragrance. *My God how long is it since I've eaten?*

'What'll you have sweet pea?'

'Silly question I guess, but what are the choices?' Spencer was ravenous. He had no idea when he'd last eaten.

'Well, pardner…you got steak…or let me see know…or…ah yes…steak.' Priscilla laughed.

'My guess is they don't cater for vegans?' Spencer nudged her in the ribs.

'What's a vegan? Is that an Australian thing?'

Spencer didn't bother explaining or inventing a lie. Priss seemed happy to mosey right past it, like the mention of LAX. He'd nearly gotten into trouble over the internet and email addresses in New York City, five years ago. He'd have to watch what he said.

They squeezed into a booth nursing their Budweiser's as they waited for the steaks. Spencer scanned the room gazing at the memorabilia, there seemed to be a lot of photos of the late movie star, Clark Gable.

'A popular boy around here?' Spencer pointed to one of the big glossy black and white prints.

'This is where the king of Hollywood was when he was waiting for news about his wife Carole Lombard.'

'What happened to her?' Spencer had heard of Gable, but not his wife.

'She was killed in a plane crash on Potosi Mountain, not far from here, in 42. She was only thirty-three. They say Gable never got over it'. Priscilla took a long pull on her beer.

Spencer gazed at the photos of the late King of Hollywood and his ill-fated wife; at the same time, he reappraised his opinion of the Pioneer Saloon. *I don't know what I was worried about, this place is ok…sure it looks a bit primitive but these are just honest working folk, a little rough around the edges but…yeah. nothing to worry about here.*

The front doors crashed open. Three more grease spattered roughnecks burst in. Big loud, dirty and thirsty.

The biggest and dirtiest, a man who appeared to be hewn out of granite, doused in oil, yelled. 'Hey there bar keep, three beers, three steaks and a bottle of Bourbon…we're hungry and thirsty, so move it, ok?'

The barman folded his broad arms over his equally broad chest. 'Skunk, you just behave yourself now. You'll get served just like everybody else. Act up and I'll throw you out.'

'Sure, Sam, sure. We're not here for trouble, are we boys?' Skunk turned and winked at his buddies.

Priscilla leaned forward. 'I hope that jerk doesn't see me. He comes to the Big Four and I've always refused to ah…'and she rolled her eyes. 'If you get what I mean.'

'Gotcha.'

# CHAPTER FOUR

# THE SKUNK LEARNS HOW TO TREAT A LADY

'Hey Skunk, tell us about the time you parked your Chevy in a tree.'

'You just hush up now, Charley Ray, or I'll tell the boys about you and that nigger lady.'

The three roughnecks were noisily drinking their bourbon with beer chasers, telling bawdy jokes. This wasn't a gentlemen's club.

Skunk turned his gaze around the room. He wiped a hand across his stubbled face. 'Well, looky here boys.' He pointed one dirty finger in Priscilla's direction.

Priscilla blanched. 'Listen, big boy,' she leaned forward, addressing Spencer in a low voice, 'whatever happens, don't get involved. This creep could eat you for breakfast. He'd steal a fly from a blind spider.'

Skunk lumbered over to their booth. Spencer cast a jaundiced eye over the apparition before him. A stained denim shirt, with the sleeves ripped off exposed massive tattooed arms burnished by the harsh Nevada sun. He had piercing coal black eyes, a long jaw and a barrel chest. He seemed built to hurt people. His feet encased in solid chunky oil-stained work boots. Spencer's eyes momentarily focussed on the boots. *What's the bet, steel tipped? And the tattoos…really?*

One tattoo was a picture of three hooded men holding a noose. *Well, well, well. A Klansmen no less…nice.*

'This is ya lucky day, honey. I got a fifty-dollar bill, that's burning a hole in my pocket. I got my truck outside, hows about you and me go and have a little fun?'

Spencer couldn't help himself; he felt the laughter about to explode. *Is this guy for real?*

Skunk leant, both hands on the table, his big toothy grin turned to Priscilla. Spencer gazed at his unattractive visage, a red sweaty face, his hair shaved to a fine stubble and just about the biggest reddest blue veined nose Spencer had ever seen.

'Go away Skunk, you're revolting.'

'I remember you once called me a vulture, you two-dollar hooker.' Skunk snarled.

'Actually, Skunk, I never called you a vulture. I said you're something a vulture would eat.' Priscilla took off her sunglasses, winking at Spencer.

'Time to go I think, Skunk. I don't think the lady wants to talk to you.' Spencer tapped Skunk on his weathered shoulder.

'I'm talkin to the whore. Fuck off, pretty boy.' Skunk glanced briefly at Spencer.

*Oh dear,* thought Spencer.

Spencer leaned forward, grabbing Skunk's impressive proboscis between his thumb and forefinger. He squeezed very hard. At the same time, he sprung to his feet, leading Skunk away from the table. Skunk resembled a Brahmin Bull being led by a nose ring.

Very predictably, Skunk howled. 'Led go by dose!'

'Now Skunk, oh yes…I think I understand how you got that name…Phew. As I was saying, I'm going to let you go, but behave, ok?'

Spencer released the nose, now even bigger and redder than before. Skunk bent down, hands on his knees. He shook his head. He sprung up. Screaming. His eyes still watering from Spencer's vice like grip. He threw a ham sized fist at Spencer's jaw. Spencer had been anticipating such a move, he turned avoiding the punch, then grabbing Skunk's fist he squeezed. Using his Kokoro training he effectively transformed his grip into something akin to a hydraulic press.

Skunk howled. Bellowing, his face contorted in pain. His words spilled out of his mouth, a jagged rasping sound. 'Lemme go, you sonofabitch. I'm gonna kill you.'

'Dear me Skunk. Wrong words…Now if you want the pain to stop, it really couldn't be simpler. Skunk dear, repeat after me, 'I'm sorry Miss, that I've acted inappropriately'…hang on a minute, that's a big word, isn't it?' 'That I've acted badly and I'll leave immediately. Now, say ten Hail Mary's and go home.'

'You, sonofabitch.'

'Your vocabulary is a little limited, Skunk. Try and remember you have an audience, and improve the dialogue.'

Spencer went on squeezing. Skunk was roaring with pain and indignation.

The bar fell silent, watching as Skunk yelled obscenities. His face red, sweat pouring off him. Skunk screamed to his comrades. 'C'mon guys, get him off me.' It seemed his buddies weren't keen on entering into the discussion.

Skunk's companions were weighing up the options when Sam the bartender leaned forward. 'Boys, I really wouldn't recommend you escalating things.'

Sam was a big man renowned throughout Nevada for running his bar with no tolerance for violence.

The two oilmen turned to see Sam with his baseball bat. The word "Pacifier" was carved into the time worn hickory. It's unlikely the pacifier had ever hit any home runs or a ball into the bleachers, but it certainly had knocked rambunctious patrons into the land of nod. Sam had both meaty hands on the bat, gently swinging it from side to side. He reiterated.

'Now boys, I don't think you really need to get involved, do you?'

'Hell no, Sam. Skunk got his self into it. And he damn well can get his self out of it.'

Without another word Sam strode purposefully to where Skunk and Spencer stood motionless. Everyone was watching the drama as the sound of Skunks carpal bones breaking could be heard above the chatter. The crunching sound was like the snapping of a chicken leg.

Sam strode towards the two men, his bat held in two hands.

'I did warn you Skunk.'

Sam's pacifier swatted across the back of Skunk's stubbled skull, at which point Skunk appeared to lose all interest in the proceedings.

Sam pointed the bat at Skunks two comrades. 'Ok boys, time to go. Pick him up. Throw him into the back of your truck. Do it now!'

Skunk's comrades drained their beers, chuckling amongst themselves as they unceremoniously grabbed their unconscious comrade and dragged him out.

'See you next week, Sam,' one of the men yelled as they disappeared out the door, still chuckling.

'Sure, thing boys,' was Sam's cheerful response.

'Sam doesn't mess around, does he?' Spencer grinned at Priscilla.

# CHAPTER FIVE

# SPENCER HAS A ROOF OVER HIS HEAD

'Tell me Tarzan,' Priscilla said with a lop-sided smile 'are there any more like you where you come from? You sure are one corn fed country boy. We got our share of tough good ole boys. But you're something else. A girl sure feels safe with you ridin shotgun.'

Spencer shrugged as he drained the last of his Budweiser.

Priscilla waved to Sam as they headed for the door.

'Good to see you again, Priss.' Sam grinned.

Two giant T-bones and mounds of French fries along with two more Budweisers had left them satisfied. Spencer was impressed with Priscilla's appetite.

'Where abouts exactly are you headed sweet pea?'

Good question, where am I headed?

'Really I've got no idea. LA I guess.'

Spencer figured that was where he Michiyo and baby Trilby had last been together, albeit almost sixty years in the future.

'Waal,' Priscilla drawled 'I've got a small two-bedroom apartment in Santa Monica, right near the pier. I'm headed there for a bit of rest and recreation. You're more than welcome to stay with me, you're gonna be a house guest, not a lover boy.'

'Priss that suits me just fine. I'm well and truly spoken for, I can assure you. I'm grateful beyond belief and I accept your kind offer. I'm not sure at this moment how I can repay you but I'm sure something will turn up.'

Priscilla pushed the big Chevrolet mercilessly through the harsh desert landscape, a whole lot of nothingness. The press button FM radio blared with songs about a lovelorn native American couple drowning in a raging river and a girl named Cathy who was making a fool of her boyfriend. Spencer enjoyed the corny lyrics of the top forty numbers.

Sacramento and San Jose passed in a blur. Priscilla pointed out the old Hearst Mansion San Simeon, on the Pacific coast of San Luis Obispo County.

Spencer admired the Spanish architecture of Santa Barbara when they made a quick fuel stop at a Texaco Gas station. He gawped in disbelief when the smiling attendant in a crisp grey uniform, peaked cap and red bow tie ran out of the office, pumped the gas and checked the oil and water. *Wow, that's service.*

Beaches with vast expanses of golden sand, kissed by the warm Californian sun reminded Spencer of Australia. He remembered when Special Agent Savannah Steele quizzed him about his future as they were returning from Japan, she asked Spencer what his plans were. 'I can just see you now. Santa Monica, Carmel, Santa Barbara. The beach, the surf. That's you to a T.' *My God. And here I am. I wonder what ever happened to that lady?*

The Chevrolet swung into Santa Monica Boulevarde, and then, Ocean Avenue. This was swinging 60's California: beach babes, T birds and hot rod coupes.

'Waal big boy, this's home.'

The Chevrolet glided into the condo car park. Spencer grabbed her bags, marvelling at the size of the Chev's trunk.

Spencer carried Prissy's luggage into the single level condominium, from the living room glimpses of the ocean and the Santa Monica pier beckoned.

*The epitome of 60's chic*, thought Spencer. He admired the beamed wooden ceiling and open fire place. The polished boards embraced the room with soft warm colours. Throw down rugs in bold Aztec designs added character. One rug had been a Kodiak Grizzly Bear, a perpetual snarl on its face, exposed fearsome looking teeth. Pride of place on one wall was a Frederic Remington painting "A dash for the timber". Spencer didn't know a lot about art but he knew in his century Remington's Art was worth serious money.

'Wow,' he gasped. 'A Remington. Is it genuine?'

'Guess so, bought it in El Paso a couple of years ago…paid…I dunno, I think quite a bit…for it…fifty bucks maybe.' Prissy shrugged.

'Let me tell you Prissy that could be your retirement fund.' Spencer gazed intently at the oil on canvas work of art.

'Hell no, it's just a little ole painting.'

## CHAPTER SIX
# COFFEE TIME

'It's just about now when I'm having a coffee at the Galley, that I feel like I'm on holiday. I tell you; I'm beat.' Priscilla smiled, taking another sip of her coffee. 'Well, Sugar, any plans?'

Priscilla and Spencer were in the 'Galley' restaurant in Main Street. This nautical themed restaurant with its model of a dinghy on the wall and porthole windows created the illusion of being on a boat. It boasted a riot of Christmas type lights suggesting the owner strung them up many Yuletides ago, deciding "Hey that looks good; I think I'll leave them there."

Spencer cast an approving glance over Priscilla, wearing fashionable 60's Bermuda pants in a vibrant sunflower yellow with an embossed rose design down one leg, an equally colourful electric blue shirt, this with her beehive hairstyle made Spencer wonder if Sandra Dee and Bobby Darin would suddenly walk on to the set.

*This girl is as uplifting as a Texan summer breeze.* Spencer couldn't help smiling at this irrepressible lady who just radiated…what exactly…well, thought Spencer, he hated the word "nice" but it was in fact appropriate. *She simply radiates niceness.*

The only downside, Spencer thought apart from being locked into another century and missing his wife and daughter, was…*the coffee is bloody awful.*

Spencer sat nursing his appalling, typically American brewed coffee. I don't think an espresso machine has found its way to 1960's California.

'Hey Dennis,' Priscilla called out to a man, who'd wandered into the Galley.

'Hi there Priss, having a break from your realtor business in Reno?' Dennis sauntered over to the table.

Priscilla turned to Spencer and winked.

*I guess maybe she keeps her profession a secret.*

'Sure am. Dennis, meet my Australian friend, Spencer. Dennis plays drums in one of our struggling local bands.'

'Drummer by night, surfer by day.' Dennis laughed.

He was average height with the taut six pack body of the devoted surfer. Paddling the long boards beyond the breakers guaranteed a physique devoid of any flab. Turned out in faded denim jeans, canvas deck shoes and a T-shirt advertising Ludwig Drums he looked as cool as a bucket of penguin shit, Spencer thought.

'Well, an Aussie.' Without waiting for further comment, Dennis went on, 'Man I really gotta go there. I believe they got some great breaks. I've heard about Bondi, Maroubra and Avalon.'

Spencer was immediately buoyed by Dennis's *joie de vivre* and bubbling enthusiasm.

Spencer shook Dennis's hand. 'I live near the beach, the surf 's great. In fact, it's just like California only we drive on the opposite side of the road.'

'Oh yeah man, I tell you, it's on the list.'

They spent a lazy hour discussing surfing and music, with Dennis trying to edge hot-rods into the conversation talking about twin carbs, extractors and other go-fast equipment. Spencer was totally out of his depth. To him a car was something you jumped into, turned the AC on and pointed it in the direction you wanted to go.

'Ok guys, I gotta go. Why don't you come down to the pier at seven we've gotta gig happening? It should be groovy. A gasser.'

Spencer and Priscilla glanced out of the porthole to see Dennis leap into his T- bucket hot-rod, flamboyantly painted in gleaming black with orange flames ducoed on the side. Its exposed V8 motor exploded with a roar. The coupe tore up the bitumen leaving a stench of molten rubber.

'That's Dennis,' Priscilla said unnecessarily.

'Nice guy…and realtor, huh?' Spencer laughed.

Priscilla screwed up her nose. 'Waal, not everybody is real comfortable with the job description so…I don't imagine you have a lot on. Do you wanna check out his band? Meanwhile let's explore Santa Monica.'

Strolling along the boulevards, they headed to the beachside boardwalk. Spencer started to lighten up. Here the pace of living was a relaxed steady rhythm, and he fell into the role of tourist, able to leave the terror of abandoning his wife and daughter behind for the moment. The spirit of California was on display with street art, murals and zany characters. A mixture of trends, bohemianism and a unique artistic climate created a scene Spencer realised was uniquely West coast.

Everything intrigued him; the painted facades of houses even the weird apparel of some of the buskers.

'Waal honey chile, I'm wore slap out. Over yonder's the pier, reckon it's time to catch Dennis and the boys.'

The atmosphere on the Santa Monica pier was happy, noisy and colourful with bikini-clad beach dolls, mums and dads, hustlers and wannabe Hollywood actors.

Against all the odds, Spencer felt relatively relaxed. He glanced sideways at the lady by his side, grateful beyond belief Priscilla had taken pity on him. Spencer had learned very quickly to be a good judge of character. His previous adventures had taught him just how important allies were in a strange world with danger never far away.

Priscilla scanned the approaching pier, hand held over eyes, the sun now sinking in the West.

'The pier's buzzing. I guess the Beach Buddies are the attraction. Don't you just love this Peach ice cream?' Priscilla laughed at the sight of a juggler with an eclectic array of objects all in the air at one time. His dexterity and humorous banter entertained his audience. An upturned top hat was half full with nickels, dimes and quarters.

Spencer and Priscilla had spent a leisurely hour strolling along the boardwalk all the way to Venice. Priscilla nudged Spencer as they paused at muscle beach where an assortment of very fit men pumped iron to the admiring glances of the assorted beach babes. 'Now that's what I call eye candy.' Priscilla giggled.

The band had just set up when Spencer and Priscilla sauntered along the Santa Monica Pier. They plonked themselves down on one of the wicker chairs, munching on their ice creams from the "Soda Jerks" ice cream shop.

Dennis gave them a wave from behind his drum kit emblazoned with an obviously hand written sign on his bass drum "Beach Buddies."

*Oh dear, I think I can see why they may be as Priss described "A struggling local band."*

The Beach Buddies sadly looked like amateurs. They stood like amateurs, when they started enthusiastically belting out Chuck Berry standards they sounded like amateurs. They did have a certain style. And some of their stuff wasn't bad. *Someone needs to sort these guys out.*

As one song finished, they would argue amongst themselves about what the next number would be. The audience wasn't a great help with an obstreperous drunk yelling, 'how about some Sinatra or Bing Crosby, c'mon guys play some proper music.' Then warming to the sound of his own voice, the heckler added, 'What about playing 'far far away,' which brought a round of laughter from the crowd.

The lead guitarist, with his sunburst Fender Stratocaster, tapped on his microphone. 'We'd like to play one of our own compositions, hope you like it, this's called' Travellin Round the USA', a nice easy ballad.'

'Everyone's gone travellin round the USA,' was the hook, also known as the chorus and then the melody mentioned various places around America.

Spencer paid close attention to the Beach Buddies. The lead guitar on his strat was capable of some blistering solos in the style of Chuck Berry and Bill Haley's Comets. The bass player with his Fender Precision Bass was playing his twelve-bar blues riffs competently, if a little unimaginatively. The keyboard player was a standout on his Vox continental organ. Dennis's drumming was solid and worked well with the bass player, but they were let down by a general lack of professionalism.

*Somebody needs to take these guys in hand. They just haven't quite got it together.*

Spencer glanced at Priscilla. 'I'm not sure their song writing is going to win any awards.'

The crowd that had already started to diminish were now leaving in droves.

After the set finished the band took a break, a disconsolate Dennis wandered over and sat down heavily on the wicker chair next to Spencer. 'We don't seem to be knocking em dead, do we?'

Dennis leaned forward his elbows on the table his head cupped in his hands. He looked a picture of misery.

'How would you feel about some input from an Aussie who knows little about the music business?'

'Sure thing, Spencer, go for it.'

'First of all, I think the band has great potential. You do some terrific Chuck Berry covers. That ballad, "Travellin Round the USA", nice ballad, but given that surfing is currently the biggest teen thing in the US, how about considering turning it into a rock and roll song along the lines of Mr Berry's "Johnny B Goode" and instead of travelling round the USA, how about "Surfin USA?"'

Dennis gazed at Spencer as if he had just had a vision of the messiah. 'Wow. Now there's an original idea.'

'And…and while we're at it, given that surfing is so big, why not see if you can simply create music directed specifically at surfers and perhaps if you could change the name of the band from the Beach Buddies which to me sounds…well I don't know, a little like a group of old guys, to maybe "The Beach Boys" and get some snappy hip, beach type clothes as a uniform. What do you reckon?'

# CHAPTER SEVEN

# FANCY MEETING YOU HERE

"Short order cook wanted, Apply Penguin Coffee Shop 1670 Lincoln Boulevard." Spencer pored over the wanted ads in the Los Angeles Express.

Morosely drinking his awful American coffee at the Galley, Spencer was down to his last five dollars. He'd found a twenty dollar note on the beach when out for an early run, but that'd dwindled. Priscilla headed back to Nevada for two weeks saying, 'Listen big boy y'all stay here while I'm gone. When I get back you can rustle up more of that Jap food. What'd you call it, booshi…dooshi?' Spencer laughed at her obvious flub.

'Thanks, Priss you're a lifesaver. And it's sushi. Seeing as you liked that, I'll knock up some other favourites when you get back.' June was nudging July and Spencer needed to find a source of income.

*This has to be a printing error. "A dollar an hour". You're kidding me.* Spencer studied the ad. Do people really work for a dollar? Spencer peered at the menu at the Galley. "Hamburger 15 cents".

*Well, I guess, if you work for an hour there's your food for a day paid for.*

Absorbed and preoccupied with the want ads and his immediate future, he'd developed a knack of pushing thoughts of his wife and child into the dark recesses of his mind. He'd noticed a conservatively clad woman staring fixedly at him, her coffee and doughnut untouched. *There's something high voltage about her. A fighter robbed of her little girl years, a long time ago.*

The lady was pleasantly if a little conservatively attired for the swinging sixties California was renowned for. The sensible dark blue suit and equally sensible court shoes suggested she may have been associated with a church group, or perhaps government. Her dress, a fraction longer than the current fashion. The dark blue leather bag, a little larger than fashion decreed. But then Spencer couldn't know what the lady carried inside was a substantial piece of metal. What you might call "a tool of trade."

Spencer, quickly glanced again. *She's watching me? Looks familiar. Hell, I don't know anyone? She's heading my way?*

Absentmindedly having a sip of the cold coffee and ignoring the doughnut, she stepped up to Spencer's table. Without asking, she noisily pulled out a chair. It made a rasping sound as it was scraped across the wooden floor. She plonked herself down, throwing her bag on the table. It landed with a resounding thump. 'Well, well well, Spencer Marlowe.'

Spencer dropped his paper in alarm and gazed at the lady again, momentarily stunned. This was the last person he expected to see. 'Savannah. My God. I don't believe it. Savannah, Savannah, I never imagined I'd ever see you again. How the hell are you?'

Spencer had found himself cast back to 1955 in Manhattan. Savannah was an FBI agent. Both Savannah and Spencer had gone to Tokyo on a mission that would result in taking down the New York mob headed by crime boss Tony Romano, with a sting involving mass importation of heroin. On their flight back to the USA from Japan, Spencer had agreed to tell Savannah, everything, all about his trips back into time.

On the flight Spencer had fallen asleep and had woken to find himself back with his wife Michiyo in Manhattan in his own century.

Savannah stared fixedly at Spencer. Her face giving nothing away. Eventually she spoke in quiet, measured tones, which to Spencer sounded like she was grilling a suspect, a wanted felon.

'Spencer Marlowe. Oh boy, I can't tell you just how much I'd hoped our paths would cross again. I can't believe it. How the hell you managed to disappear all those years ago had everybody baffled.'

She leaned back in her chair, arms folded. 'I always thought you'd turn up again like the proverbial bad penny. Well, I've damn well got you now. And let me tell you, there's no escape. You…are going to tell me everything. No 'It's a long story. No bullshit. I mean everything.' She flashed her FBI badge. 'And just to let you know. I'm now a Senior Special Agent. And as much as I only have good memories of you, unless I get answers, I swear I'll run you in. Let me assure you if I want, I can keep you in custody on charges regarding national security that I haven't even dreamed up yet. So…talk to me. Oh, and before you do. Just to let you know I…or we, that is Special Agent Fletcher and I, know rather more about you than you could possibly imagine.'

'Savannah, my life is an open book.' Spencer was worried, but he smiled disarmingly.

'Yeah, well as John Wayne said, "That'll be the day."'

Spencer hadn't questioned his disappearance from the flight back in '55, since he was just glad to be back in his own time, with his own wife, in his own life again. As far as his wife Michiyo was concerned he'd never been away, so it was easy to pretend nothing had happened. No deli in Manhattan, no mobsters trying to extort him and then trying to murder him, no yakuza operation to divert millions of dollars and illicit drugs out of the hands of organized crime. No, once he was back, he tried to put the past behind him.

Now though, he wondered what Savannah and Dale of the FBI had thought of his mysterious disappearance. Had they opened an investigation? Into little ole him? They couldn't possibly have found anything about him, so how long had they kept searching for him?

Savannah retrieved her doughnut and with her mouth full, spoke again, 'Spencer, I tell you this is serious. Now talk. Ok hang on…just so we 're talking about the same time and place. You fell into a coma on the flight from Tokyo…now, do you in fact remember that?'

Spencer shrugged; all he remembered was going to sleep and waking up sixty-five years in the future. He'd been happy to finally be home again.

'Ok let's start with the flight…you fell into a coma. We were offloaded at San Francisco you went to hospital. I went to a hotel to get some sleep. When I returned to the hospital four hours later, they said you'd simply disappeared. Disappeared, for Christ's sake. How did that work? Where the hell did you go? Luggage untouched. I mean seriously? Why? How? Now I run into you again…so…where have you been and exactly what's going on? I warn you; we know more than you think.' Savannah's face was a fierce scowl. Her jaw taut. Her fingers tapped relentlessly on the table.

Spencer felt trapped he could see no other way but to explain his time travel experiences. 'Well Savannah, what I have…'

'Before you start, just think long and hard about what you're going to say. Because it could mean the difference between freedom and being locked away for a long stretch in a federal pen.'

'Yes…sure…ok'

Savannah interrupted again. 'I have to tell you after what that scumbag Riko said before he decided to swallow cyanide, we have followed up on everything to do with Spencer Marlowe. We know you were in Hawaii in 1941 and you were involved in an important mission with a photographer…what was her name?'

'Roxanne.'

'Yeah, that's the one. Tell me was she in on all this?'

'On all of what?' Spencer enquired the picture of innocence.

By and large Spencer had done a good job of compartmentalising his experiences but at the mention of "the photographer" the memories of Roxanne flooded back. Waves of guilt combined with a gut wrenching feeling of loss threatened to overwhelm him. He remembered with frightening clarity the feelings he had for that remarkable woman, at the same time the feeling of guilt that he had somehow betrayed Michiyo. As always, he had to deal with the unfairness of never being able to unburden himself.

Roxanne, I wonder whatever became of you. What did you think when I disappeared out of your life? Move on, you can only deal with the cards you've been dealt.

'Alright let's move on. I told you we know a lot. We've spoken to the two operatives you were working with a…Matt…'

'That would be Matt Spinetti.'

'And,' Savannah consulted some notes. 'Walter Crabtree.'

'Wow, Walter and Matt, how are they?'

'Moving right along.' Savannah snarled. 'Spinetti and Crabtree who are now CIA. That stands for…'

'I know what that stands for.'

'Yeah, well they spoke very highly of you and the photographer lady and someone called…Horse?'

'My God. I wonder what happened to him?'

'Yeah yeah. Well, this isn't exactly reunion time. Spinetti and Crabtree say you simply disappeared at the time of the Japanese attack. They figured you had just been one of the many casualties. Obviously not. But regardless. You up and disappeared…again…bit of a habit wouldn't you say?

'Now do you remember when you were in the hospital in Manhattan after Romano's thugs had beaten you within an inch of your life?'

'Oh yeah, I remember, "Are my testicles black?"' Spencer guffawed.

'Yeah, I know…I was…a little embarrassed.' Savannah had the good manners to blush.

'A little.' Spencer chortled. 'You thought I asked you if my testicles were black, then you conducted an intimate examination. I took my mask off and asked "Are my test results back?"' Spencer couldn't help it as he collapsed into peals of mirth.

'OK ok, let's get on with it. While you were drugged up and babbling you had rambled on about internet, dot com, hot mail and someone called Google, remember that?'

'Well, no, not exactly,' Spencer said pedantically 'I actually don't remember anything I was drugged up, as you know.'

'Sure.' Savannah snapped testily. 'But you know what you said because I read it back to you.'

Spencer nodded.

'Anyhow' Savannah announced triumphantly 'We made inquiries with the Australian Government. There was no internet fishing company. There were no fish called gigs. So, there were no gigabytes…and guess what…there was no Dot Com. You said her name was short for Dorothy Comopolous…and there was no Mr Google. We figured that was some sort of code name. So, smarty-pants, we know a little more than you could have imagined. Am I right?'

Savannah had her arms folded, a look of triumph on her face, a lady in control. 'Now…at last…I'm going to know the full story. I warn you. We think we more or less have you figured out, so shoot.'

*I can't imagine what they've figured out, but?* Spencer didn't know whether to be alarmed or amused.

'Ok.' Spencer cleared his throat, just then the manager padded up to the table, a tall lumpy disagreeable specimen who'd been watching Spencer and Savannah talking and not ordering anything other than a coffee and doughnut.

He removed a toothpick from his mouth, pointing it at Spencer. 'This isn't a public park; the idea is if you're here, you order something, got it?'

Savannah glared at this untidy jerk, with his stained apron, white shirt resplendent with an artistic, Jackson Pollock array of food stains, a florid unattractive visage, a greasy comb over and what was worse, attitude.

Savannah turned to Spencer and smiled. A half-smile that took him back to their adventures in 1955.

*Oh, dear pal. You really shouldn't have.*

Grabbing her FBI badge, Savannah shoved it in the face of the unfortunate restaurateur. 'Beat it. Or I will find a way for you to be shut down for the next month while the health authorities, the IRS, and anybody else I can think of, makes your miserable life a living hell.'

The man gazed at the badge; his face paled. 'Sorry ma'am, sir, would you like a refill? On the house of course.'

Savannah dismissively waved him away.

Spencer had to smile as the man scurried off. 'I'm surprised you didn't just shoot him. I suppose you're still carrying that bazooka?'

Savannah opened her handbag.

'Yep. There it is. My God, if it was any bigger it'd need wheels.' Spencer immediately recognised the impressive Magnum with its walnut grip. 'Still using those hollow point rounds?'

There was a momentary flash of the old Savannah as a grin struggled to crack the fierce façade. 'Do you remember in Tokyo, when I shot that guy and you were coated in his blood and brains?'

'Ugh, do I remember? How about in Spencer's restaurant when you bloody well shot the hit man, Isaac the Jew at point blank range…in the head?'

The dam now broke and the laughter cascaded out of Savannah. She slapped a palm on her thigh. Tears were running down her face. 'I was sure you were going to throw up your breakfast.' Savannah chortled.

For a time, there was nothing but the raucous sound of laughter reforging the bonds that had been severed those years ago when he vanished. She hadn't changed a bit, and he was glad of it.

Spencer pointed a finger, his laughter almost preventing speech. 'Oh Savannah. It's great to see you, it really is.'

'Yeah,' she said softly, 'you too Spencer.'

CHAPTER EIGHT
# GET ON WITH IT

'Spencer, we still need to know.' Savannah gazed around the restaurant and again started drumming her fingers on the table. 'Both Dale and I have been completely baffled by you. But…we think we have pretty much figured things out.'

Savannah started nervously twisting a handkerchief. 'I guess what's important is neither Dale or I ever for one minute thought of you as potentially a criminal…someone who had changed his name to evade the law or anything like that.' Savannah paused to take a sip of her now refilled coffee. 'I guess really, we were both disappointed you had come up with what turned out to be a completely bullshit story, when whatever the truth was, we both would have backed you all the way…so please,' she implored softly, 'tell me the truth, the real truth.'

*At last,* Spencer thought, *a chance to tell another person my story.* There was an intense feeling of relief to finally tell all. He liked and admired Savannah and the idea of having her as a confidante. To tell her about the fears he lived with, how he so desperately missed his wife and Trilby, his beautiful daughter. How entranced he was with her, the joy of being a father, to explain his biggest fear that he may be locked into the past forever.

'Ok, this is the whole truth. Nothing but the truth.' For the next hour Spencer poured out his story. His mission in Singapore, the sabotage of the Japanese ships, the beautiful heroine Trilby Lim, his comrades Sam Albert and Irwin, meeting the now Singapore Prime Minister Lee Kuan Yew and then when he had found himself once again cast back in time to Hawaii in 1941. The villainous Lee Tai, his attraction to Roxanne. And then on the eve of the fateful Japanese attack on Pearl Harbour, once again waking up with Michiyo prior to their wedding in Hawaii.

He explained how when he and Michiyo had travelled to New York on holiday, he'd woken up on the Manhattan subway in 1955, initially with no idea how he got there. And then his fateful altercation with crime lord Tony Romano and his subsequent introduction to Savannah's boss Special Agent Dale Fletcher.

Savannah sat back in her chair, only moving to motion the now very compliant waitperson to bring more coffee.

'And then on our trip back to the States from Tokyo when I went to sleep and you thought I was in a coma, I was once again transported back to the next century and Michiyo.'

Savannah listened to the whole story in silence. When it was clear he'd finished, she sat bolt upright, folded her arms and suddenly erupted into peals of laughter, causing other patrons and the untidy waiter to stare at her in alarm. 'For chrissake Spencer, how long did it take you to come up with that heap of crap? Seriously you razz my berries. I will say this, top marks for creativity. You could make a movie about all that. Singapore and Lee kuan who?'

'Yew.' Spencer stared at Savannah in dismay, feeling both very stupid and profoundly disappointed.

'Now you just listen to me. I told you both Dale and I had put a lot of work, manpower and energy into figuring out the enigma of Spencer Marlowe, didn't I?'

Spencer nodded.

'We know you were in Hawaii in 1941. As for that damn Singapore story, well who knows? We know you were apparently in your late twenties when you were in Hawaii and about the same age in New York in 1955 when we first met, and that was what…fourteen years after. So obviously that threw us. Well, we finally figured out the mystery of Spencer Marlowe.'

'Go on.' Spencer was intrigued.

'And we now know, why you kept on saying "It's a long story" and now this stupid time travel nonsense.'

Spencer shrugged.

'There is only one possible answer, only…one.'

'And that is?'

'You've managed to get your hands on some sort of miracle drug, or potion, elixir, call it want ever you want. Both Dale and I can understand why it's such a closely guarded secret. If the world got to hear about it there would be rioting in the streets everybody would want it; hell I want it for chrissake. So, if you were say, thirty years old in 1941, you'd have been born in about 1910 or 1911, but…and this is the big but…for all we know you could be one hundred years old. This is the bit that we have no way of knowing. But certainly, you would have to be at least fifty at the moment. And you sure as hell don't look fifty. Well?'

Spencer certainly hadn't seen this one coming, but he could see their logic. *You can only play the cards you've been dealt.*

Spencer looked suitably sheepish. 'I take my hat off to you both, that's pretty damn smart. I have to tell you, I can't go into all the details, there are still problems. I have a recurring problem with amnesia for instance. But…well…you sure figured things out.'

Savannah sat motionless for a couple of minutes; she then daintily picked up the last morsel of the doughnut and munched thoughtfully. 'What's going on in your life at the moment? Oh, and while where on the subject, what about Maggio, was she bullshit, or does she…'

'I'm quite sure you remembered her name is Michiyo and she's not some bloody baseball player.'

'I guess if you were going to make up the name of a fictitious wife or girlfriend you wouldn't say she was a Jap now would you?' Savannah laughed.

Spencer noticed her twinkling eyes and knew no offence was meant.

'But seriously what exactly are you up to at the moment? You have to be in LA for a reason. God damn I just need to know what's going on with your life right now.' She shook her head and muttered, 'How hard can it be?'

'Well,' Spencer couldn't help himself as he broke into laughter. 'It's a long story, but in fact I'm at a loose end, sort of foot loose and fancy free and unfortunately broke.'

# CHAPTER NINE

# COME ON HOME. MEET THE WIFE

'How would you like to work for me?'

'Doing?'

'I've been tracking a lowlife involved in trafficking underage girls and supplying them with heroin. Also making and distributing child pornography of the most disgusting type imaginable. I want to take this creep down, destroy him and his organisation.'

'Have you considered just shooting him?'

'I'll just ignore that. Well, what do you think?'

The Galley was cloistered and close, so many tables and so little room, now empty but for the waiter who'd retreated behind the counter, listening to a ball game on the radio.

Spencer couldn't help thinking. *Why do I get the feeling that I'm being thrown in at the deep end again?*

'Why me? You must have other agents?'

Savannah ignored him; reaching into her bag she pulled out a photo and handed it to Spencer. 'Look at this.'

'Yeah, ok tall, good looking, distinguished so?'

'This is the Spencer I remember. C'mon seriously, you don't recognise him?'

Spencer shook his head.

'That's Zachariah Colchester.'

'Really?'

'Spencer,' Savannah snapped, 'he's only the most famous director in Hollywood.'

Spencer shrugged. 'Sorry, never heard of him.'

Savannah rolled her eyes. 'Is this the amnesia thing?'

Spencer shrugged again. 'I still don't see exactly where I fit in. As I said, you must have other agents.'

'The problem is this guy is so well connected you couldn't begin to imagine. I need someone who is a cleanskin. Unfortunately, my team of agents look like agents. J Edgar insists on a certain presentation. All the agents look like they came out of an assembly line marked "Clean Cut Agent." What I need is someone to pose as a buyer of the porn and the heroin. We believe Colchester has connections in Mexico that could be supplying him with both the H and the girls. Sort of a package deal. Now you with your Australian accent you should throw off any suspicion.' Savannah stared hard; her eyes gleamed with the fanaticism of a zealot. She glanced at her watch, drumming her fingers on the tabletop.

Spencer smiled at the chunky unattractive time piece, and wondered if it was some sort of 60's chic that had passed him by.

'This's probably enough for one day. I think Boris Karloff wants to shut the joint. Tell me Spencer, where are you living?'

Spencer told Savannah about Priscilla.

'Well, this has been quite a day, and very entertaining. Come on Mister Marlowe, lord give me strength. Time travel. Don't that just beat all you ever stepped in. We'll get my car. I'm taking you home. It's not that I don't trust you, but I want to see where you live. You're not going to disappear on me again, are you?'

'Savannah, I promise you I'm not going anywhere.' Spencer felt like a fraud making that promise. He decided to change the subject.

'You haven't told me anything about what you've been up to since our trip to Tokyo. I imagine you and Seth are now an old married couple?'

'It…ah…didn't work out with Seth. You didn't like him, I know.'

'Look Savannah, you know how it is, sometimes you just don't click with someone. I'm sure he was basically a good guy, y'know working with kids and all that. What was it, you caught him playing around? I mean, he wasn't a bad looking guy. I can imagine being surrounded by all those pretty nurses. Heck, any guy would be tempted.'

Savannah frowned, shaking her head. 'Spencer, I…I really don't want to talk about him. Ok?'

Spencer had an uneasy feeling. 'The trouble is I know you only too well. Out with it.'

Savannah glanced around her. 'Spencer your gut feeling was 100% correct. He was bad, very bad.'

'What on earth happened? What did he do to you?'

Savannah was looking distinctly uncomfortable, fidgeting with her hair and glancing around the room. I'm…I'm…damnit, look, Spencer, 'I'm not sure I really want to talk about it, but let's just say he was…evil…evil beyond belief.'

'Oh dear…I can see this might be more of a case of "What did you do to him?" What exactly happened to Seth?'

'Oh, well…We had an argument and he…ah…disappeared.'

'Savannah! Disappeared?'

'Yes Spencer…he…just…disappeared…and now the subject is closed, ok?'

It was Spencer's turn to laugh. He tapped the side of his nose and winked.

'Well, you know how I feel about bad guys. One day I'll tell you all the details, ok?'

'Savannah, Savannah, this is too juicy. I gotta know.'

'Hell's bells,' Savannah muttered, 'Same old Spencer, like a God damn dog with a bone. I have my own office. You know, run my own race so to speak. I'm no longer the green bunny from Hicksville.'

'Savannah, hold it right there. Great about your office, I'm delighted your career is obviously going well. Wonderful. Seth?'

'Ok, what do you want to know?'

'So, Seth is no more, literally and figuratively. Is there a new man in your life?'

'Spencer, I have to tell you, yes there is someone in my life. I've never been happier, life is wonderful. I had no idea just how good things could be.'

Spencer was delighted to see Savannah so happy; he had always had the impression that she was never really in love with Seth. 'Well, when do I get to meet him?'

Savannah started to look distinctly uncomfortable; twisting her handkerchief, her eyes downcast. She then gazed at Spencer. He had the feeling that she was weighing things up. 'It's not a he.'

'Oh, I see.'

'You're shocked, aren't you?' She uttered in a voice laced with bitterness. 'I really am stupid. I don't know…I just thought perhaps you, you of all people would understand.' Savannah now dabbed at her eyes with the handkerchief. 'Just forget about us working together. I've made a mistake, a stupid mistake.' She dabbed again at her reddened eyes. 'Do you know? You're the only person I've told. Not even my mother. I know she'd be horrified. If the FBI found out, that'd be my career gone. It's so bloody unfair.' Savannah sprang up, and went to leave.

'Whoa for Christ's sake, hold on, damn you.'

Spencer actually felt tears welling up in his own eyes. *If only you knew, in my century no one would bat an eyelash. You could be the head of the FBI. You could even be president of the US.*

'Savannah,' he said softly, 'I'm not in any way shocked or disapproving. I'm genuinely happy for you and…'

'Inez.' Savannah sniffed.

'I'm sure Inez is a wonderful person. I'd like to meet her…but?'

'What do you mean, but?' Spencer saw raw suspicion in Savannah's eyes.

Spencer laughed as he pointed a dagger finger at her. 'Don't think you're getting away with, "It's a long story" where Seth is concerned.'

It was Savannah's turn to laugh. 'One night, perhaps when we've had a couple of Asahi's I might tell you the story.'

'Asahi?'

'My God Spencer, you wouldn't believe it, but since you and I were in Tokyo I've fallen for Jap food, hook line and sinker. I've introduced Inez to it as well and she's turned out to be a great Japanese chef. Not only that she's been learning Japanese. I tell you Inez soaks up languages like a sponge. How about you come around tonight, meet the wife. Oh lord,' Savannah said with a giggle, 'that's the first time I've ever referred to Inez as a wife.'

# CHAPTER TEN

# SAVANNAH'S BETTER HALF

Spencer used some of his rapidly dwindling funds to pay for a cab. Savannah and Inez's comfortable Californian bungalow in Marina Del Rey was fortunately only a five-dollar fare including tip. Spencer was still entranced with LA 1960's style. As the gold Chevrolet Checker Cab rumbled noisily along Lincoln Boulevard, the affable Hispanic driver was extolling the virtues of President John F Kennedy. 'I tell you buddy; JFK will sort out that gilipollas Castro.' His running commentary accentuated by the waving of a giant-sized stogie.

Not at all sure what to bring, Spencer had bought a bouquet of tulips from a street vendor. Flowers certainly are cheap in the sixties, fifteen cents for a bunch of freshly cut, sweet smelling blooms.

For the first time since Spencer had arrived, so to speak, he felt completely at ease and relaxed. There was a moment of awkwardness when Spencer met Inez. Clearly Inez was initially uncomfortable this tall stranger should be privy to their guilty secret. Once the ice was broken the evening was a joyous occasion. Spencer had the feeling both Savannah and Inez were delighted to have their domesticity and their obvious love for each other on display. Once again Spencer could only reflect on how much the world had moved on since 1961.

Spencer found Inez captivating. Her hair, black and straight gave contrast to her face, sweetly dark upon soft brown skin with striking black eyes. To Spencer, she looked like a Spanish aristocrat, tall and graceful, in a word, refined.

Inez had that delightful lilt to her voice that sounded both sophisticated and beguiling. Her mother tongue, Spanish, but her English was perfect. Inez had been teaching Savannah Spanish, they'd made a point of speaking it when together at home. Savannah now spoke Spanish like a Columbian as that was where Inez was from.

Savannah and Inez were complete opposites; it was immediately obvious this relationship was harmonious and loving. Spencer basked in the warm glow that seemed to suffuse the room.

Savannah had made the miso soup, Inez the rest of the dinner. Spencer sat back feeling as if he was sliding into 1960's life, and the next century was just a dream. *Perhaps this is where I'm meant to be.* Seeing Savannah and Inez so comfortable and happy with each other was the catalyst he needed to accept this was real and he had to carve out a life for himself. 'How did the two of you meet?'

Inez glanced at Savannah, who nodded and smiled, as if to say, 'It's ok.'

'I was married. Unbeknownst to me, my husband had been dealing in drugs, which he'd been shipping to other US states. That of course brought him to the attention of the FBI'. Inez hesitated; Spencer could see tears welling. 'He'd become violent. I think he'd been sniffing too much cocaine and was paranoid…suspecting me of…of having affairs, talking to the police. Why would I talk to the police? I'd no idea he was

dealing. I thought the money came from his antique business.'
Inez was wringing her hands. Savannah put an arm around
her.

Spencer was horrified this graceful, statuesque woman,
with her lustrous black hair and olive complexion and who
wore her Latin background with pride, could have been
married to a violent criminal.

'When we first met, he was charming, considerate,
sophisticated. He looked just like Victor Mature.' Spencer had
no idea who Victor Mature was. 'It was just a veneer. It was
not long after we were married that the beatings started.'

'Did you go to the police?'

Savannah cut in, 'Spencer, sometimes I actually believe you
really must be a time traveller. Unless the husband beats a
woman halfway to death the police simply don't want to know.
And…and just what do you think the damned options are?
Inez would have been kicked out onto the street with nothing.
Truly the laws are just barbaric.'

'What brought things to a head?'

'It's strange how things turn out. I'd been sitting outside
their home in an unmarked FBI Chevy. I had a tip. A dealer
was about to drop off some heroin, when I heard screams
from the house. Inez was being beaten. I heard a male voice
yelling and threatening to kill her; that was all I needed. That
was probable cause. So, I banged on the door, screaming at
the top of my lungs, FBI, FBI open the door. When the
bastard saw I was alone and a woman, all of a sudden he
became brave again. Stood on his dignity and told me to fuck
off.'

Spencer almost felt sorry for the husband. 'Then what?'

'I cocked the God damn Magnum. Shoved it into his face and told him to sit down on the lounge.'

Inez was staring at Savannah with a mixture of awe and love.

Spencer could well and truly envisage the scene. *You poor bastard. Of all the FBI agents, you had to cross Savannah.*

'Terrific story. Then what?'

Inez then spoke. 'I'd gone to the bathroom to clean up. My dress was torn. I was bleeding. My nose was broken…I was a mess. I'd only been there for minute when a shot rang out.'

Spencer's eyes ratcheted onto Savannah. Her face was inscrutable.

'Apparently my husband had a gun. My God I'd never seen a gun in the house. I can't imagine where he'd kept it hidden. Anyhow, he'd drawn his gun and Savannah had shot him…oh…it was awful…horrible. When I rushed back into the lounge, he was dead. There was blood everywhere. He had the gun in his hand. I'm just so glad that Savannah wasn't killed. I'm sure that she probably feels in some way guilty.' Inez gazed at Savannah her eyes glistened. 'Just remember darling, it was him or you. You simply had to do it.'

Spencer glared at Savannah, who winked and smiled.

CHAPTER ELEVEN

# BUTTER WOULDN'T MELT

'We have to find a way of getting closer to Zachariah Colchester.'

Spencer straddled a particularly uncomfortable government issue grey steel chair in the FBI field office in Wilshire Boulevard. Spencer's life seemed to be now entrenched in the swinging sixties. The weather in October, Spencer decided, was definitely balmy. *I guess there are a lot worse places I could be.*

Spencer contemplated Savannah's little kingdom. The old wooden floor was more cinnamon where the varnish still held and washed out in the regions that had had more wear. Splotches of what Spencer suspected was gun oil that had accidently leaked, evident under a cluttered work bench. His eyes were drawn to a sturdy bookcase, shelves full, with cracked spines, and foxed dustjackets packed as tight as teeth. *The Illustrated World Encyclopaedia History of Rifles and Machine Guns, Professional Gun Smithing,* and lo and behold, *The Mary Thomas's Knitting Book.* Spencer grabbed the slim tome waving it triumphantly above his head. 'My God, there's hope for you yet. I knew it. The hard-bitten FBI Amazon is just a façade.'

'Get real. It was a present from Mum. I think she had visions of Seth and I having kids and I'd be knitting booties. Jesus, can you imagine?'

Behind the plain oaken desk with its untidy scrabble of wanted posters scattered haphazardly, Savannah sat tapping a pencil on her teeth. She threw the pencil down, picking up a framed photo of Inez standing in the doorway of their bungalow, holding a large black and white tabby cat.

Spencer admired the photo. 'I thought you wanted to keep this relationship under wraps?'

'That's a photo of our cat Capone. Inez just happened to get in the way.'

'Subtle, Savannah…subtle.'

Savannah leaned forward on the desk her hands steepled under her chin. 'Isn't Inez just wonderful? Can you see why I love her so much?'

'She is a lovely lady and a polar opposite of you.'

'Really? How so?'

'Inez is gentle, thoughtful and if you don't mind me using that word again…subtle.'

'You arrogant son of a bitch, that's insulting.'

'Ha ha…my point exactly. Would Inez have responded like that?'

'You might be right.'

'A word of warning perhaps.'

'That being?' Savannahs eyes narrowed.

Spencer leaned back on his chair. 'You successfully fooled Dale Fletcher, who, as your senior officer should have known better. And chances are you've fooled a lot of other people. But you didn't fool me.'

'What on earth are you talking about?'

'You know bloody well what I'm talking about. When you got dear old Isaac the hitman to go for his gun so you could shoot him.'

'Yeah, well he didn't have to reach for it.'

'And while where at it. You simply murdered Nick the mob lawyer in cold blood.'

Savannah snarled. 'The guy was a God damn wife beater.'

'I suppose I shouldn't mention the four you rather disposed of in Tokyo?'

'Four…it wasn't four, that thug Riko swallowed cyanide.'

'Ok three.'

'Wait just a minute. One of them had a knife at your God damn throat. And if I remember correctly, he was going to cut your head off.'

'Savannah, for that I am eternally grateful, but if you remember the next guy you shot had in fact surrendered, and after I told you he wasn't a threat.'

'Yeah well…I guess you have a point with that one, but he was yakuza. A Japanese gangster. Certainly not a good guy.'

'This is like banging my head on a brick wall. You don't seem to get it. You can't just go on being judge, jury and executioner.'

'Really, why not?'

'I seem to remember having this conversation once before.'

'Well, you'll be pleased to know, I did take your advice.'

'This I gotta hear.'

'Yep…I stopped using those hollow point rounds. You were right, they were so damn messy.'

'Oh, hallelujah the Lord be praised, peace on Earth and goodwill to men.'

'Shut up Spencer.' She hadn't missed the wry tone or the unimpressed expression after all.

'Any how I was in the middle of issuing you a word of warning.'

'Go on,' Savannah groaned.

'What I was trying to say is that if the love of your life finds out about your homicidal tendencies, it may put a strain on your relationship.'

'Actually, you may well be right.'

'I don't think that Inez's late husband actually had a gun.'

'He did too.' She mimed taking a gun out of her pocket, held by the thumb and forefinger. The whole while she grinned like a kid at Christmas. 'Right after I shot the bastard, I put a nice nickel plated 0.38 into his hand, that I just happened to have in my pocket.' Savannah chortled.

'I give up.'

'You should have seen what that animal did to Inez. My God. If it had been a different time and place, he wouldn't have got off so damn easy,' Savannah hissed.

'I'm sure he was grateful.'

'Look, Spencer, you and I have had differences of opinion from day one and I'm sorry if you see me as some crazed gun happy psychopath, but try and remember we live in different worlds. From the day Henry Kelly murdered my dad in cold blood, I've devoted my life to taking down bastards like that. So…'

'So, you're trying to say you're going to go on being judge, jury and executioner.'

'Spencer, I'm going to do what I have to do, get over it. If you'd seen what Inez's husband had done…' Savannah's eyes blazed as she plonked back down on her chair; suddenly she burst out laughing. 'The creep's dead. I wound up with Inez. What in hell have I got to be upset about?'

***

The office reminded Spencer of Spinetti and Crabtree's headquarters in Hawaii, only this time the photo of the president was different. Dwight Eisenhower's photo beamed down from the wall, managing to look like Ford's salesman of the year. Right in the middle of the wall was a photo of Savannah being handed an award from Hoover himself. Next to President Eisenhower's framed photo was a larger picture of J Edgar Hoover, his scowling visage screaming, "Come on you Commie bastards, we'll get you."

'He sure looks like a scary guy.' Spencer grinned.

Savannah turned to run an approving eye over the man who struck fear into the hearts of criminals and politicians alike. It was rumoured he had something on everybody; his position was secure, as every politician and bureaucrat knew whatever transgressions that had occurred in their life, J Edgar would know about it. His scariest line was, "Don't worry senator, I'll personally make sure your arrest for soliciting that prostitute on Hollywood Boulevard will be quashed. Your secret will always be safe with me."

Savannah laughed. 'Yeah, I met him a couple of years ago. I'd been trying to take down some communist agitators who'd been trying to gain influence at one of the major studios.

57

Would you believe it, this commie shmuck actually pulled a gun on me?'

'And…Let me guess…you shot him?'

'It was a righteous kill, everybody said so.'

'Savannah, not for a moment would I suggest otherwise.'

'Well, he really was a bad guy. No loss to society.'

***

Spencer had just made a coffee in his temporary office next to Savannah's; he screwed up his nose at the tasteless excuse for his favourite beverage. Savannah had managed to get him on a temporary salary with an advance of one hundred dollars which although initially disappointing Spencer discovered it went a long way in 1960's America.

It had taken a little time for Spencer to learn the intricacies of what on the surface appeared to be just your average government office. The windows were crafted from the latest bullet proof glass, and at the press of a button solid steel shutters would ratchet into place. There was a room that was effectively a huge safe, big enough to fit five people comfortably inside, airconditioned with basic provisions to last several days. Inside a veritable arsenal of shotguns, long guns, hand guns. two specialist sniper rifles, a crate of fragmentation grenades and tear gas cannisters.

'Spencer,' Savannah bellowed as she stormed into his office. 'I reckon we've got it.'

'Got what?' Savannah laughed as she caught sight of Spencer eying off his foul-smelling brew.

'Oh, dear poor, poor Spencer, I know how seriously you take your coffee and the FBI rubbish is awful…do you remember that wonderful coffee machine we had in Spencer's Restaurant?' she said wistfully.

'Don't remind me. Got what?' he repeated.

'Zachariah is having a shindig at his pad on Loma Vista Drive. All we have to do is somehow get invited to it.'

'Great idea; how about I contact his staff and just say the FBI would like to come to his party so they can chat to the guests and ask who's into kiddie porn and underage girls…yep…that'll work.'

'Alright Mister Doubting Thomas. I admit at the moment it presents a logistical problem. But the Lord favours the righteous.'

'The Lord favours the righteous? Have you got religion since the old days?'

'You probably don't care to remember, but when that slant eye in Tokyo was about to remove your head from your shoulders and I made that impossible shot, killing the son of a bitch, I actually recited a prayer, and well, it worked. So, if I choose to get religion temporarily, I will. But meanwhile on a practical note, there's something we need to attend to.'

Savannah leaned forward, opening her desk drawer, she grabbed a Colt 0.38 revolver in a well-worn leather shoulder holster, shoving it across the desk.

'What's this?' Spencer eyed the weapon as if it was the harbinger of a noxious disease.

'That,' Savannah sighed, 'is what is known as a gun. A gat. A pistol. Or if you prefer, a *pistola* in Spanish.'

'I know what it is,' Spencer testily replied, 'I want to know…why it is?'

'Spencer even though you are only an auxiliary in the FBI you are required to carry. Although in your case I'm not so sure it's such a good idea.'

'Hey, hang on, I'm not quite as bad a shot as you think.'

'Really? Anyway, Spencer you have to wear it. That's an order…got it?'

'Ok, boss. Got it.'

'Ok, Spencer, before we try and figure out how we get closer to Colchester I'd like to at least give you some basic instruction on how to use a weapon.' Savannah picked up the revolver, flicking the cylinder open with a practised motion, she inspected the load.

'In case you hadn't noticed, I'm quite capable of defending myself.'

'Not against some thug with a firearm. There's a shooting range near here. I want to take you there tomorrow.'

'So, I'm going to embarrass myself with a whole lot of FBI hotshots having a laugh? You are one tough lady. Whatever happened to that sweet innocent FBI novice I remember so fondly?'

'For God's sake Spencer, you have to carry a firearm and you have to know how to use it. Are all Aussies so difficult?' '

'No, but the difference is, in Australia, women don't bully their menfolk.'

'So, Maggio never argues with you? The man is always right, huh?'

'No Savannah…it's in fact a very equal partnership, Michiyo…MICHIYO is a very strong-willed woman, a lot like you in fact.'

'Really?'

'Yes,' Spencer said coldly, 'but she doesn't habitually go around shooting people. I would add that she would never accept anything other than absolute equality. And…all jokes aside, neither would I. And I don't think Inez would be a pushover either. Oh, and one more thing…'

'Uh oh.'

'Yeah, uh oh indeed. It's Michiyo as you well know, not that bloody baseball player.'

'A truce, I think. What do you reckon?

Spencer nodded. 'Truce.'

'Anyway,' Savannah insisted. 'I reckon you'll enjoy it. Where we're going is a terrific club, great atmosphere. We can get something to eat if you want. It's in a rough part of town but I've never seen any disagreements. One thing I will say: shooters always seem to behave themselves.'

'Well, 'I wouldn't be at all surprised if with a bit of practice, I could become an expert marksman. What's the name of this place?'

'It's called the Southern Belle.'

# CHAPTER TWELVE

# THE SOUTHERN BELLE

It was a typical cloudless LA day, the days were cooler, reminding Spencer so much of Western Australia in Autumn. Savannah whistled a Mitch Miller tune as she loaded the weapons into the trunk. Making a right onto Seventeenth Street, she grinned as she floored the big V8 onto Olympic Boulevard.

'Goes like a God damn rocket. Do you know Spencer, I can't imagine cars ever getting better than this? It's got heaters, a press button radio. What more could those Detroit whiz kids possibly come up with?'

Spencer was still fascinated by the automobiles with their extravagant fins. He smiled to himself as he thought of his BMW with air-conditioning, cruise-control, ABS, sat-nav and so much more.

'Yep, they've thought of everything.'

Spencer enjoyed reading the billboards in 1960's America, as they rocketed down the highway, he couldn't take his eyes off the extravagant hoardings cluttering every available space.

He noticed the advertising signs were mostly for cigarette brands, Lucky Strikes, Players. And one that had him intrigued, Red Man Chewing Tobacco.

'Gas.' Savannah pulled off the interstate into a Shell station, a two island four pump affair with a small pay hut made of bright white boards, it looked like a kids' playhouse. At the far end of the spacious lot Spencer saw a hamburger joint with a line of people.

'Wow, I don't believe it, McDonald's.' Spencer was intrigued by the sight of the McDonald's decked out in red and white but without the distinctive golden arches from his century. He slotted the nozzle into the tank, pumping six bucks even, nudging above full.

Savannah, peeled a ten dollar note, from a roll in her pocket and paid the attendant with his cop like peaked cap, white shirt and red bow tie.

They climbed back into the car, Savannah started the engine, glancing out of the window. 'What's so special? It's just another hamburger joint. If you're hungry we can stop. I don't reckon their burgers are anything wonderful. I will say, they're quick. But seriously Mel's is way better. We can join the line. Shouldn't take long. They sure knock em out quick.'

'No, it's ok. It's just that I was…um surprised to see a McDonald's I guess.'

Savannah glanced sideways at him. 'Why is it that I still find you a bit of a puzzle? I mean, what is it about a hamburger joint? McDonald's is just another burger place. If you ask me, they'll be here today and gone tomorrow. They don't have what it takes to be a stayer in LA I'll guarantee you that.'

He could invest in McDonald's. Make a fortune. Perhaps return to Michiyo a multi-millionaire.

Spencer studied the McDonalds and wondered as he so often did, would the future be as he had already lived it or would the world change? Was this his mission? Maybe when and if he returned to his century, there would be no McDonalds.

'I'm not sure that would be such a tragedy.'

'What was that?' Savannah asked.

'Nothing. Just talking to myself. I remember when we were in Japan, all you wanted was a burger and a Bud. 'I'm so glad I introduced the country girl to a slice of Asian culture. I couldn't believe it when you told me you and Inez were into Japanese food.'

At the mention of Inez, Savannah's expression softened. 'Inez and I like nothing better than curling up in front of the TV eating sushi, or whatever and watching Ben Casey.'

'Ben who?'

'Casey, dagnabbit, you know the God damn miracle doctor.'

'Oh yeah him. I forgot.' Spencer had no idea who Ben Casey was.

'Yeah. And soon, he'll be coloured.'

'You mean, he was a white guy and he's going to become a black guy?' Now Spencer was completely confused.

'Spencer, you razz my berries, seriously. Colour TV, Colour TV. It's coming soon.'

He tried not to sound too nonchalant about the miracle advent of colour TV, or too amused for that matter. 'Oh yeah, of course colour TV. Yep, that'll be great.' It hadn't occurred to Spencer that television had ever been anything other than colour. As far as he remembered he'd never seen black and white TV.

'I saw a demonstration the other day. You won't believe it. It was fantastic.

It was at the Broadway Crenshaw centre. I tell you Spencer, Inez and I are getting a set as soon as they hit the market. But ouch, I've heard they're going to be expensive.'

'Really? How much are they likely to be?' Spencer was intrigued.

'I hear tell, about $1000.'

'Wow, how about that?'

'What'll they think of next?'

There was a comfortable silence as the big V8 gobbled up the miles. They were two friends that didn't always need conversation. Spencer reflected that he regarded Savannah as his closest confidant other than Michiyo, he was saddened that she hadn't believed his story. In all honesty, he didn't mind too much. If he could get through this newest trial, he would simply love his wife and daughter, and count himself lucky.

Savannah became more vigilant as they drove slowly into Success Avenue and then made a left into East Ninety Sixth Street.

'So, this is Watts. It looks ok.'

Spencer glanced at the endless clutter of untidy LA stucco homes. Suspicious black faces eyed the unfamiliar grey car, easily recognisable as Government and Government meant trouble. They clattered over the potholed road. Spencer started to feel the beat and rhythm of the suburb, the boarded-up buildings, groups of sullen black and Hispanic youths, scowling and talking amongst themselves, pointing at their vehicle, almost daring them to pull over.

'I see what you mean about Watts. I'm not sure I'd want to be a pedestrian here.'

Savannah glanced at a group of youths who were reclining on a torn, discarded blue velvet sofa, lying on the side of the street, a resting place for thugs and wannabes.

'Well, I guess all cities have their problem areas. The southside of Chicago is worse. But hell, LA is different things for different people. For Inez and I, it's perfect.'

'You and Inez are certainly LA ladies. I can't imagine you going back to New York.'

'I tell you Spencer, I just love California and LA. What is it you Aussies say? I wouldn't go back to New York for quids.'

'So, the nice people of LA don't object to Agent Steele shooting their citizens?'

Savannah glanced sideways at Spencer, ready to attack, when she noticed he was smiling.

'You and I will never see eye to eye on my methods, I guess. Anyway, here we are at the gun club and I promise not to shoot anyone.'

The Plymouth turned into the grimy car park in the LA suburb of Watts.

Spencer glanced around at the boarded-up shopfronts, there was an early fifties Chevrolet Styleline up on blocks with its bonnet missing, next to it a ragged black man spooning beans from a can. Spencer guessed that the old Chevy may well have been his home. 'Not all of LA is wonderful, is it?'

'Every city has its down and outs, I guess. They have programs…various initiatives but at the end of the day you're going to have those who slip through the cracks. It's not good to be black and poor.'

They were in the carpark of a row of run-down businesses, a liquor shop, a beauty salon, empty apart from a coloured girl leaning back in a chair, smoking as she watched a black and white TV. Waiting for the next customer, Spencer thought.

The only spark of glamour was the Southern Belle shooting range, big and brash a two-story breeze block building with a bold Los Vegas style illuminated sign, of a saucy Southern gal with a short skirt and sequined shirt. A Stetson at a rakish angle and carrying a musket. There was a collection of pickups in the car park, some sporting Alabama and Mississippi plates.

'Have you been here before?'

'Yep, it's a pretty rough neighbourhood but it's the best club by far, and the FBI doesn't have a range anywhere close.'

Spencer was pleasantly surprised; the club was also a very well-appointed saloon and restaurant. There were customers eating and drinking at a long bar that ran the length of the room. The bar was constructed of an impressive polished oak slab. Behind it, a full-length mirror and a counter was laden with mostly bourbon, but in keeping with the tastes of the hip Californians, there was gin and vodka and a blackboard sign listing all the popular cocktails.

Spencer glimpsed through an open doorway a kitchen with a bevy of chefs turning out typical comfort food, hamburgers French fries. They advertised the newest taste sensation…pizza! The bar staff was composed of mostly very pretty girls dressed exactly like the neon sign on top of the building: short skirts, sequined shirts and Stetsons. A juke box in the corner poured out the plaintive love song "Crazy" sung by everyone's favourite, Patsy Cline.

There was no getting away from the fact it was a gun club. At one end of the barn-like building a group of men earnestly fired a variety of handguns at paper targets, hauled out on wire runners at varying distances. Whoops and hollers could be heard from a group of good old boys who appeared to be competing with each other while emptying bottles of bourbon. The crack of gunfire and the smell of cordite and black powder from old muzzle loading pre-Civil War pistols permeated the air.

Spencer smiled at these country guys in their jeans and boots, so different from the Californians with their slim fit trousers and pointy toed shoes. He nudged Savannah. 'Do you think it's a problem mixing alcohol with guns?'

'This is America. We love our guns and people who go to gun clubs are very responsible citizens.'

Savannah strolled up to the counter, purchasing boxes of 0.38 calibre Remington cartridges. 'If you shoot here you have to buy your ammunition here, they charge a premium, but it's a small price to pay for the use of the club, I reckon.' She pulled on a pair of glasses and a clunky pair of earmuffs. 'Put the earmuffs on and load the pistol. You do know how to load it don't you?'

'Did I detect just a trace of sarcasm there?'

'I'm going to roll the target out to twenty feet. Now this is a pretty easy shot.'

Spencer glanced at the square bit of cardboard fashioned as a bullseye. 'Wow,' he said hesitantly, 'that's a pretty darn small target.'

'Fire at will.'

Spencer frowned that was a smirk, a dead set bloody smirk. *I'll bloody well show her.*

Spencer confidently fired off the six rounds.

'You missed…for Christ's sake, Spencer not one slug hit the target.'

Spencer squinted at the offending piece of cardboard. 'Maybe not, but I think some of the rounds went pretty darn close.'

One of the good ole boys in the next alley laughed, a rasping unpleasant sound. 'Well little lady, I don't think your boyfriend is gunna protect ya from the muggers in Watts.'

'When I want your advice redneck, I'll ask, ok?' Savannah eyed him coldly.

One of his buddies threw fuel on the flames. 'Well Billy Bob, I guess that's tellin ya.'

Hank Williams was wailing "Your Cheating Heart" on the juke box.

'You just keep yore trap shut Jim Bob' he snarled to his companion.

'Jim Bob, Billy Bob, are these guys for real?' Spencer turned to Savannah.

***

Spencer fired the revolver until his trigger finger was sore, the cordite hurt his eyes, the air was thick and heavy. Even the earmuffs failed to drown out the constant boom of the many weapons being fired nonstop.

'Yeech…I think I can see some improvement,' Savannah grudgingly accepted, 'and there is certainly one great big positive.'

'Oh, I can't wait. And what would the positives be?'

'Well,' she chortled, doubling over with laughter 'you haven't shot me or any of the customers, although' and she cast a disdainful eye on the Southerners 'I wouldn't have minded if you had managed to shoot 'Silly Bob.'

'I suppose you meant Billy Bob; the other Bob was Jim Bob. Hey you don't think the third guy is also a Bob?'

Savannah shook her head. 'I know I shouldn't be critical but seriously some of these yokels, their ideas and attitudes belong in the dark ages. Did I tell you about the hurricane that tore through Arkansas?'

Spencer grinned, shaking his head.

'Yep, it did a million dollars' worth of improvements.'

The last bullets had been fired. Spencer and Savannah were in the carpark. Savannah remarked. 'There's nothing more relaxing than shooting a few rounds, I tell you.'

'Each to his own,' Spencer retorted. 'A lot of people actually enjoy a good book or going to the movies.'

'Sounds God damn boring to me.' Savannah chuckled. 'You may be right. Inez doesn't care for guns and she always has her nose in a book.'

Savannah and Spencer leant on the Plymouth, savouring the mild sunshine. Spencer swigged the last of a bottle of Coca Cola trying to drown the acrid taste of the black powder. The doors of the Southern Belle swung open, out spilled the three Southern boys, a little drunk and still angry. Billy Bob pointed a dagger finger at Jim Bob, at the same time giving Savannah the evil eye.

*Something tells me we're being discussed and it's not a friendly discussion.*

'These guys are wearing their weapons on their hip. Is that allowed?'

'If they've got a licence to carry…then why not?' Savannah shrugged.

Spencer did a quick appraisal of the potential threat; he'd already figured the hulking Billy Bob was likely to be an instigator. Spencer couldn't help smiling at this lumbering bully of a man. This's someone who wins through intimidation Spencer had decided, big…certainly, powerful…you bet, but slow. In other words, easy meat. A walk in the park. *Billy Bob you're out of your depth here.* Spencer accepted what Savannah had said about people being allowed to carry guns but these southern boys were angry and a little drunk.

Spencer cast his eye over the youngest and so far, unnamed guy and quickly dismissed him. *This one will turn tail and run as soon as the odds are against him.*

Spencer's gaze lingered for a few seconds on Jim Bob. *Different odds here.*

Jim Bob had the stance of the accomplished street brawler, average height but lean and hard muscled. He stood relaxed with his thumb and forefinger linked in the belt of his working man's blue coveralls with his remaining fingers pointing downwards. His curled upper lip displaying amused contempt. Spencer glanced at Savannah who nodded in acknowledgement at the sign of the Klan, the three fingers representing the three K's.

As far as a threat level, Spencer rated Jim Bob a three out of ten. But considering he had never rated anybody higher than a five out of ten it meant that the lovable Jim Bob was still a threat to be reckoned with.

Billy Bob strolled up to Savannah standing a fraction too close, his stained Stetson pushed back on his head.

'Hey there sweet thing, how's about you and me get a little better acquainted?' He smiled an ingratiating smile. 'We got off to a bad start inside.' He turned, winking at his buddies, adding, 'But I reckon after a few drinks, we could have some laughs. Whadya reckon babe?' His manner was not one of a potential suitor. Spencer suspected he was deliberately baiting Savannah.

Spencer drank the last of his Coke, thinking, *I don't think this'll end well.*

Billy Bob was as tall as Spencer with massive arms that indicated years of hard manual labour. His protruding stomach overhanging his belt suggested years of hard drinking.

Savannah sneered as she looked him up and down, shaking her head, she turned to Spencer. 'What woman would want a fat slob like him?'

'I don't like being insulted, bitch.' The lecherous smile evaporated from Billy Bob's face.

'I wasn't insulting you. I was describing you. And tell me Billy Bob, just out of curiosity, are your parents, siblings?'

Savannah, will you ever learn to keep your trap shut?

Ignoring Billy Bob, Savannah turned to Spencer. 'Hey Spencer, do you know what the definition of a virgin is down South?'

Spencer mouthed to Savannah, 'Enough already.'

Spencer took Savannah by the arm, attempting to lead her away from the angry Southerners. She was unstoppable, chortling. 'Yes, that's a girl who can run faster than her brothers.'

'Sorry boys, nice chatting, but we have to go.' Spencer tried steering her away from the three rednecks, but she was clearly not having it.

'I haven't finished,' Billy Bob snarled.

'Yes, you have, Billy Bob. Cos we're out of here.' Spencer whispered to Savannah, 'Please keep your big mouth shut.'

Billy Bob made the mistake of grabbing Spencer's arm; Spencer sighed and gazed at the offending limb. 'Billy Bob, you really don't want to do this.'

Spencer grasped the hand of Billy Bob and using a manoeuvre favoured by law enforcement he bent the hand back and at the same time grabbing his arm, twisting it, forcing Billy Bob to bend at the waist. 'Billy Bob, that's it. It's over. We're going home. You and the other Bobs are going to walk away and you're not going to be a problem, now, are you?'

'Son of a bitch.'

Spencer turned to Savannah. 'This guy's a slow learner. Billy Bob, we're done.' Spencer raised his foot and gave Billy Bob a kick in the behind sending him sprawling.

It seemed Billy Bob wasn't about to move on with his life, yelling out. 'Jim Bob don't let em go. I aint finished with em.'

Jim Bob thought this might be a good time to draw his weapon; his hand was on the butt of his gun, when Savannah barked, 'FBI, freeze!' She held her revolver in one hand and her badge in the other.

'Well, Jim Bob you ever see one of these before?' Savannah's gaze was clear and hard, she now stood face to face with the southerner.

'Yes, ma'am, that's a 357 Magnum.'

'Then you have some idea of what sort of damage it would do.'

'Yes Ma'am,' he said with a slow smile. 'Why that'd kill me deader'n a nigger at a Friday night lynching party.'

Savannah cocked the hammer and jammed the barrel into Jim Bob's mouth, shattering his two front teeth.

'You fucking bitch!' screamed Jim Bob as he held a bandanna up to his bleeding mouth. For a moment Spencer thought his rage might get the better of him and he might make a grab for his firearm, but Jim Bob really did understand the power of the Magnum. Spencer thought it'd filtered through the murky recesses of his grey matter that the Magnum's owner was very far removed from the sweet subservient ladies of Mississippi or whatever Southern backwater he came from.

'You dumb redneck cracker. You're God damn lucky I don't pull this trigger.' She turned to the other Southerner, who had so far remained silent. 'Hey you.'

'Yes ma'am.'

'I don't suppose your name has a Bob in it as well?'

'No ma'am, it's Earl.'

'Earl, I want you to very carefully pick up all of your pals' firearms, I mean, very, very carefully, by your thumb and forefinger. Place them on the ground, kick them towards me. I'm confiscating your weapons.'

'You got no God damn right to take our guns.' Billy Bob had clambered to his feet, as belligerent as ever.

'Yes, I can, sub section 538, paragraph 18, an agent can confiscate weapons when public safety is threatened. If you don't like it Billy Bob, I suggest you go to our head office for California in Sacramento and plead your case.'

'I really think it's time to go.' Spencer scooped up the handguns.

'Yep, not a bad result.' Savannah smiled.

Spencer gazed quizzically at her. 'Sub section 538 paragraph 18, really?'

'Sounded pretty legal didn't it.' Savannah giggled.

# CHAPTER THIRTEEN

# A PALL OF GLOOM

'God damn. How hard can it be? Come on Spencer, think of something.' Savannah frowned at her FBI coffee mug.

Spencer and Savannah had racked their brains trying to figure out how to get invited to Zachariah Colchester's love in.

Savannah was silent as she paced up and down like a caged tigress. 'It's bloody hopeless.'

Spencer frowned; he was sprawled untidily on the steel office chair. 'This shindig is for movie people, music people, movers and shakers and wannabes. I just can't see where we can fit in, or why we'd be invited. The thing is, everybody's connected. I can't imagine just what we could come up with to convince people that we're music or movie people. Hang on. I may have it!'

'I know you, you smart arse Australian funny man, you're going to come up with one of your hilarious "let's poke fun at Savannah" routines. Let's hear it.'

'How about I'm an Australian movie maker, about to make a film about a rogue female cop who goes around shooting bad guys, without resorting to things like judge and jury.'

'And let me guess. Starring yours truly?' Savannah rolled her eyes.

Spencer reclined in his chair, hands behind his head, smirking. 'Y'know, I reckon it'd work. I've come to America to find an actress for the lead role.' He warmed to his theme. 'Yep, I come to LA. I discover this unknown; hell there's heaps of unknowns in this town. And I come across this lady. You that is. Now let me see. Yep, you, working in a drugstore. One glance and I'm smitten. You're an out of work actress. I gaze into your eyes across a crowded room.'

'Drugstore.' Savannah interrupted.

'Yeah, of course, drugstore. I order a banana split. And the moment you open your mouth I can hear the voice of a cop.'

'Are you for real?'

Spencer laughed. 'I suppose it's a bit farfetched. But, let me tell you, you look like a cop, you talk like a cop. Heck you even smell like a cop.'

'Smell like a cop?'

'The perfume you wear it's, it's, well. I mean it's nice and all that but it's, well it's sorta masculine. I'd wear it.'

'That, my Australian yokel, is Kiehl's Musk. Inez gave it to me.' Spencer knew when he was defeated.

'Well, it was an idea and right at the moment that's the only idea we have.'

'If you think I'm going to pretend to be some actress floozy you can just think again. "Their eyes met across a crowded room?" Really?' Savannah snorted.

'Drugstore.'

'Spencer.' Savannah yelled. 'Forget it. All right already. No cotton pickin drugstore, no banana splits. Got it?'

There was a subdued silence as Spencer and Savannah gloomily considered their prospects.

Savannah scowled. 'You can guarantee a lot of those guests will be a part of the porn thing and the soliciting of underage girls. I have to stop this bastard. There simply has to be a way.'

One of the two phones on Savannah's desk rang, a harsh jangle, shaking them out of their thoughts of doom and despair. Savannah grabbed the phone. 'Who…Spencer Marlowe? Yes, he's here.'

Savannah handed Spencer the phone, mouthing, 'Who in hell is this?' Then came the quick smirk and in a loud voice. 'Well, well. A lady for you!'

'How's my Australian koala bear?'

'Prissy, nice to hear from you. What's up?'

Spencer held his hand over the phone, whispering to Savannah. 'This is the lady I told you about…Priscilla.'

'I'm back in town, I got your note saying you have a job. Something about an old friend. I gather that was she who answered the phone?'

'The very same. And Priss, the good news is I'm in funds. How about I buy you lunch. I'll twist Savannah's arm and invite her along. She's an old friend and my new boss.'

***

Priss, Spencer and Savannah relaxed in one of the red leather booths in Rae's Restaurant in Pico Boulevard. Not fancy, but good home-style cooking, all the favourites.

Rae's was something of an institution, a diner not a lot different from thousands of diners around the US. Its faded art deco fluorescent sign, its hastily applied green paintwork layered again and again over cracked concrete walls was tawdry but also welcoming, like a quaint rundown cottage.

There was a traditional long counter that seemed to go forever Numerous cooks scurrying, with their tall white chef's hats, worn as a badge of pride. Noise and cheerful banter accompanied the heady smells of real American food. The servings generous, verging on preposterous. A menu that hadn't changed in thirty years. Steaming, brewed coffee served in chipped enamel mugs. Clam chowder, burgers, waffles, biscuits and gravy, steaks and seafood. Ketchup. mustard and other condiment bottles adorned every table.

This was a restaurant for truckers, cab drivers, and cops on a break. And in the wee small hours the drunks, tarts, pimps and general riff raff. If you were looking for trouble it was a bad idea go to Rae's, where cops had been getting free food for decades and considered it a duty to nip any in the bud.

Savannah and Priscilla got on like a house on fire. Spencer watched with amazement as the two ladies chatted as if their friendship spanned years.

'I tell you Savannah, you should've seen Boy Wonder here giving this horrible guy Skunk a lesson on how to treat a lady.'

Savannah laughed as Priscilla retold of the encounter at the Pioneer Saloon.

'Don't worry, Priscilla we're old friends and yes I've seen Spencer's impressive street fighting skills up close.' She turned her gaze to Spencer, saying softly, 'We go back a long way don't we pardner?'

Spencer smiled back, momentarily he felt a wave of emotion sweep over him. He realised that Savannah, in spite of her homicidal ways meant a great deal to him. He reflected that if he were to be whisked back to his century, just how much he'd miss Savannah, Inez and of course Priscilla.

'Yep, the restaurant, Tony Romano.' Spencer had a swig of his Coke.

'Japan, yakuza party night. My God, that was something, wasn't it?' Savannah chuckled.

'What on Earth is all this?'

'Sorry Priss, just a bit of reminiscing. Savannah and I were involved in an FBI sting operation back in the fifties.'

'Really, I had absolutely no idea you two went back that far. Wow, Spencer I'd really like to hear your life story. You've actually told me very little.' Priscilla motioned the waiter for more coffee. 'When I first met Spencer, he was in the desert, disoriented and didn't know who he was. I guess the heat would do that to you.' She chortled. 'Well honey child, you sure got your memory back alright. So, how about it? Tell me the whole story, how come you're in the States. You married, kids? I mean give! What are you? Who are you?'

Spencer felt his heart pound, his mouth went dry.

Savannah glared at Spencer. 'Actually, I'd love to hear it also. How about it, Boy Wonder?' She smiled sweetly.

'Umm, well, it's ah…' Spencer's mind raced. What the hell, I'll just have to trot out the same old, same old. What's she going to do. Shoot me?

Spencer couldn't help himself; he laughed out loud. Pointing a finger at Savannah he chuckled. 'Well, it's a long story.'

Savannah grabbed an ice cube from her glass and threw it at him. 'One day. One day, you're going to damn well fill in the gaps.'

Prissy drained her coffee, 'How exactly did the two of you meet up again after your last, what would you call it? Adventure, mission, escapade or whatever?'

Spencer turned to Savannah. 'Well would you…'

Savannah interrupted, 'My God, it was something wasn't it. Talk about a small world. After we'd sorted out the yakuza, I remember asking Spencer where he was likely to go when we got back to the States. He said he wasn't that keen on New York, he was more a beach sorta guy. Do you remember that, Spencer?'

'I do.'

'I can remember saying to him, "I'll just bet you'd be a San Diego or Santa Monica sort of man." Surfing, the beach, all that stuff.'

Priss still looked puzzled. 'So, ok. But I still don't get the connection.'

'I'm…God damn. The hell with it.' Savannah grinned. 'Waiter, may I have a slice of the pecan pie. With ice cream please. Yeah, where was I? Well anyway, Spencer just disappeared from the hospital perhaps never to be seen again. But…but, do you know, I always had a funny feeling we'd see him again. After I returned to New York without Mr Wonderful here, I was a bit of a star. Anyway, Dale Fletcher offered me my own branch. He gave me a choice of Arkansas. Yuk. Texas. Double yuk. Or da…dah! Would you believe it? Santa God damn Monica.'

Priss laughed. 'And as they might say, "the rest is history."'

'May I speak?' Spencer eyed off the pecan pie replete with an avalanche of vanilla ice cream.

'By all means. But don't think I'm sharing. Get your own.'

'What I was going to say was…in fact, it was just a bloody coincidence. Prissy picked me up. She lives in Santa Monica, so your theory is shot full of holes. How about just a tiny bit, with just a smidgeon of ice cream?'

Savannah handed Spencer a spoon 'I'm watching. Just a touch. Ok?'

'You can trust me.'

Spencer carved a large wedge of pie and ice cream and popped it into his mouth.

'Jesus, that was half the God damn plate full. No, I win. I figured you would turn up like a bad penny, or a damn pecan pie pirate. And I was right. That's all that matters,'

They'd finished their lunch of hamburgers, and fries, washed down with bottomless cups of coffee.

'I guess that's about all we'll get about Spencer's mysterious past. So, you see Priss, what we want is to get to Colchester's party and well…we can't figure out how to go about it,' Savannah said.

'I might be able to help.' Priscilla turned to Spencer. 'You remember Dennis from the Beach Buddies? I think they're playing at that party. Dennis knew Zachariah before Zach hit the big time. This's how Dennis got the gig playing there on Saturday night. And by the way he wants to thank you. They've been making the switch to playing sort of surf-oriented songs. That ballad they did, do you remember? "Travellin round the USA" 'they changed the words to "Surfin USA," and it's been very popular…and…although it's early days, a record company has indicated if they can develop a bit of polish, there could be a recording contract. The record company thinks anything to do with surfing could be a winner.'

'That's great.' Spencer was delighted for the band. 'But how does that help us?'

'I'll have a word with Dennis, I reckon he could cook up a story that you're a recording company executive from Australia and he wants you…and of course Savannah to be at the party, to hear the Beach Buddies live.'

# CHAPTER FOURTEEN

# LET'S HAVE A PARTY

'Well, Spencer, shut the front door. God damn Priss is a miracle worker. We're going. I tell you Spencer, Colchester's days are numbered.'

'Whoa, hold it. That's one hell of a jump from going to a party and then arresting one of the biggest names in Hollywood.'

'Jesus H, you're one negative son of a bitch at times, Spencer. I tell you, I'll find something, or someone that's going to spill the beans. Yes!' Savannah triumphantly punched the air.

'All I'm saying is, tread warily. Ask too many questions and we'll be shown the door quick smart.' Spencer held up a warning finger. 'And?'

'And what?'

'If this guy is as big a wheel as you say, I'd imagine he could make your life pretty bloody difficult if he made a complaint to the Feds or the local senator, or probably even the damn governor, if he so chooses.'

Savannah scowled as she threw herself onto her oak swivel chair. 'Hell in a handbasket. I just hate it when you're right, you Australian know it all.'

'We'll be in the lion's den, that's a great start, but what I'd suggest is that once in we do a bit of networking.'

'What on Earth are you blathering about? Networking indeed. I'm going to subtly poke around and ask some questions.'

'Savannah and subtle are two words that don't exactly go together.' Spencer laughed.

'Ok, dear. What exactly is this networking bullshit?'

'All I can do is gently, softly, persuasively, chat to likely looking guests, or even better Colchester himself about porn, drugs, you know, all the nasty stuff?'

'Hey, just you hang on a minute. Who's the genuine solid gold FBI agent here and who's just the hired help? Eh? Tell me that. I'm going to ask the questions. God damn. This's my job, it's what I'm trained for. I mean what are you trained for? Hell, when it comes right down to it, I still don't know what you actually do. I know you speak Jap and you kill people with your bare hands and all that crap, but what is it that you actually do?'

Once again Spencer felt uncomfortable delving into his past. He tried to smile as he waved a hand in the air. 'Well, I have many talents but really it's, it's a…'

'Oh yeah, I know. It's a long story, right?' Savannah rolled her eyes.

'I think this might be time for some more Australian words of wisdom.'

'All right, let's have it.'

'Here's the thing. Yeah, I get it, you're the FBI agent and all that, but I can't get my head around a woman asking about porn and girls, and all that sort of stuff. It just wouldn't wash. I reckon it has to be me asking questions.'

'Well then smarty pants, how do I fit in?'

'You are going to be my assistant, that's what. A humble and I might add obedient assistant.'

'Yeah, well you can stick the obedient rubbish where the sun don't shine, I'll tell you that for nothing.' Savannah grunted.

'Savannah. We do it my way or not at all, ok?' Savannah could be stubborn and need more than anything to be in charge, but this time he knew he had the right of it. He also knew she could listen to reason, hard head or not.

Savannah hunched forward in her chair, her arms folded. She was silent for a few minutes, then wearily relented. 'You're right, I know you're right. Well then, it's all sorted, we have a plan, I guess.'

Spencer leaned onto the desk, steepling his hands under his chin. 'There is one more thing.'

'Let's hear it.' Savannah grimaced.

'Do you remember when we…ah…had the chat about…um…fashion?'

'I remember you were about as subtle as a sledgehammer. So, c'mon out with it.'

'Savannah I wasn't about to criticise, it's just that this is going to be a groovy, swinging party for hip people and you're going to have to look the part.'

'What's wrong with what I'm wearing?'

'There's nothing wrong with what you're wearing. In fact, your outfit looks quite arresting.'

'Very funny.'

'What you are wearing makes you look like exactly what you are; I'm not going unless you get some suitable gear. I would suggest you ask Priscilla to get involved. She seems quite excited about the chance to be involved in a bit of FBI drama; did I tell you she has wangled an invitation for the three of us? One thing I would say, that monstrosity of a watch you're wearing, that has to go.'

Savannah held up the watch for a closer inspection, then with a sly smile, explained, 'It's an FBI special.'

'What's so special? It's big masculine and unattractive.'

'Get over it,' she said sharply. 'The watch stays.'

# CHAPTER FIFTEEN

# BE THERE OR BE SQUARE

The black Cadillac Fleetwood limousine swished onto the circular driveway of 16 Loma Vista Drive. The uniformed driver opened the rear door with a flourish, out stepped Special Agent Savannah Steele, now Executive Assistant Savannah Steele, and Australian promoter and recording company executive, Spencer Marlowe.

Spencer thought he looked pretty cool in his light grey tapered trousers a navy-blue cashmere sports jacket, burgundy shirt and cravat, his stylish black kid leather pointed toe shoes polished to a dull sheen. He whispered to Savannah, 'I know I said wear something different, but I confess I didn't expect…awesome.'

'Is it ok?' she hissed. Savannah was wearing a fitted black sleeveless dress with a multilayered pearl necklace and elbow length black gloves.

'You look fabulous, just like Audrey Hepburn in Breakfast at Tiffany's, and those gloves hide that awful bloody watch.'

Spencer and Savannah stood awkwardly at the entrance. Two more limousines silently rolled up. A bevy of laughing tricked up ladies with their tuxedoed companions piled out giggling, their excited high-pitched chatter had a cocaine edge.

'Well here goes. Nothing ventured…' Spencer steered Savannah to the impressive entrance where a huge bald unsmiling man waited.

'G, day mate. Spencer Marlowe, from Australia and my, ah…assistant Savannah. Zachary is expecting us.'

'Zachariah, you idiot,' Savannah muttered.

The limo people pushed in front of them.

'C, mon Milo. Open the God damn door. This lady needs a drink.'

'Certainly, Miss Taylor.'

Savannah nudged Spencer, whispering 'I don't believe it! That's Elizabeth Taylor. Oh, and look, that's Gregory Peck. I'm going to ask for an autograph.'

'You bloody well aren't. Cool it.' Spencer grabbed Savannah's arm and pulled her into the foyer.

Zachariah Colchester's mansion was everything an entertainment potentate's home should be. Extravagant, with everything on a grand scale, a fifteen-car garage, a pool that could have been used for an Olympic event, only now it seemed to be the playground of a nude and semi-nude fairy-tale that had come alive. Beautiful people in a beautiful setting, this was LA on display.

Spencer felt an involuntary shudder at what was on view. *All the glitz and glamour in the world, but what about the unseen underbelly?*

Spencer and Savannah were ushered into the presence of the great man.

By any definition Colchester was imposing, his silver-grey hair longer than the current fashion. His leonine features, aquiline nose and coal black eyes, like trapdoors, magnetic and unnerving. Power with a hint of brutality emanated, subtle but unmistakeable.

'Well Spencer, Dennis tells me that you're a record company man from Australia?'

Spencer shook the proffered hand, the grip vice-like. Spencer returned the favour. Momentarily tempted to employ his Kokoro training. *Think you've got a strong grip?*

He started telling the story he had rehearsed. 'That's right Zachariah, I'm here looking at a variety of entertainment options. I thought Dennis's band the Beach Buddies had some potential; you see one of the things I'm looking for are musical acts that are on the cusp of fame that…well frankly that we can get on the cheap to do an Australian tour.'

'Well music is not really my big thing; movies are where the money is.' Zachariah nodded.

'Well, that's another aspect to our business.'

'So, you're looking at movies as well?' Zachariah studied Spencer with a cool stare.

Spencer moved closer to Zachariah. 'I've heard you might be able to put me in touch with someone who could help me source some…ah…special movies.'

'We have a variety of big budget films in the works,' he said. 'Actors and actresses on the lips of every movie-going man and woman in America. Everything's special in Hollywood, Mr Marlowe. We're putting millions of dollars into dozens of movies every year, it seems.'

The big shot was playing coy. 'I was looking for something a bit more special, Mr Colchester.'

He leaned in, smiling huge. 'Why, we're in talks to spend somewhere in the neighbourhood of thirty million on a special project we're dreaming up. A period piece about ancient Egypt. More if it goes over budget, like so many end up. Can you imagine what thirty million dollars even looks like? I can't, and I live here!' He gestured around to his enormous house, grinning and laughing.

*No doubt about it, this bloke's been powdering his nose with the expensive stuff.*

Spencer decided to go for broke. It seemed like Zachariah Colchester wanted to impress him, so he didn't mind dispensing with the subtlety a bit.

'I've got a bit of a different taste in films. I'm actually looking for the type you can't find in the theatres,' he said. 'Know of anywhere I can set eyes on that sort of thing?'

Zachariah only paused to study him for a moment before apparently deciding Spencer could be given access. The movie mogul nodded to a big man in a dinner suit that didn't quite fit.

Spencer glanced at the man. *My God, he looks like an extra in The Sopranos.* He had to be at least six foot six, Spencer estimated, and with his shaven head and unsmiling watchful visage he looked like he was designed to inflict pain.

'I think we should have a chat in private.' Zachariah smiled an easy smile. 'Milo.'

'Yes, boss.'

'Show Mr Marlowe to the den.'

Spencer turned to Savannah who had an arm linked in his. 'Ok Savannah, go and mingle. There's a good girl,' he said, patting her butt.

It was all Spencer could do to not burst out laughing. Savannah glared at him, turned on her heel and stormed off.

'Women, huh?' Spencer turned to Zachariah, winking.

'Yeah, fuck em, then fuck em off I say.' Zachariah sneered.

*Wow, you really are a sweetheart.*

'Savannah's my personal assistant while I'm in LA. I made the mistake of screwing the silly bitch. Now she thinks it's going to be marriage and kids.'

'Yeah buddy, we've all been there. Give 'em a bit of cock and you never get rid of them.' Zachariah slapped Spencer on the shoulder and laughed.

'Isn't that the truth.'

*Oh, Savannah I'm sure glad you didn't hear my bit of improvisation; you would have shot the both of us.*

Spencer breathed a sigh of relief. His misogynistic line of chat seemed to have won over Zacharia.

Spencer followed the verbally challenged Milo down a long passageway, its walls adorned with photos of prominent movie stars, all inscribed with warm greetings.

"Good luck Zach" signed Tony Curtis, another with the unsmiling visage of Yul Brynner, Cary Grant and others that Spencer hadn't heard of.

'Wow Milo, this is some pad, you've sure got a great job here working for Mr Colchester.'

Dead silence from Milo, until they'd reached their destination. In a flat dead voice, 'In here.'

Milo opened the door, motioning for Spencer to enter.

Spencer gazed around at a beautifully appointed office. Deep pile tartan carpet, added a bizarre touch of Scotland. Heavy drapes blocked what would have been an expansive view of LA. A small movie screen on the other wall seemed to be the focus, this room was about movies, as Spencer was about to find out. Nasty, unpleasant, brutal movies.

Set up on one side, a 16mm movie projector.

Spencer was focussing on two paintings on the wall next to the desk. *Picassos, both of them, unbelievable.*

All of a sudden Milo's ham like hands had unceremoniously grabbed him, slamming him against a wall, breath was forced from his lungs.

*You may be big pal but.* Spencer's immediate instinct was to retaliate, but he hesitated; Milo started frisking him.

'Open coat.'

Spencer decided instead to play the aggrieved innocent. 'Hey what'd I do? what's going on?'

Milo didn't answer, but expertly searched Spencer for weapons, and Spencer assumed some sort of listening device.

Milo finished and pointed to a chair. 'Sit. Boss comes. Ok?'

Within a few seconds Zachariah entered the room full of bonhomie. 'Sorry if Milo was a little rough.' He laughed. 'No hard feelings I hope, but I've got to be careful.'

CHAPTER SIXTEEN
# CHARLIE

Savannah had indeed stormed off in a fury, a waiter passed by with glasses of champagne. 'Hey, give me one of those.' Savannah poured the contents down her throat in one quick gulp.

She placed the glass back on the tray and grimaced. 'Christ, that's lolly water. Hey pal, is there any chance a girl could get a beer?'

'Certainly, madam.'

Savannah decided to go exploring. She found herself in a barn-sized room complete with a fully stocked bar and of all things, pinball machines. Savannah gasped at the sight of a floor to ceiling glass wall. On view outside she could see another swimming pool, lit up, with rotating colours, swirling enticingly, and beyond, laid out below them was LA, a glittering constellation of lights.

'What a view,' she murmured. 'All of this, Zach, but it's not going to save you from Savannah Steele.'

The big room was abuzz with chatter. Savannah had lost count of the famous names she'd seen. Minor film star Ronald Reagan was arguing with Marlon Brando. Popular actor Glen Ford had a young starlet hanging on his every word. The heady smell of marijuana laced the air.

She found Priscilla chatting to a long-haired man in floral shirt and tight black trousers and meandered over.

'Priscilla, you're a sight for sore eyes.'

Priscilla gave Savannah a hug and introduced her to Dennis. 'Dennis is the drummer for the Beach Buddies. They're on a break.'

In the corner of the room was a compelling looking individual playing guitar, perched on a low stool, surrounded by a group of young female admirers.

Dennis nodded at the guitar player. 'That's Charlie. He's a bit weird, but he's not a bad player. He's written some cool songs he wants us to play.'

Charlie finished his song, putting the guitar down he sauntered over to where Dennis, Priscilla and Savannah were standing.

Savannah eyed off Charlie and Charlie eyed off Savannah. She saw a short man with long lank black hair, the sleeves of his rolled-up shirt displayed identical tattoos of a woman's face on each forearm. 'How ya doin girls…Dennis.'

Savannah was taller than Charlie; she felt a slight shudder wash over her as she stared into his eyes, eyes that glowered like hot irons on the forge, scorching with the hate of ages. It was almost as if there was an immediate understanding between the two of them; it certainly wasn't mutual attraction.

'Y'know.' Scowled Charlie. 'I reckon I can smell bacon.'

'Where does bacon come from, Charlie?' Savannah's gaze was unflinching as she moved closer.

'Well Ma'am,' he whispered with a slow drawl. 'I reckon it comes from pigs.'

Savannah smiled, a smile that didn't reach her eyes. 'Yep Charlie, but do you know it also comes from razorback hogs. You know those hogs with those sharp tusks. Tusks that can rip out a man's intestines and just gobble them up as he screams and bleeds out.'

# CHAPTER SEVENTEEN
# MOVIE NIGHT

Zachariah opened a box of Monte Cristo cigars. Selecting one, he carefully nipped the end off, with a cigar cutter made of polished steel and fashioned in the shape of a lady with her legs wide apart. The cigar was placed between her legs which were snapped shut cutting the end off. Milo sprung forth a lighted match at the ready.

Leaning back in his chair Zachariah drew back on the cigar and exhaled, a plume of blue smoke eddied its way to the ceiling. His intense unblinking gaze focused on Spencer as hard and malignant as a Cobra about to strike.

'Well buddy, I hope you have deep pockets, what I'm going to show you is the best. Milo.'

Milo turned the lights. The projector whirred.

The next half hour Spencer would later reflect was one of the most difficult in his life. He witnessed depravity involving very young girls that made him feel physically ill, and then pretend like he enjoyed what he was being subjected to. As he watched the unspeakable horror unfold, he for the first time understood what men and women of law enforcement had to go through in being forced to watch such films in the line of duty.

Spencer had to not only watch, but come up with suitable comments. He was having trouble keeping his dinner down, at the same time trying to laugh and come up with ribald remarks. The only thing keeping him sane through the ordeal was the thought that either he or Savannah would have to put an end to this vile creature and for the very first time he identified with Savannah and her cavalier attitude to justice. *My God, if Savannah were to see this.*

Finally, the ordeal was over; Milo turned the projector off and turned the lights back on.

'Well Marlowe, how did you like that?'

'Well Zachariah, that was better than I expected.' He shook his head. Spencer was trying hard to focus and come up with some convincing throwaway line. He felt dirty, unclean and dispirited, he was in no way a religious man but he felt as if he needed to confess his sins. He realised his overwhelming emotion was depression, that there were many men who would pay money, good money to witness this barbarity. *Play the part, damn you, you have a job to do.*

'That little blonde in the last clip, wow…very tempting, I will say.' He winked at Zachariah.

Zachariah laughed an unpleasant sound, but his next comment chilled Spencer to the very core. 'Yeah Spencer,' he said quietly, 'tempting…and disposable.'

Spencer forced out a laugh that he hoped sounded genuine.

'Zachariah, how about you and I work out a deal. My people would be prepared to buy all that you can rustle up, and maybe even work out a recurring deal…what, monthly?'

Zachariah pursed his lips. 'What we've got is expensive merchandise, Spencer And there's demand. I can't just sell you everything.'

'I'd like to get together in the cold hard light of day and work out the financials. What do you say?'

'Call my office on Sunset, to arrange a time.' Zachariah stood up putting his hands on the desk, closing the matter. 'Is there anything else I can help you with?'

All of a sudden it seemed as if Zachariah might have been having second thoughts. He wondered if the phone call to his office tomorrow, might be met with a polite brush off. *Time to dangle another carrot.*

Spencer nodded to where Milo stood impassively, motionless as if carved in granite.

'Zachariah, there is one other thing. But it has to be in strict confidence.'

'Don't worry about Milo, he knows a few of my guilty secrets. Don't you Milo?' Colchester laughed.

A grunt from the man mountain.

'Out with it, Spencer, you're amongst friends.'

'Heroin Zachariah, I want heroin, a lot of heroin.'

'How much is a lot?' Colchester gazed thoughtfully at Spencer.

'Initially if you could supply a kilo, I want to do a quality check, I'm sure you understand.'

'And then?'

Spencer waved his hand expansively. 'At the right price,' He laughed. 'Enough to supply the whole of Australia, enough to make you a very rich man.'

'Well,' countered Zachariah, 'I'm already rich, but until my bank manager phones me and says my account is full, I can always use a bit more.'

Zachariah turned to Milo. 'Get Charlie.'

Without a word Milo exited the room.

Milo and Charlie entered the room a short and uncomfortable time later. Spencer glanced at Charlie, noting first how out of place he looked here. Unprepossessing, short, scruffy, Charlie looked like an ex-con.

'Charlie, Charlie,' Zachariah's voice boomed. 'How are you enjoying the party, how are the Beach Buddies going? Keeping the crowd entertained?'

Without waiting for an invitation Charlie flung himself down on to one of the antique Spanish Oak chairs. 'Get me a scotch and ice Milo.'

Milo hastened to obey, going to a drinks trolley set up next to the desk.

Spencer's eyes narrowed as he watched the interchange. *Clearly Charlie has some clout. Evil looking bastard.*

'Beach Buddies are doin just fine and dandy, with a bit of work I reckon they're gunna be a hit. They're starting to put surfing stuff into their act, going down real well.'

'Good, good, glad to hear it. Spencer, I'd like you to meet Charlie. He's my fixer.'

Charlie nodded at Spencer, not offering a handshake.

'Spencer wants to buy some smack. I thought you may be able to help.'

'Might be able to do that. How much?'

'Initially a kilo.'

Charlie drawled. 'That'll cost you ten G's'

Spencer couldn't wait to leave. It felt like this place and these people were going to infect him somehow. Wriggle under his skin and lay eggs. He summoned reserves of willpower and tried to force himself to stay nonchalant. 'When can we do business?'

'Tomorrow soon enough?'

'That works for me.'

CHAPTER EIGHTEEN
# MOSAIC CANYON

'Those bastards, I knew they were evil, but…' Savannah shook her head in disgust.

Spencer had recounted his movie night with Zachariah and his meeting with the malevolent Charlie. She nodded along when he mentioned Charlie, and he saw that remorseless killer come out in the tightness of her eyes. She'd clearly met him.

'Ok Savannah, what do you want to do about the purchase of the heroin?'

'I guess we have to focus on the business at hand. I've spoken to Dale Fletcher in the Brooklyn office, they're keen to bring down Zachariah Colchester and everything he's involved with. But, And this is a big but, the problem with buying the heroin through Charlie is, it's keeping Colchester at arm's length. And it's unlikely that we can pin it on him, but if you don't go ahead and buy the drugs, he's not likely to want to proceed with the movie deal; he'll smell a rat for sure. Anyway, the long and the short of it is that Dale has authorised the ten grand for the heroin, so run it by me again. What's the arrangement?'

Spencer had his hand in his pocket grasped around the cornicello. *I do so hope you're really a lucky charm.*

'I have to go on my own to a ghost town in Death Valley called Shoshone Springs. Do you know it?'

'I do.' Savannah nodded. 'It's often used as a movie set for westerns. It's pretty darn authentic. It's in…let me think…I think it's in Mosaic Canyon Road. Inez and I have driven out for the day. It's a long drive from here, it would have to be…I reckon at least four hours. Maybe a bit more. Yes, it's quite something. Overlooking the town is a rock outcrop called, if I can remember correctly, the Devil's Knob. That's about a half a mile from the town. If you climb up you get a spectacular view of the desert and what's left of the township. Spencer, are you sure you want to do this?'

'I don't think I have a choice. I'm not real comfortable carrying ten grand of Uncle Sam's cash but I can't think of an alternative. Anyway, Colchester wants to sell me his movies so there's no reason why they would double cross me.'

Chapter Nineteen
# CASTING ASPERSIONS

'Well Charlie, what do you reckon?'

'C'mon Milo, a man could die of thirst here.' Charlie waved his glass. 'This place ain't a desert, is it?'

Charlie thought the office was pretentious with its tartan carpet and priceless artwork, without asking he opened the heavy drapes and stared at the vision below of a sprawling Los Angeles and its constellation of lights.

Zacharia rose from his desk, a work of art in timber, perfect in its imperfections made more striking by the passage of time and the age in its wooden swirls.

'There's a lot of money down there, Charlie.'

'Yeah, Zach, and I want my share. You already have yours, and then some. Sonofabitch.' Charlie grinned as he waved a hand at the desk and the Picasso. Zachariah and Charlie went back a long way.

'Stick with me, Charlie. Your day will come.' Zachariah patted Charlie's shoulder.

Charlie took a healthy swig of his recharged scotch. 'Yeah, I know it will Zach. But there is one thing we gotta discuss. Have you met this guy's supposed personal assistant?'

'No…she was with Marlowe when I met him, we weren't exactly introduced…but who cares? Marlowe says he's fucking her and now she hears wedding bells. So, what's so unusual about that?' Zachariah shrugged.

'Zach you're a smart guy, but I think he's leading you down the garden path.'

'Jesus Charlie, you really are fucking paranoid. How in hell did you arrive at that conclusion?' Colchester gazed at Charlie with an expectant look on his face. He knew the man had an innate sixth sense when it came to summing up people. For Charlie there was only two species in the world, those who could help him, and those who could be exploited. There are winners and losers. Give Charlie an inch and he'd beat you to death with a claw hammer.

'She ain't no fucking PA. She's law I tell you. I've been in enough prisons and dealt with more pigs than you've had hot breakfasts.'

'What do you suggest?'

'Marlowe is driving to Shoshone Springs tomorrow. He's going to see Tex, they'll play a little "I'll show you mine if you show me yours," cash for kilo. They do the exchange…now it's going to take him at least four hours to get there. Marlowe's shooting for two pm. What I suggest is, phone Australia. I know a guy who's in the rackets in a place called Kings Cross, which is in Sydney. He knows everyone who's anyone. If Marlowe is the big shot he claims to be, someone will have heard of him.' Charlie took another long pull on his scotch. 'Zach,' Charlie implored, 'we've got a sweet setup here. It's fucking cherry: the girls, the movies, the drugs. Let's not end up ass over teakettle because of some damn Aussie we've never heard of, and this Savannah bitch.'

# CHAPTER TWENTY

# LOVE THAT CAR

'I'm not real happy with you going to meet this guy Tex on your own, Spencer. How about if I tag along, they couldn't object surely?'

Spencer reclined on the steel chair in Savannah's office, manoeuvring to try and get comfortable. *This chair has to have been designed for someone with a body shaped like a pretzel.* He climbed to his feet and stretched, gazing through the window at bustling Wilshire Boulevarde. Spencer watched as red turned to green and vehicles started to move like crawling snails eager for inches of space to slide through.

He turned and faced Savannah, 'Don't worry. They want to sell the heroin, we want to buy. They believe I'm going to pay big bucks for their movies. What could go wrong? I'll head off about ten in the morning, apparently this guy Tex will be waiting; I'm expected sometime around two in the afternoon. The only thing concerning me is that bloody Government issue battleship grey car of yours. It just shrieks law enforcement.'

'Come out to the car park, I've got something to show you.'

Savannah's office was nondescript with nothing to suggest it was FBI. There was a sign emblazoned on the opaque glass of the front door saying, "Community Intervention

Programme" and a slogan, "This is your community, and we value your input."

'What on Earth does the sign refer to?' Spencer waved a hand at the door.

Savannah gazed at the sign as if she hadn't noticed it before. 'Do you know, I actually have no idea, but it was Dale Fletcher's idea to keep a low profile. He wants to have agents, more or less incognito.'

A motley collection of vehicles in the car park contributed to the picture of an average slightly down at heel suburban strip mall. A pre-war Chevrolet and some other vehicles Spencer didn't recognise sat parked. But there, in all its glory, sat poised as if it was just waiting for someone to trigger it, was a gleaming red convertible. Spencer was speechless; this sleek low slung Detroit masterpiece looked like a cruise missile on wheels. 'My God, what is it?'

'That, my dear, is the latest model Ford Thunderbird complete with a 390 cubic inch v8.' Savannah chuckled. 'And get this, it has the trio of two-barrel Holley carburettors and...' Savannah threw her hands in the air. 'Are you listening?'

'Of course. Riveting. Umm, is that for me?'

'So help me. Pearl before swine,' Savannah muttered. 'We figured that you had to turn up in something befitting your status as a big-time movie, rock and roll promoter type of guy. Oh, and it develops 340 brake horsepower. Jesus, I give up.'

'No, seriously, I love it. I mean, Hoddy carburettors, well everyone...um loves them. Anyway, it sure doesn't look like FBI. Whose is it?'

'We confiscated it from one of the local hoods who'd been involved in drugs, prostitution and general sleaziness. And by the way, that's Holley, not Hoddy'.

Spencer ran his hand over the gleaming paintwork. He stepped back, admiring its classic aerodynamic design, with its chrome hubcaps, looking like the wheels on a Roman Chariot. A chariot with white sidewalls and lashings of chrome, a masterpiece in steel.

'And what happened to the bad guy? I suppose you shot him?'

'Spencer,' she snapped, 'I don't shoot everyone. For your information he's doing ten years on the Rock, ok?'

***

A cobalt blue, cloudless California day greeted Spencer when he climbed into the T Bird, checking his wrist for the Rolex. *Damnit, I miss that watch.*

'Hey how about this?' The trim was Town Red. It had bucket seats with a wide chrome finished centre console. The white Bakelite steering wheel was twice the size of those in later model cars.

'Now let's see. Instrumentation. A speedometer and a clock. Well, I guess there's no such thing as AC or cruise control.'

Spencer opened the driver's door with a click and gently slid the steering column to one side. 'My God, cars from my century don't have a movable steering column. Cool, very cool. Surprise surprise, it has a clock. 9:12 am, perfect.'

The big V8 came to life with a gentle burble. Spencer smiled at the not unpleasant odour of leaded petrol; the automatic transmission was smooth as silk.

'Oh boy, I'm going to enjoy this trip.' Spencer grinned from ear to ear as the Thunderbird glided out of the car park. He tentatively put his foot down, revelling in the rich sound of the exhaust as he shot onto highway US 395. The sleek convertible leapt forward like a rocket sled, leaving all other vehicles in its wake. With the wind in his hair, he was able for a minute to take his mind off the mission and its possible dangers.

Spencer was still absorbing all the interior of the T Bird had to offer as he stretched out in the cockpit, like red leather seats. He glanced at the ribbed chrome dash and noticed the tank was full. He instinctively reached for non-existent seatbelts. Although bright and flashy, there was little in the way of instrumentation. 'I think aircon might have come in handy. Cruise control, no bloody cruise…archaic.'

Everything was still new for Spencer, a world looking like an endless rerun of old black and white TV shows. He saw a billboard for Nabisco biscuits with a wholesome looking boy wearing a Nabisco hat and holding a cookie in his hand. Another billboard boldly screamed its message, "Hacienda Airlines Champagne tour to Las Vegas, only twenty-four dollars."

He watched the hot brown morning light through his recently acquired aviator shades. Palm trees. Palm trees everywhere. More billboards, and for Spencer a most astonishing array of cars. Not the generic bland offerings from his century but sleek finned Cadillacs old Chevys, a Ford V8 woody station wagon, its roof piled high with surfboards and of course a Volkswagen Kombi hand painted in bright colours, emblazoned with the sign, "Peace not War."

Spencer rapidly left the suburbs behind; he was soon approaching the charter city of Lancaster in the Antelope Valley on the edge of the Mojave Desert. Spencer was enjoying himself. The yellow poppies were blooming, with the unique peppery scent teasing his nostrils. There were numerous Joshua trees named by early Mormon settlers. The tree's role in guiding them through the desert and its unique shape had reminded them of a biblical story when Joshua reaches his hands up to the sky in prayer.

Lancaster, he decided, was a pleasant city: orderly, neat. This was small town America. It was hard to imagine big city crime in this quaint Marty McFly kind of burg. This certainly appeared to be a city of homespun values, with every second home displayed the Stars and Stripes. A town with war veterans raising kids, going to church and living the post-war American dream.

As Spencer cruised slowly through Lancaster, he observed a little league baseball team in El Dorado Park all yelling excitedly, with proud parents watching on. When they spotted the Thunderbird, play stopped. The team all waved. Spencer waved back, honking the horn. He smiled at the sight of these youngsters playing the national game. *I don't think they see too many T Birds in Lancaster.*

For a brief moment he dwelt upon his childhood in Australia and the impromptu cricket matches he and his friends played in the blistering summer sun. Spencer had been a pretty fair fast bowler, sending the red leather six stitcher flying down the pitch with deadly accuracy.

The beauty of the Lancaster countryside with its poppies and fields of alfalfa, onions and carrots had now morphed into the forbidding Searles Valley, harsh dry and brutal.

The barren valley with its featureless terrain had the effect of jolting Spencer into reality. *Perhaps Savannah is right, maybe things won't go as planned.*

He felt in his pocket for the reassurance of his lucky silver cornicello. Finding it he placed it to his lips.

CHAPTER TWENTY-ONE
# THE LADY GOES A HUNTING

Savannah had risen at dawn. Inez was already bustling around the kitchen preparing breakfast and coffee. 'Inez darling, you didn't have to get up this early,' Savannah protested.

'I wasn't about to let you go without a decent breakfast and by the way I saw what you placed in the trunk. You thought I didn't see, didn't you? Now, sit down, eat!'

Savannah didn't answer as she sat down to a plate of eggs over easy, crispy bacon and a short stack with maple syrup. She attacked the breakfast with relish.

'That was great. Now I have to go.'

'I know you don't want to talk about your job. I know you don't want to worry me. Please be careful.' Inez put her arms around Savannah.

'I'm always careful, don't worry.' Savannah kissed her lightly on the lips.

The sun was rising like a flower opening as Savannah fired up the Plymouth and headed northeast to face the day. She punched in a local station on the press button radio. Jim Reeves was warbling 'He'll Have to Go.' Savannah turned up the volume and muttered. 'Yes Zachariah, you'll have to go, you sonofabitch. Savannah Steele's coming for you.'

Inez gazed out their living room window at the rapidly disappearing Plymouth, she crossed herself. '*Vaya con dios*, my darling.'

# CHAPTER TWENTY-TWO

# I WENT TO THE DESERT ON A HORSE WITH NO NAME

Sweat rolled down Spencer's face as the heat started to intensify. The Thunderbird gobbled up the miles as it entered Death Valley. Spencer shuddered involuntarily at the very name. *My God, I can see how it earned the title.*

The rolling sand dunes at Mesquite flats spread out in front of him like a yellow and brown rippled carpet. *This's what the Sahara would look like.*

Surprisingly, it wasn't devoid of life; there was an abundance of wildflowers and a few big horn sheep that looked like they were probably wild. This was the unsmiling desert. How many early pioneers perished in this God forsaken wilderness, he wondered. He then passed the sign for Furnace Creek and Red Rock Randsburg Road. Finally, he made a right into Mosaic Canyon Road. The blistering black top seemed to radiate heat. The horizon, a shimmering wavy brown mirage.

'I reckon you could just about fry a bloody egg on that tarmac.' Spencer grabbed a colourful bandana Inez had given him, wiping his face and neck. The sweat was running in rivulets. His hands slippery on the wheel.

In the distance dominating the landscape, squatted the brooding sentinel, the rock formation, Devil's Knob.

Death Valley is one of the hottest places on Earth. It occurred to Spencer that driving with the top down probably hadn't been such a good idea.

And then, there it was, the ghost town Shoshone Springs. *Well, this is it.*

Spencer idled the Thunderbird sedately down the main street, in fact the only street of Shoshone Springs.

This looks like Dodge City. Where's Wyatt Earp?

Spencer could see the livery stable, the general store, the bank and the saloon. What he couldn't see were any people. Tumbleweeds gently rolled as if searching for lodgings. Everything looked old, decaying, and neglected. Spencer was taken aback at the sight of a gallows erected in front of the courthouse.

'Now that has to be part of the movie set.' Spencer still thought this particular relic was a bit confronting.

A lone flagpole with a faded Confederate flag sat resolutely in front of the old courthouse. The Gold Nugget trading post had a wooden sign advertising Bull Durham Tobacco, creaking in the wind, as it swung gently on rusty hinges. Shoshone Springs had in fact been resurrected many times to be used as the set for western movies. John Wayne, Kevin Costner and Gary Cooper had all been in gunfights on this piece of western real-estate.

As the Thunderbird slowed to a crawl, there was a shout. 'Hold it right there, pardner.'

*This has to be Tex.*

Strolling out of the saloon was a lanky man, tall with a stained, fringed western shirt, blue jeans, black Stetson, riding boots and…*I don't believe it.* Tex was also equipped with a very businesslike Colt 0.44 six shooter in a holster, low slung on his hip as if he was expecting the Clanton Brothers to come out shooting.

Tex shook a Marlboro cigarette from a soft pack, carefully lighting it with a chrome Zippo, his cupped hand shielding the flame from the breeze. Standing with his Stetson pulled low and his legs apart Spencer thought he looked like a gunfighter waiting to draw.

Spencer climbed out of the T Bird grateful for the chance to stretch his legs. 'You're Tex?' Spencer felt that he was stating the obvious. Tex stared his unsmiling visage, displaying no emotion.

'Did you bring the ten G's?' Tex clearly wasn't one for small talk.

Spencer nodded. 'Do you have what I came for?'

'Waal,' Tex sneered with a mean chuckle sending shivers up Spencer's spine, 'there's been a bit of a delay, so if you just hand over the ten big ones you can come back later for the smack.'

Tex now leaned against a hitching rail, his right hand resting on his Colt. A venomous sneer on his face.

'If you don't have what I came for, I'm heading back to LA.' Spencer started to have a sinking feeling; Tex was too far away for him to unleash his karate skills.

Tex demonstrated the 0.44 wasn't just for show, he sprung forward. the gun appeared in his hand with a speed Spencer thought was very impressive. He threw the smouldering cigarette butt to the ground. 'Hand over the cash, sucker.'

## CHAPTER TWENTY-THREE
# A ONE-SIDED GUNFIGHT

She was hot and sweaty; there were ants, probably unused to human flesh and very keen on exploring every exposed piece of edible meat. Perspiration ran in rivulets down her face.

'Jesus H Christ, you little bastards leave me alone.' She squashed an ant that decided the interior of her ear presented interesting possibilities.

Lying in a prone position high up on Devil's Knob, she had her M14 7.62 MM Garand Rifle with its Lyman Alaskan fixed power telescopic sight, complete with a rubber eyepiece to block out ambient light. This particular weapon had been the sniper rifle of choice for the US Army since the Korean War. In the hands of an expert this was a devastating weapon. She was such an expert. She lay patiently, trying to ignore the ants, the sun and the perspiration, part of her FBI training was to lie motionless for hours in all weather conditions. She could live with the ants. This lady was the perfect killing machine. 'Come on baby, just you wait and see what Aunty Sav has for you.'

***

*What to do? This's going downhill rapidly.* Spencer turned to the Thunderbird. The cash was in the glove compartment. His mind raced.

'Real slow now, pardner.' Tex grinned as he barked his command.

With heavy heart and a feeling of dread Spencer removed the bag with the cash and held it out to Tex. *Just come a bit closer, sunshine.*

'Throw the bag over here.' Tex laughed, a hoarse unpleasant sound.

Spencer threw the bag at Tex's feet; a little cloud of dust eddied and quickly settled. Tex raised the 0.44. The pistol was now at waist height. Spencer felt as if time stood still. He was waiting for the handgun to explode and propel its lethal chunk of lead into his waiting body.

In those few seconds his life and adventures actually did flash through his mind at breakneck speed like a movie on a fast wind. He had a vision of wartime Singapore, of his ally Horse, in Hawaii, sneering, and muttering 'Dey was cream puffs, boss.' He saw the smiling ebullient mobster Tony Romano the arch villain in the Dale Fletcher dubbed mission, "The Manhattan Sting." Was this where it all ended, a bloody corpse on a movie set western street? He saw the smiling face of Michiyo and his beautiful baby daughter Trilby. *Can it really end like this?*

There was no sound. Tex's head exploded. In that millisecond it looked like a watermelon shot at close range, but instead of red fruit with black seeds there was bone, flesh and grey brain matter.

The sonic boom of the lethal 7.62 mm round followed a split second later.

Spencer stood motionless, aghast. His chest heaved; he was weak at the knees. The absolute realisation he must have been literally a split second from death, hit home with a vengeance. But who…? *Savannah, has to be.*

As the flies descended on the corpse, Spencer swivelled around trying to get an idea of where the shot came from. He glanced at Devil's Knob. *Can't be. That has to be at least a half mile away.*

Spencer was suddenly distracted by a chorus of voices calling out. Young voices. Female voices. '*Ayuda, por favor Señor, por favour.*'

Spencer didn't speak Spanish but his reasonable Italian was very similar to the Spanish and the distress in these young voices didn't need an interpreter.

He tracked down the sound, which originated from the livery stable. He flung open the old slatted oaken doors, gasping in horror. A large very modern and very businesslike steel cage stood in the centre of the room, and inside were a dozen young girls. The stench was horrific. A few buckets had been provided for the human waste, but the heat was intense and not helping. The girls looked like they at least had been fed, but there was no water in sight. A very young girl no more than thirteen thrust a slim brown arm through the bars, her big black eyes radiated a mixture of fear and hope. '*Señor, agua. Por favour agua.*'

Now there were more arms thrusting out of the cage, the terror on the girl's faces was heartbreaking. 'I'll get you out of here,' he said lamely.

Spencer stood without moving for several moments, trying to push past his horror and actually do what they were begging for.

A vehicle in a hurry. Clouds of dust created a mini tornado as an automobile in the distance sped towards Shoshone Springs. *Friend or foe?*

After a moment of panic, he found water and placed buckets filled with the precious liquid not far from the cage. '*Vado a liberati*' Which was Italian but close enough to Spanish for the girls to understand.

*Now, the keys, where are the keys?*

Spencer decided a quick search of the dead Texan's pockets might reveal the whereabouts. Grimacing as he delved through Tex's blue jeans, Spencer's stomach lurched as he saw the swarm of big black flies descending on Tex's blood and bone. One of Tex's dead eyes appeared to be resolutely watching Spencer as he foraged through the dead man's pockets.

The dust cloud now a mini tornado, the full-throated roar of a V8 motor shattering like glass, the desert silence.

Relief surged through Spencer as he identified the welcome profile of the Plymouth, its sharklike fins making it immediately identifiable.

Spencer located the keys in the late Tex's jeans; he tried to keep his eyes off the bloody, pulpy mess, once a man's head. The flies continued to descend en masse. Spencer made a half-hearted attempt to shoo them. The powerful sweep of flapping wings diverted his attention. The vulture descended gracefully onto a disused water tower. Hooded eyes focussed on the repast waiting like a banquet for kings. Spencer shuddered at the entire scene; death he could see was good news for some.

Spencer grinned as Savannah's automobile tore down the street and screeched to a halt, she gazed approvingly at the corpse 'Not a bad shot. What do you reckon, Spencer? I hit the sonofabitch exactly where I intended.'

'Well, I'm grateful you've given up on those hollow point rounds it's a big enough mess as it is. Anyhow we have a more urgent problem at the moment. Follow me.'

Savannah held a hand to her face as she saw the horror of the imprisoned and petrified girls. 'We have to get them out.'

Spencer held up the set of keys that he had taken from the Texan.

*** 

Shoshone Springs now had more visitors than it had had in the last fifty years. Savannah had driven to a homestead and telephoned for backup, and a collection of no-nonsense police and FBI agents from LA, Bakersfield and even Las Vegas had swarmed the place.

The scene looked like a cop convention with police cruisers from several counties, hard-eyed men with aviator glasses, some with Stetsons, some with the traditional peaked caps, all appalled at the plight of the girls. There were ribald comments about the corpse that lay on display until the crime scene was secured.

'Son of a bitch sure got what he deserved.' Another pointed at the growing number of vultures waiting patiently.

'How's about we leave him? Our feathered friends will have him picked clean in no time.'

Through an interpreter the girls told their tale of horrors. Recruited in Badiraguato, a small town in Mexico by a man named Emilio Bustillos they'd been seduced by the promise of lucrative jobs.

The true horror started to unfold when the girls told of what they had been subjected to.

A young girl no more than fourteen took Spencer and Savannah to the set. In the back of the saloon a large room set up as a bedroom, cameras and lights still in place. Here Bella explained in a matter-of-fact tone how she and the others were violently raped by a number of men while being filmed.

'These men Bella, did you hear a name?' Savannah asked in Spanish, gently holding the girls hand.

'I think one was Charlie. he was a short man.' Bella started to cry. 'He said "do what I want or you will wind up like the others." I didn't know what he meant but I knew I had to pretend to enjoy what he did. One of the other men was a big man, a very big man, I think his name was Milo, he wasn't as cruel as Charlie.'

Savannah was in tears as she listened to Bella. She whispered to Spencer. 'If ever you criticise me for shooting the people who did this…I swear.'

'You swear…what? You'll shoot me as well?'

'I'm sorry Spencer, but this is just about the worst thing that I've ever seen and we, that is you and me, know absolutely that Zachariah's dirty fingerprints are all over this and that little psychopath Charlie and…and obviously that creepy manservant Milo. And let me tell you that animal Zachariah has enough money and influence to stay of jail probably forever. Do you know what Zachariah Colchester's biggest problem is?'

Spencer shook his head. Savannah whispered, 'Me.' She jabbed a finger at her chest. 'Me. Savannah Steele, I will not rest until the bastard is dead, along with Charlie and Milo. And guess what? I don't give a fuck about due process.'

Savannah rarely swore, for a fleeting moment Spencer almost felt sorry for the perpetrators of these evil crimes. *If you only knew what was coming after you.*

## CHAPTER TWENTY-FOUR
# IT GETS WORSE

'*Señor, Señor.*' A little girl, perhaps the youngest, tugged Spencer's sleeve. '*Ven, vent e maestro.*' Spencer's basic understanding of the language, and the plaintive expression on the girl's face was easy to read.

Spencer and Savannah followed this diminutive child to the town's Boot Hill where yesterday's outlaws were buried.

Boot Hill was indeed a hill, the girl strode confidently up the mound holding Savannah's hand firmly in hers. '*Sigueme Mama.*'

Savannah glanced at Spencer the tears running down her face. Spencer was grim faced knowing exactly what they would find, the only question rampaging through his mind. *How many?*

On the lee side a mechanical digger squatted with the jaws of its mechanical mouth open, poised like a mythical beast waiting to pounce on its unsuspecting prey. The whole scene looked like a horror movie set. It was graphic. It was unmistakable.

'I was hoping against hope that it wasn't going to be this.' Savannah grabbed Spencer's arm.

In front of them were eight identical holes in the ground, next to it at least a dozen freshly heaped piles of dirt. This picture of horror was as descriptive as it was obvious.

***

In the days that turned into weeks, gradually piece by piece like a giant jigsaw the ghastly magnitude of the crime unfolded.

The girls were recruited from poor families from rural Mexico, lured to the US with the promise of good jobs and a better life. From the moment they arrived in Shoshone Springs their lives were brutal and short. The girls were subjected to hideous inhumanities, all recorded in glorious technicolour before they were summarily executed.

'*And so disposable.*' Zachariah's words rang in Spencer's ears.

As Spencer and Savannah pored over what in fact turned out to be minimal evidence in her FBI building, Savannah threw her arms up in disgust. 'Do you know, there's not a God damn thing we can use against Colchester. The bastard would laugh us out of court.'

'What about Charlie…and Milo?' Spencer asked. They meant nothing to her without getting Colchester, he knew.

She sprang to her feet, and without a word Spencer began to follow her. He made it a point to give his cold cup of God-awful coffee an accusing glare as he left it behind. 'Do you know what I think?' she asked.

*No but I bet it involves killing someone.*

They left the nondescript room where the evidence was splayed out on a large conference table, and tacked up on the walls with labels. Savannah made straight for her office.

'How do you feel about a trip to sun drenched Mexico?' Suddenly Savannah's face was wreathed in a beatific smile.

'What do you hope to achieve in Mexico?' Spencer countered.

'Well…I would really like to have a chat with Señor Bustillos. And well…you know have a little tour of Mexico. See the sights. That sort of thing. But primarily that little chat with the Señor. Maybe we'll get him to see the error of his ways.'

'A chat…c'mon Savannah, seriously.' Spencer couldn't help himself. He broke out into raucous laughter.

'Honestly Spencer, I really want to have a chat, I want him to give us all the evidence to put Colchester away.' Savannah managed to look self-righteous.

Spencer wiped tears from his eyes. 'I can see it all now: good morning, Señor Bustillos, we're with the FBI from California and if it's not too much trouble could you please tell us all about your business dealings with Zachariah Colchester? Hell's bells Savannah, this guy would have to be a powerful warlord, drug baron, call him what you will. He'll be surrounded by gun toting thugs. You have no jurisdiction. Get real, woman. This sounds like a bloody suicide mission. Even if we could get to this guy, do you think for one cotton picken minute he would tell you anything and let you walk out of there alive?'

'Ok I admit we would have to be…ah… persuasive.'

'Savannah, weren't you listening? The FBI has no jurisdiction in Mexico.'

'Details Spencer…details, I'm sure that I can appeal to the Señor's better nature and get him to help with my enquiries.' Savannah was sprawled on the wooden chair at her desk absentmindedly swivelling it from side to side on its rotating base. The unsmiling faces of past Presidents and J Edgar Hoover himself presided over the scene in their framed black and white photos.

Spencer sat quietly for a moment pondering the situation. The plight of these innocent children and those that had already been murdered had disturbed him more than anything that he had encountered on his previous trips to the past. Maybe, just maybe?

The tumultuous events since he'd arrived in 1961 California had helped to compartmentalise his life in the next century, but seeing the plight of these innocent Mexican girls forced him to dwell upon his young daughter Trilby and he quickly came to the conclusion that this evil had to be stopped, he thrust his hand into his pocket and felt the reassuring outline of the cornicello. 'I'm in.'

# CHAPTER TWENTY-FIVE

# WHO THE HELL DO YOU THINK YOU ARE?

'Where are we going?' Spencer awoke to the sound of Savannah knocking on the door of Priscilla's condo. He'd barely managed to slip on some board shorts and open the door, sure Savannah was going to bust it down.

She frowned at his sunny t-shirt and shorts. 'Do you own a suit?'

'What? No, I don't have a suit.'

'All right, trousers, white shirt and a tie. I know you have those.'

'Like I said, what's happening?'

'I rang Dale and told him all about the girls, Tex, Charlie, Milo, Zachariah. He said we have to go to the FBI in Roseville Sacramento. We have to see the Special Agent in charge, a David Biddy. It's a courtesy thing, we have to fill him in on all the details. Dale's called him. He's expecting us.'

Some twenty minutes later, Spencer piled into the car carrying a mug of coffee. 'You're kidding me, it's at least a six-hour drive.' Spencer remembered part of the route from being with Priss on the drive from Nevada.

The car roared onto US 101. Big finned Chevrolets, Ford station wagons and pre-world war Buicks, Cadillacs and

Chryslers seemed to scatter as the Plymouth barged through with its horn blaring.

'In a bit of a hurry, are we?' Spencer closed his eyes as Savannah squeezed between a lumbering K model International truck and a Willy's Jeep.

'What? It's not my fault everyone's so God damn slow.' Savannah sounded the horn at a two-door Pontiac Catalina with smoke billowing from its exhaust.

Spencer cast his mind back to when Michiyo would chide him about driving too fast in his BMW. 'Spencer, just remember you have a little daughter in the car.'

'I guess you're not telling this guy Biddy about our planned little trip to Mexico?'

Savannah rolled her eyes.

Just after two o'clock they arrived at the three-story grey and white stucco FBI building in Roseville, Sacramento. Savannah wound down her window, flashing her badge at the security guy.

'By the way, what exactly is my job title?' Spencer asked.

'Would you believe, "office manager" is what Dale has you classified as?'

The secretary ushered them into David Biddy's office.

Savannah and Spencer exchanged glances at the sight of Agent in Charge, David Biddy. His sparse winter-white hair, alcohol ravaged pouchy eyes and red-veined cheeks made him look like a man who'd given up on life.

Lighting a cigarette, wheezing and coughing, he didn't stand.

'Have a seat. Fletcher told me about it all, but let's hear it from the horse's mouth, Agent Steele.' He directed his question to Spencer.

'This is Special Agent Savannah Steele.' Spencer pointed at Savannah.

'Oh really? Yeah, I guess I forgot. A female agent…isn't that nice? Who the hell are you then?' he glared at Spencer.

'I'm the office manager. I've been appointed by Dale Fletcher.'

'I see. Ok, Steele, I really don't know why I need to hear the story again; it doesn't sound like it's that important.'

Spencer could almost feel Savannah's anger rising to the surface. 'With all due respect sir, this is a major crime. Young girls taken from Mexico, then filmed being raped and murdered. This is a heinous crime that in my opinion is unprecedented and I respectfully request the full resources of the FBI are brought to bear in catching the perpetrators. I already have…'

'You listen to me, little lady, I well understand how all of this offends your female sensibilities…'

'Just wait one…'

'Don't interrupt. What I see plain as day, is a gaggle of wetback prostitutes who are bitching that they didn't get a square deal from their pimps. If some of them have died you can bet your bottom dollar they've overdosed on heroin. For Christ's sake woman, why would they kill them? They're worth more money alive than dead. Now that's it. Leave it alone. If the cops from that jurisdiction want to get involved that's up to them. This meeting is over. Hettie!' Biddy yelled. 'Show our guests out, would you please.'

***

'Charlie, what the fuck happened?'

Zachariah paced the lounge room, a glass of malt scotch with ice in hand.

Charlie sauntered over to the drinks trolley and poured himself a large bourbon.

'Well, as you know, nobody in Sydney has heard of this guy Marlowe. So exactly who the fuck he is, I don't know.'

'What about this Savannah broad?'

'So far we got bupkis on her too.'

'You still think she's law…FBI maybe?'

'Jury's still out. I know the feds have been planting some agents in unmarked offices and they keep a low profile. Could be one of those. Though why the feds would have an Aussie working for them? Beats me.'

'Tell me how much you know for sure.' Zachariah gulped a mouthful of scotch.

'I have some contacts in the cops but they've got fuck all. They couldn't rub two brain cells between them to make a spark. Tex is toast.' He chuckled at his own joke. 'The girls have been released, obviously.'

'Hell, Charlie this is serious.'

'Get a grip, Zach. Nothing links us to Shoshone Springs; I made damn sure of that. Ok, we've lost the town, the film setup and some equipment. A handful of Mexican girls. That's all she wrote. It seems Marlowe must have blew Tex's head clear off, which is a bit of a surprise. He was no fool and I tell you he was as quick as Billy the Kid with that 0.44 0f his. Tex wasn't carrying any smack because he was going to shoot Marlowe and take the 10 G's Marlowe was packing. So, what the fuck are you worried about? It's a blip on the radar. My bet is the cops or the feds won't come knocking. If they do, just throw one of your high-priced lawyers at him.'

# CHAPTER TWENTY-SIX
# FAREWELL

'Waiter, another round of Coronas please.'

Empty bottles, jostled for space on the worn timber table, next to the remains of yellow fish tuna and halibut. There was an undercurrent of trepidation; Spencer and Savannah were going to journey into the unknown. Spencer mentally kicked himself for so readily agreeing to this absurdly dangerous trip, Savannah's blithe gung-ho enthusiasm didn't stand up well to scrutiny in the cold hard light of day.

Spencer, Savannah, Inez and Priscilla were having a farewell dinner at the Albright seafood restaurant on Santa Monica pier.

'Savannah won't tell me why exactly she and Spencer are going to Mexico; do you have any idea, Priscilla?' Inez held a handkerchief, nervously screwing it into a ball.

'Inez, I've seen this Aussie warrior in action. I think Savannah will be in safe hands.'

If you had seen Savannah in action, you might wonder who was protecting who. Spencer laughed to himself.

Spencer couldn't help reflecting on the absurdity of life. Here he was sharing a meal with Savannah, who he first met in New York in 1955 when they were both involved in a perilous adventure to bring down Mafia crime lord Tony

Romano, then there was the utterly charming and delightful Priscilla who saved his bacon, picking him up in the middle of a very inhospitable desert, and of course Inez, the statuesque Colombian beauty who was Savannah's soulmate. *Unless I'd seen it, I wouldn't have believed it. Inez is absolutely the yin to Savannah's yang. This lady will be the one to temper Savannah's impulsive desire to singlehandedly wipe evil off the face of the Earth.*

The more Spencer engaged in conversation the more he realised Inez was a lady of enormous depth: she was fluent in several languages and surprisingly she had decided to learn Japanese when Savannah had introduced her to the cuisine. Inez and Spencer would chatter away in this complex language until invariably Savannah would yell, 'Enough already!' Inez and Spencer would laugh until Inez would put a consoling arm around her. 'Sorry Savannah, but I don't get a lot of chance to practice.'

***

The light of dawn cast a rosy hue, glimpses of the ocean and the gentle sounds of waves breaking created an atmosphere of normality. Spencer could make out the early morning workers arriving at the pier, a day like any other.

The Plymouth rolled quietly into the parking lot of Priscilla's condominium; Spencer watching from the courtyard. He grabbed his holdall packed with the essentials. Savannah had assured him it would be a quick trip. Casting a backward glance at this comfortable apartment that had become his oasis in a sea of turbulence, he shut the door quietly, and strode to the waiting automobile.

*Why do I get the feeling this isn't going to be quite as straightforward as Savannah likes to make out?*

'Good morning intrepid FBI agent Steele. Are you ready to fight evil in sunny Mexico? Oh, and I hadn't actually given it a lot of thought, but what about weapons? Surely we can't just waltz through Checkpoint Charlie with a pistol or two?'

'Good morning to you, Spencer. And…um…yes weapons. Well, I guess that's my department, isn't it?' She smiled nervously.

'Whoa girl, just hang on a minute. I'm in this vehicle as well as you. Now, come clean about any guns. It's my neck on the line as well. I don't fancy a few years in the hellhole of a Mexican jail because you've brought a treasure trove of weapons with you.'

'Spencer dear, don't worry about a thing. You're allowed to carry a small handgun for protection. In any case if there's any problem we can bribe the border guards. Hell, they wouldn't particularly care what you took into Mexico so long as the bribe was big enough. So, bleeding heart Marlowe, just sit back and enjoy the ride, ok?'

Spencer and Savannah were lost in their own private thoughts as she powered the big sedan to San Diego, then on to Tijuana. The early morning traffic was sprinkled across the blacktop, as if the roads were a playset that only came with a few cars. LA was yet to come alive.

'What time do we get to Mexico?' Spencer settled back, and tried to enjoy the drive.

'Couple of hours.'

Spencer couldn't help having visions of moustachioed Mexican officers finding the weapons, pistol whipping them, then bundling them off to an unspeakable prison. But as he glanced sideways at Savannah his mood lightened. Her fingers tapped time to the drumbeat of a trite pop record, 'Running Bear', as the song blasted from the radio. Spencer had been intrigued by '60s music and the stories woven into the lyrics.

'You ok?' Savannah tilted her head quizzically.

'Yeah, I guess. I was thinking about a song I heard the other day; it was by The Kingston Trio it was all about the Tijuana jail. It was just a song, but, well you know…'

'Spencer, believe me, this is the easy bit. I'll smile sweetly, bat my eyelashes and they'll be like putty in my hands.'

'Smile sweetly, bat your eyelashes? This I gotta see.'

The border crossing was uneventful as bored US officials waved them through. The equally bored Mexican officials looked in their car briefly. When Savannah started gushing about their honeymoon, they quickly told them to move along.

'Here we are in Mexico, where to from here?'

Savannah finally snapped out of her subdued silence. 'This is just great, isn't it?'

The transformation from the US was like a time warp; old cars, horse and carts, men wearing wide-brimmed sombreros, baja jackets and ponchos. Women mingled, chatting amongst themselves, their colourful ankle length skirts and intricate embroidered and beaded blouses adding a vibrant splash of colour.

'You wouldn't guess in a million years what first triggered my love affair with Mexico?'

'You're absolutely correct, Savannah, no idea. Hang on, I know?'

'I know you. You're going to come up with some liberal criticism of me and my methods. Ok let's hear it funny man.'

'You got me. I was going to suggest you had some fond memories of killing some poor Mexican brigands. Perhaps you caught them stealing the hubcaps from your car.'

'Really this's so silly, but when I was a girl, I used to go to the movies and my absolute favourite was the Cisco Kid.'

'I think I remember, and he had a fat jolly sidekick, what was his name?' Spencer vaguely remembered seeing reruns of the old movies on television.

'That was Pancho. I just loved it. After Cisco and Pancho had saved the damsels in distress they'd ride off into the sunset. Of course, the Cisco Kid had to have his wonder horse just like all of the western heroes, his was called…oh…let me think, Diablo. Yeah, that was the name of his black stallion.'

Savannah spent a few minutes obviously reminiscing about Cisco, Pancho and their exciting adventures. She then awoke from her reverie exclaiming. 'Look, look Spencer, aren't they just gorgeous?'

Savannah pointed at a pair of macaws; these giant birds with their multi-coloured plumage really were quite spectacular. They reminded Spencer of the parrots in Australia. 'These macaws are like the dinosaurs of bird life, they're huge.'

They had left the urban sprawl of Tijuana and were now motoring through Mexican farmland; Spencer admired the colourful stucco buildings soaking in sunshine. Houses regularly spaced in lots, most of them modest, painted in a riot of colours. Fences were haphazard, made of unfinished boards nailed vertically with large gaps in between.

The fauna seemed to be uniquely Mexican, Spencer thought, although there were common varieties of trees like Oak and Cyprus.

'I've never seen a tree like that Savannah, what is it?'

Savannah obviously enjoyed showing Spencer all that Mexico had to offer.

'That's the *ahuehuete*, also known as a Montezuma cypress. Spectacular, isn't it?'

This unusual specimen reminded Spencer of the Moreton Bay fig trees in Australia. He admired the majesty of the weathered boughs and the well anchored roots.

'Magnificent,' he murmured.

'I wish Inez could be with us. Now…down to business. Our first stop is Hermosillo, which is in Sonora. We're booked into the Holiday Inn. That should be about seven hours, then another ten hours tomorrow to Badiraguato.'

Spencer was immediately struck by the obvious signs of poverty and just how primitive Mexico was compared to the US. There were ragged urchins everywhere holding out hands for money.

'*Pidiendo dinero Señor, por favor.*'

Then there were the donkeys, everywhere. Donkeys laden with produce being led by sombrero wearing men all in plain cotton shirts and trousers and sandals hewn from car tyres. Their multi-coloured ponchos adding a splash of colour.

'How about some food? I'm hungry.' Spencer hadn't had breakfast.

Savannah grinned. 'Oh boy I just love Mexican food, how about you?'

Spencer hadn't had a lot of Mexican, but what he'd had, he'd enjoyed. Savannah enthused. 'Keep your eyes open for the *antojitos.*'

'What?'

'That's a street vendor, you'll just love it. Do you remember when we were in Japan and I didn't have a clue about their cuisine? I think the boot may be on the other foot now.'

'Where approaching, let me see, yep, I think it's the village Pilar.' Their car bounced over the primitive road.

Spencer could see a sprawl of food stalls, colourful and inviting.

'Spencer, just get a whiff.' They car juddered to a holt, one wheel resting in a pothole. Savannah was like a child in a chocolate factory.

They ambled from stall to stall, Spencer had to admit it was mouthwatering.

'Look they sell stuffed *gorditas!*'

'Stuffed what?'

'*Gorditas, gorditas.*'

Spencer shrugged.

Savannah approached the smiling vendor, a happy rotund man who looked like an extra in a Zorro movie. Sporting the inevitable wide brimmed *sombrero* and a stunning white shirt with elaborate embroidery painstakingly stitched, featuring the flowers of Mexico and the fearsome Jaguar. He greeted them with a friendly wave,

'*Americano. Beinvenido.*'

'*Dos gorditas, por favor.*'

Spencer was drooling at the sight and smell of this pastry stuffed with cheese and meat.'

'*Oh, ademas dos agua frescas, por favour.*' Savannah asked the vendor in her fluent Spanish.

'What was that about?'

'That's two fruit drinks, you'll love em, trust me.'

They went back to the Plymouth to eat their feast.

Savannah spread her lunch over the back seat. Spencer sat behind the wheel and balanced his food on the armrest, admiring the dash of the American vehicle. It was nothing like the cars of his century. Heaps of chrome, big round dials, a chunky radio with white plastic station selector buttons. Not equipped with seat belts, he wondered what would happen to a head that smashed into all of that pretty metal if the car had an accident.

'Isn't this just great?'

'Great,' he echoed. Spencer had to admit this was Mexican like he had never had before. Savannah's description, he decided, didn't do it justice.

'Well, time to roll.' Spencer drove while absorbing all around him.

He'd been entranced with the Mexican countryside the colour, the clamour and the vibrancy.

'*Hermosillo.*' Savannah pointed to a sign. Spencer had been expecting a village.

'This is a major city.' Spencer's hand tightened on the wheel, eyes darting from left to right as he stared at the frenetic traffic that appeared from nowhere.

'You're kidding,' he mumbled as he swerved, just avoiding a lunatic with a handcart full of melons.

Spencer was taken aback as they drove into chaotic late afternoon traffic. Buses with exhausts belching blue-black smoke, passengers clinging to luggage racks and anywhere there was a hand hold. And the noise? A cacophony of sound as a multitude of horns blared their discordant message. Worn brakes screeched and the tinny clatter of the two stroke *Mirabella* motorcycles as they weaved perilously added to the chaos. Smartly uniformed officers calmly directed traffic at intersections. Diesel and petrol pumped through the air. Spencer felt the pollution wrapping around his body like a second skin. *Federales* patrolled in old American Chevrolets and of all things, Volkswagen Beetles.

'Well, that was an experience.' Spencer sighed in relief as he made a right, squinting at the discoloured sign advertising The Holiday Inn. Even the air seemed to clear as they turned. into the quiet boulevard leading to their hotel.

'Check this out,' he said, and gestured to the bellboys. They bustled out dressed as *toreadors*. The Plymouth rolled into the sweeping circular drive of the Holiday Inn; Spencer winked at Savannah.

'Well,' Savannah retorted, 'what did you expect, Santa Claus costumes?'

The bellboy struggled with Savannah's suitcases. 'Are you sure you needed to bring so much stuff?' Spencer shook his head at the amount of luggage.

Savannah stayed close to her suitcases like a mother hen guarding her chicks. 'Spencer dear, everything has a purpose. I didn't come for a fashion shoot. What I bring, I bring for a reason.'

They decided to meet in the lobby at six after they had freshened up.

The shower water was hot and ample, the towels white and fluffy. After drying himself, Spencer padded into the bedroom, smiling at his surprisingly pleasant accommodation. It was the perfect array of homey hues, giving a sense of home away from home, a place of nurturing safety. He mentally took his hat off to Holiday Inn and their ability to create an illusion of Midwest American hospitality in the wilds of Mexico.

Opening his suitcase, he selected a short sleeved plaid pattern shirt, a pair of high waisted brushed cotton charcoal trousers and soft leather Italian loafers.

Spencer had taken a seat at the bar, nursing a Coke, when Savannah joined him, refreshed and relaxed.

'Look at you.' Savannah rolled her eyes.

'What's with the eye roll?'

'You look like you're going to dinner at the country club.'

'I didn't know what you had in mind for dinner. This's a nice hotel. But obviously…'

'Obviously, what?' Savannah sneered. 'You obviously have an issue…'

'I don't believe this. You look…fine… seriously.'

Savannah's saddle shoes were worn and scuffed. The dungarees and white poplin shirt were tired and creased.

'Actually, smart arse, where we're going isn't a God damn high fashion destination. It's the real Mexico.'

'Ok. Lead on. So, I'm intrigued. What's this place called?

'*La Campana*,' she announced.

'*La…Compana,*' he repeated, making sure she didn't miss the sarcasm. The word meant nothing to him.

She nodded. 'It's a hawkers food area. It's in a slightly dodgy part of town, but…well. Should be ok. We'll leave the car, it's a nice night for a walk. Mind you, dressed in those duds, they'll probably think you're a Texan oil millionaire and…'

'Let me guess, you'll have to defend my honour?'

'Truce, Spencer. Truce. There won't be a problem. I damn well hope not,' Savannah muttered.

Strolling through *Hermosillo* Spencer was surprised to find a well laid out modern metropolis with wide boulevards and well-maintained parks and gardens. They paused to admire the *Cathedral De La Asuncion*.

'I can understand why you like Mexico. There's a lot of history.'

'Love it.' Savannah nodded. 'We're now entering the dodgy part of town. There won't be a problem, but…well…just keep your eyes open.'

The streets were narrower, the signs of poverty were there. The street urchins now more insistent, hard eyed men cruised by driving old American automobiles. Prostitutes brazenly offered their services.

'There it is, just as I remember. Honestly Spencer, the food here is terrific. You're going to love it.'

The colourful stalls were raucous, with tempting aromas wafting across the compound. The range of different dishes was amazing. Spencer had no idea Mexican food came in so much variety. They sat at a rough wooden trestle table, sharing with a boisterous Mexican family; the children clearly entranced by the exotic *gringos*.

They munched away happily on tamales, tostadas and tacos washed down with Corona beers.

A smiling little boy sidled up to Spencer, pointing a finger as he babbled something in Spanish, to his mother and father at another table.

'*Lo Siento, Señor.*' The mother smiled as she hustled the little boy away.

'*Esta bien, Señora,*' Savannah replied.

'What on earth was that all about?' Spencer demanded.

'That was just great, wasn't it?' Savannah stuffed the last of a *tamale* into her mouth.

Spencer drummed his fingers on the tabletop.

'Oh yeah, the little boy. He said, "Why are you so funny looking?"'

Spencer grinned, giving the family a friendly wave.

Savannah clearly wasn't paying much attention to four men sprawled at another table, eyeing the *Americanos*. Spencer cast a sidelong glance at Savannah, who eventually noticed them.

Spencer cast a surreptitious gaze in their direction. Sizing the men up wasn't difficult. Three were young, late teens perhaps, or early twenties, scruffy, with a hungry look. The fourth was older, maybe early thirties, portly verging on obese. The men whispered.

Savannah and Spencer strolled off into the night; Savannah in high spirits. 'I just love Mexico; some people say it's dangerous but I've never had a problem.'

The four men also left, spreading out unseen, flanking Spencer and Savannah. silently, sneaking into position. One at the front. One at the back and one each on either side.

Right on cue Spencer noticed they were in a dimly lit area, surrounded by the desperados.

'Hey *gringo*, give me your wallet.' The older man had planted himself squarely in front of Savannah and Spencer, a very large knife in his hand. An unpleasant smile, erratic dentistry, discoloured in mostly green and brown added to his thuggish appearance.

Spencer glanced at the motley assortment of villains, figuring the hierarchy. The older guy obviously their leader. A modern-day Fagin.

Spencer guessed the older guy was the *El Patron* to the younger guys, determined to stamp his authority on his admiring proteges. To Spencer he looked like a cartoon character waiting for a caption.

*C'mon guys really, you're out of your depth.*

The big chief's three amigos were an uninspiring lot; one, a skinny youth with furtive rat like eyes darting from side to side, giving the impression it was a toss-up whether to flee or fight. He had a smallpox scarred face. Long lank hair hung like an oily rag over his stained poncho.

The next villain wore a black and silver American cowboy shirt, a black Stetson and torn black jeans. Exuding an air of confidence and an unhealthy interest in the American *señorita*, he nudged his short, rotund, companion wearing the typical Mexican pyjama style cotton shirt and trousers. leering, he whispered. '*Buena chica, eh?*'

Spencer's impression was they had a lot more than *dinero* on their collective minds.

'You spoke too soon.' Spencer glanced at Savannah, a smile on his face.

'Really, can you believe these guys?' Savannah had the temerity to laugh.

The older man and his gang seemed confused; this wasn't the way things worked. Spencer felt as if he could read the *bandito's* mind. You thrust a large knife in *gringos* faces. They screamed. They yelled. Maybe the ladies fainted, or cried, "don't hurt me. I'll give you all my money." They definitely didn't laugh.

Their leader had a problem, Spencer knew. He had to demonstrate to his youthful followers he was a killer, a *bandito*, a man to be feared. This tall *gringo* and his *puta* had him off balance.

Spencer drew his wallet, stuffed full of *pesos*, and waved it enticingly.

The fat man's eyes gleamed; it was the classic situation, the desire for gain, versus the fear of loss.

'C'mon Pancho is this what you want?'

'How you know my name, Pancho?'

'Just a lucky guess.'

'Well, he certainly isn't the Cisco Kid.' Savannah giggled.

Savannah's laughter was the last straw.

*'Estas pero si bien pendejo,'* Pancho screamed. Loosely translated as, "You fucking idiot."

Spencer wasn't concerned, he'd already figured the lumbering Pancho was, as the Texans would say, "big hat and no cattle." Only in this case a *sombrero*. He also knew the three apprentices would almost certainly have knives and they needed to be discouraged. *This guy doesn't have a clue.*

Spencer easily sidestepped Pancho, grabbing his knife arm, at the same time propelling his considerable bulk forward. He brought the edge of his right hand down with catastrophic force. Spencer didn't hold back, a hand that could destroy house bricks and roof tiles had little resistance on a vulnerable neck. Pancho's carotid artery was immediately ruptured, his death following in seconds.

The three would-be *banditos* watched in horror as *El Patron* expired in front of them. One, the skinny youth with the long lank hair made a grab for Savannah's bag, she obligingly held it out in front of her. As he went to grab it, she kicked him very firmly in the groin. He sunk to the ground, not screaming, his breath coming in short rasping bursts. His remaining *compadres* turned tail and fled.

Savannah cast a practised eye over the corpse of Pancho, while Spencer felt for a pulse. The *hacienda* in which the Mexican had lived was vacant the tenant had left.

'A bit of a shame that El Bandito is dead. I probably shouldn't have hit him so bloody hard.'

'Oh yeah, tragedy. Absolute tragedy. Hell in a handcart Spencer, you just did Mexico, in fact the whole world a God damn favour.'

'It's ok for you, I'm still not quite used to indiscriminately killing people.'

'Give me a break. They had knives. And let me tell you they weren't just for show, diddums.'

'Diddums?'

Savannah broke out laughing. 'Spencer you're a riot. How about next time you kill somebody you say three Hail Marys and request forgiveness from the Lord above?'

'As it happens,' Spencer said, grinning, 'I'm not actually a great believer in the man with the snowy white beard, presiding over all. And, hopefully I'm done with killing people.'

'Spencer dear, If I may, I'm about to make a prediction, call it a prophecy if you like.'

'Ok, oh wise one, predict away.'

'Yeah babe, here it is. You're not getting out of Mexico without a few more violent deaths under your belt.'

'I've got no one to blame but myself. For some silly reason I had visions of sunny Mexico, a nice jaunt through the countryside a civilised chat with *Señor* Bustillos and then home again with some cute souvenirs for Inez and Priscilla.'

'Well, kiss my go to hell. You didn't really think that did you?'

'No, not for one cotton picken minute.'

Savannah punched Spencer playfully on the arm. 'Do you know I could just sit there all day and watch you kicking, punching and whatever the hell else you do, despatching the bad guys into the great beyond? It's…I'm not sure what the word is. But it's sort of poetry in motion. You never did tell me where you learnt that stuff.' Before Spencer could answer Savannah rolled her eyes and clapped her hands together, then in unison they both said. 'It's a long story.'

They were back on to the crowded streets, there was no sign of the police, or wailing sirens in the distance. Savannah grinned at Spencer. 'I really don't think a dead Pancho is going to interest the *Federales* that much. So how about we head back to the hotel?'

'Ok, but one thing puzzles me.'

'And that is?'

'I'm surprised you didn't just shoot them.'

'I don't know, sometimes you just want to get physical. I mean they really were such God damn amateurs and in any event, I didn't want to attract the attention of the cops. We don't want an international incident. Besides, Dale Fletcher would get all excited and ask some annoying questions.'

# CHAPTER TWENTY-SEVEN
# HOLIDAY TOYS

Dawn's early light displayed the burnished copper of a distant mountain range. In front of them stretched a verdant field of corn. The hee-haw of donkeys and the whimpering of mules was a reminder this was primitive Mexico. Hermosillo was on the move; the peasant's day was a long one.

The sun already a golden orb as the Plymouth accelerated bumpily onto the dusty rutted Mexican highway, the big V8 gobbling up the miles on the long journey to the home of *Señor* Emilio Bustillos.

'Savannah, please tell me you've got a plan.'

'Not really, the odds are already stacked in our favour.'

He took a moment to give her a long, hard look to really drive home how much he didn't believe this. 'We're heading to the lair of a Mexican kingpin with a proven track record of brutality and the odds are stacked in our favour? That really is a relief. Exactly…how…are they stacked in our favour?'

'It's obvious. I would've thought…we have the element of surprise on our side.'

'Silly me. Why didn't I think of that? So, the fact he will be no doubt surrounded by maybe…what, a hundred *desperados* all armed to the teeth, is as nothing compared to the element of surprise?'

'Spencer, any books on military tactics will tell you that surprise is half of the battle.'

'Half, really? what about the other bloody half? Losing is half the battle. The other bloody half will have…Christ knows what, machine guns, *pistolas* and God knows what?'

'I'm glad to see you're learning a little Spanish. Anyway, it's not as if we haven't come prepared.'

'Oh really, how are we prepared?'

'You haven't looked in the trunk, have you?'

'Don't tell me you actually drove through customs with that damn sniper rifle?'

'Do you mean that damn sniper rifle that saved your miserable life?'

'Umm…I guess I mean that one.'

Savannah fist punched the air, 'Yes! I did bring the Garand with its sniper sight and,' she reached into her pocket and pulled out a gleaming black snub-nosed revolver, 'this's for you.'

'Wonderful. Feel better already. If the good Señor knew I had this he wouldn't be able to sleep at night. Hang on, what else did you bring?'

'Oh just a few…bits and pieces.'

'Like?'

'I managed to get my hands on a Heckler and Koch machine pistol, it fires 9mm rounds, 500 per minute, how about that eh?' Savannah's eyes lit up like a child on Christmas morning.

'Do you know, there are a lot of women that get excited about things like…oh…babies… fashion…new recipes.'

'I've heard that,' Savannah replied coldly. 'But a Vogue fashion magazine isn't much protection when the bullets are flying.'

'Is there anything else?'

'Well seeing as you're asking, I managed to get a dozen fragmentation grenades.'

'Just what every girl needs on an overseas holiday,' he commented wryly.

'Well…you just never know.'

The Plymouth kicked up dust, it swirled and eddied, finding its way into the vehicle, exploring every nook and cranny of their sweaty bodies. Spencer remembered wistfully his BMW 330 I with its cocoon-like body, air conditioned and keeping the elements at bay.

They were now in the state of Sinaloa, bandit country, primitive and basic, but obviously very fertile. They'd passed flourishing fields of tomatoes, eggplants, cantaloupes, cucumbers and strawberries.

'I can't believe what grows here.'

'I've never really understood Mexican politics or their economy.' Savannah drove, keeping a wary eye open for anything out of the ordinary. A late model American sedan guaranteed to attract attention. The attempted robbery by Pancho and his gang had them on high alert.

'They seem to be able to grow anything, yet there are still more poor people than wealthy, that's for sure.'

The next hour was uneventful, repetitive. *Burros*, mules, carts laden with produce.

'Hey Spencer, there it is.'

Big and bold, the famous arched entrance to Badiraguato lay in front of them, emblazoned with the sign '*Bienvedos a Badiraguato.*'

'Let's just hope the sign means what it says,' Savannah murmured.

'Any ideas about accommodation?' Spencer gazed around at a collection of seedy hotels and *pensiones*. Savannah dawdled the car through a maze of multi coloured adobe buildings. Power lines were strewn haphazardly from building to neglected building with no pattern or rational. The road, now unpaved. Mangy dogs lounged and scratched. They rolled into the town square, featuring a bronze sculpture of a deer. Groups of men in a cantina drinking beer seemed to be paying close attention to the *Americano* vehicle. Their uniform: blue jeans and white T shirts with either Stetsons or *sombreros*.

Lurking in the half shadows of the veranda, staring like a cobra, wide eyes black as ink, leaned a swarthy man with hardened features, grasping a Winchester rifle. He yelled at the men as he pointed at the Plymouth. One of them, a tall man with a gaunt face and slicked backed hair, jammed a sombrero on his head and sauntered towards them. '*Hola, Americano.* Join us for a drink.'

Spencer glanced sideways at Savannah. 'Perhaps not?'

'Give em a big smile, Superman. Jesus, just check out the *bandito* with the Winchester.'

Spencer gave the men a friendly wave, eliciting no response.

'How about we move out of town a little way? I'm not really happy about leaving the auto unattended overnight anywhere around here.'

'I think we'd wake up in the morning with more than the hubcaps missing.' Savannah grunted. She turned and gazed back down the mean street, the sombrero man stood, his scowl fading in the distance.

'I just want to get out of this place.' Spencer glanced in the rear vision, half expecting to see a cavalcade of vehicles in hot pursuit. 'There is a subtle, but distinctly unnerving air of menace about this town.'

The road, now wider and paved as they powered out of the village into the countryside. Once again, they were in the Mexico of abundant produce. Spencer gazed at an endless green quilt of corn stretching as far as the eye could see.

The fields that had been swathes of rutted mud were now softly verdant, the new stems being ruffled by a slight breeze. The distant hills rolled like a casually laid eiderdown.

'I think I'd sooner slept in the God damn car than spend a night in Badiraguato.' Savannah grinned. There was an immediate spirit of optimism, the countryside glowed green, bathed in the light of the bright sun.

'Yeah, well if we don't find something soon, we might just be doing that,' Spencer declared gloomily.

Spencer smiled at a little boy waving from the front of a rundown clapboard farmhouse, painted in a bilious green. 'What is it with Mexico? They seem to want to outdo each other to see who can have their house painted in the most revolting colour.'

Then around the next bend. 'Hey, have a gander at that.' Spencer pointed a finger. At a large, freshly-painted sign reading, *"Cabanas el Puertecito."*

'That's a bloody sight for sore eyes. That'll do me Savannah.' It looked like a new housing estate that had sprung up in the burbs. They both wore wide grins at the sight of the cluster of rustic cabins. White washed timber with neat grey slate roofs, just as fresh as if it was grand opening day. The spick and span buildings, all freestanding, with secure parking under the main roof and more importantly a security guard standing watch, armed with a carbine and a very businesslike Colt Revolver on his hip. His unsmiling demeanour and military style uniform of khaki trousers and shirt adorned with some sort of badge of office seemed to add legitimacy to his presence, a curt nod and a salute completed the scene.

Savannah turned to Spencer. 'That'll do.'

The check in was brisk and professional. Once in the lobby they both felt the stress of travel dissipate. The bright office was adorned with a collection of coloured brochures. A stunning painting of a glaring toreador with a swirling red cape dominated one wall. The US dollars proffered by Spencer were accepted gratefully by the smiling clerk. His slick backed hair gleamed like patent leather. The key to their cabin was handed over with a bow. Spencer wouldn't have been surprised if the man had broken out into song.

'*Señor, Señor...ra.*' He paused as if he was a game show host about to hand over a new Cadillac. 'Your cabin...the third on the left'. And once again, '*Gracias, gracias.* Enjoy.'

Savannah chuckled as they climbed back into the car. 'That guy's wasted out here. He should be at the God damn Waldorf.'

'This is it.' Spencer eased the Plymouth into the parking bay. He grimaced as he grabbed Savannah's case.

Spencer kicked the door shut, hefting Savannah's suitcase into her bedroom and dropping it with a resounding thump on the polished pine boards.

The two-bedroom cabin was clean, spacious and comfortable. It could easily have been part of a mid-range North American hotel chain. Spencer appreciated the welcoming wrap around veranda with a small table and four wooden chairs painted in colourful Aztec designs.

'I would just love to bring Inez here; she'd absolutely adore it.' Savannah smiled as she gazed at the charming, homely cabin.

They deposited their bags into their respective bedrooms Each had a double bed with a multi coloured peasant style doona. The walls were adorned with vintage pictures of "Santa Anna" with the title in Spanish, "The hero of the Alamo." Spencer smiled as he deciphered the caption and thought to himself.

*I wonder what John Wayne would think.* Next to that was an old photo of the famous Mexican revolutionary Pancho Villa. Spencer grinned when he saw it. *Another Pancho. I don't believe it.*

At their last stop Spencer had thoughtfully purchased a bottle of *Casa Madero*, a local Mexican wine, he rummaged through the painted wood kitchen hutch, finding two glasses and a corkscrew. He took an appreciative whiff of the deep burgundy liquid. 'This's a real aromatic drop.' He had a sip. 'You'll enjoy this Savannah, it's very similar to an Aussie Cab Sav.'

Savannah rolled her eyes. 'C'mon Spencer you know I'm a cold beer kinda gal, but what was that you said? Just like an Aussie Cab Sav? Is that an Aussie Savannah?' She grinned.

'Bloody philistine,' he muttered as he handed her a glass.

'Hey, y'know this isn't bad at all.' Savannah smacked her lips. 'Actually, I must confess Inez has been introducing me to wine and, you know, gourmet stuff.'

'A moment of relaxation, boy o boy I needed a chance to just sit down and sort of catch my breath. Umm, we…should have a bit of a chat.' Savannah took another sip.

They flopped onto their bentwood chairs. Savannah's hands steepled under her chin as she leant onto the table. 'I didn't say before…but there is more of a plan than I'd indicated.'

'And…You choose now to tell me. Ok out with it.'

'Welllll I wasn't entirely sure you'd approve. You do really have excellent taste Spencer. This wine's great.' She took another sip.

'Savannah, as I've said before, you're not subtle. Why do I get the impression you're buttering me up?'

'God no, Spencer. Not at all. You're a man of taste and breeding,' she muttered in a stage whisper, 'and bullshit.'

'Now, that's more like the Savannah we know and love. Ok. Give.'

'Yes ok. I have in fact been in touch with Señor Bustillos, or at least one of his hirelings.'

'I can see where this is going.'

'No no, there isn't going to be a problem honest.'

'Ok, out with it.' Spencer shook his head.

'Alright then, tomorrow we head to the village of La Tuna. From there we will be met with one of his…ah…PR men.'

'For Christ's sake Savannah, this isn't corporate USA they don't have bloody PR men. We'll be met with one or more low life thugs carrying an assortment of weapons and I might add if he or them don't like what they see…'

'How about she.' Savannah sniggered.

'Savannah, you may well find this offensive but I'm quite sure in the Mexican bandit rule book, women don't get a mention apart from the obvious.'

'As I was saying, *he or they* will certainly search us and if they don't like us, we could come to a very sticky end. I might add, I don't think I need to paint you a picture of what they might do with you.'

'I know what the bastards will do. We know what they're capable of and that's what were here to stop. And by Christ I'm going to stop this animal or die trying.'

***

'Rise and shine, Agent Steele. Time to vamoose.'

After a quick breakfast of burritos and coffee in the restaurant, the dusty Plymouth glided out of the compound. No longer encased in the safe cocoon of the cabanas, they were again in sunny dangerous Mexico. There were few cars. The now commonplace Mexican buses crammed to the gunwales, were heading mostly in the opposite direction. Whole families travelled with their donkey or mule loaded with produce.

'Two hours to La Tuna. Mexico sure is a big place.' Spencer glanced at Savannah.

Savannah flashed him a half smile. She appeared to have things on her mind.

'Penny for them.'

'I know I may appear to be casual.'

'And gung-ho,' Spencer interrupted.

'Call it gung-ho, call it foolhardy, but you tell me, how in hell do you take these bastards down. They have the police and the judiciary in their pocket. The good old U S of A can't or won't do anything about it. I mean, that idiot Biddy. What a joke he was. For Christ's sake Spencer, you saw at firsthand what these creeps are doing. You told me about Zachariah's home movies. The rule of law, that's a God damn joke and you know it. I might add you didn't have to come along; nobody was twisting your arm.'

Spencer gazed out of the window at the lush fields, pondering as he'd done so many times about the evil that seemed to envelope him, the twists and turns that led him into these dangerous adventures. He felt the hard outline of the cornicello in his pocket.

'I'm hungry,' Spencer announced. 'Over there, that'll do, pull in.'

Savannah nodded. 'Yep…breakfast tacos.' The Plymouth drifted slowly into the small village, accompanied by small dogs barking and ragged children running alongside the car, giggling and waving. It was still early morning; the taco stand was doing a brisk trade. Grinding to a halt and throwing up a clatter of pebbles and dust, the big car made its entrance. The waiting customers cast curious eyes over the Yankee automobile, the tall, good-looking *gringo* and his *la muja*.

At the sight of the taco stall, Savannah seemed to snap out of her melancholy. 'Just look at that, here we are in the middle of nowhere and people are lined up to buy. Just look at this guy, he's poetry in motion. I didn't think I was hungry but, my God just get a whiff.'

The vendor had a large block of wood scarred and stained, where he expertly chopped meat, onion, peppers, cilantro and other ingredients Spencer couldn't identify. His cleaver wielded as dexterously as a surgeon's scalpel. At the same time his colourful banter kept the customers amused, waiting for the mouth-watering tacos and burritos.

'*Dos tacos, por favor.*' Spencer handed over some *pesos* and they received their delicious treats.

'I'm impressed,' Savannah said through a mouthful of taco. 'Spoken like a Mexican.' The vivid colours of the food spoke to its freshness and the bold flavours to follow.

'This is something else, isn't it?' Spencer had demolished his taco in few swift gulps; juices ran down his chin.

They wiped their face and hands on the pieces of brown paper the food was wrapped in.

Spencer smiled at Savannah. 'I think wow, is the best description. I find it hard to get my head around this food,' he paused, momentarily lost for words. 'Here we are in this Mexican backwater and I've just had a simple meal that would put five-star restaurants to shame. Amazing, just amazing.'

'You can see yet another reason why I love this country: the people are friendly the food is terrific.' Savannah laughed.

'Hang on just a minute before we get all starry eyed.' Spencer screwed his paper wrap and threw it into a bin.

'You can be a picky bastard, Spencer. The food, the people. What's not to like? Ok it's a bit backward, so what?' Savannah eyed him coldly.

Spencer shook his head, reminded once again of Savannah's mercurial qualities.

'Friendly people huh? Have you forgotten the late unlamented Pancho and his *tres* companions?'

Spencer could see the beginnings of a smile as it valiantly tried to override the scowling visage.

'Clever boy. You've done it again.'

'Done what?' he snapped.

'Pancho and his *tres* companions, see,' she said triumphantly. 'You're slowly but surely learning Spanish.'

'Stop changing the subject. As I was attempting to say, Mexico isn't just a land of happy laughing people; this is also a country where the likes of Emilio Bustillos and a lot of other assorted bad guys thrive with police and political protection.'

'I think we've had this discussion before. We have to go, if we want to get to La Tuna in good time.' Savannah cast a quick glance at her watch.

As they settled into the Plymouth with Spencer behind the wheel, Savannah resurrected the conversation. 'Spencer, I'm not oblivious to the crime and corruption in Mexico, far from it. But we have crime and corruption in the States. And if you remember, that's what's led us here in the first place. Remember the meeting we had in Sacramento with that FBI idiot Biddy? That was a guy who just wanted a quiet life until he retired. As I said before there are somethings we can't really change. But for me I'm happy to just do my bit. And when I come across this…this such well organised criminality, I just know I have to do what I'm good at.' She gazed out of the window at the endless fields of vegetable crops. 'The thing is, I see so much unpleasantness in my job. I guess I want to grab hold of the beauty along the way.'

'Well until you end up shooting another bad guy anyway.'

'Spencer. Let me tell you, I sleep well at night. I've no regrets whatsoever about the lowlife I've removed, ok?'

Spencer glanced sideways at a now scowling Savannah. *I think we might leave that alone for now.*

It had been obvious to Spencer ever since Savannah executed the hit man in the restaurant in their last adventure that the rule of law was simply a minor obstacle for her. It was like a holy crusade to rid the world of bad guys with scant regard for due process.

They made good time, pulling into the tiny village of La Tuna mid-morning. It seemed as if it was *siesta* time; nothing moved.

La Tuna was a village time had forgotten. It reminded Spencer of the movie The Magnificent Seven. He could imagine a black clad shaven headed Yul Brynner or Steve McQueen to come ambling up the dusty street, six guns in hand, awaiting the *banditos*.

Spencer observed the typical white down at heels stucco buildings and the old church with its belltower.

'Hey Savannah check out the horse trough.' The rough and ready horse trough fashioned from oak planks supporting a discarded metal bath, filled with a grey slimy fluid. 'I don't think town planning has much of a future,' he added.

La Tuna was a village with no discernible pattern. Every building was different, borrowing ideas from different eras. Like granny's quilt, a mishmash of styles. Nothing moved apart from a disinterested mangy dog, stirring briefly, wagging a tale, then deciding to go back to sleep.

'Is it my imagination or do Mexicans seem to sleep a lot?'

'Yeah, well not everybody's sleeping. Over there look,' Savannah hissed.

Savannah had already seen two hard-eyed men in an open top World War Two Jeep. Both were fairly daunting prospects. These men were nothing like the late Pancho and his comrades. Both had bandoleers over their shoulders. One had a Colt 0.45 semi-automatic pistol in a shoulder holster, the other a wicked looking revolver also in a holster, slung low on his hip. They both wore *sombreros*, flared leather trousers and cuban heel boots.

'I hate to say it, but I hope your gun is at easy reach,' Spencer muttered.

My God these guys look like extras in a Clint Eastwood spaghetti western.

'Hey gringo,' the shoulder holster man motioned them over. Spencer idled the car in their direction. As they ground to a halt, the other man leaned on the passenger door sill, his beard long and matted, his breath putrid. Leering at Savannah, he addressed his partner. 'Hey Francisco, this is one pretty Señorita, we could have some fun with her.'

'*Idiota*,' the man called Francisco snarled. 'They're here to do business with Señor Bustillos. You want to get us both killed? Keep your dick in your pants.'

Francisco was at the driver's door. Then in guttural English, 'Sorry *señor*, this man is an idiot. Would you mind very much coming with us in the Jeep? I'm sorry, but I'll have to pat you both down for weapons.' Francisco smiled an oily smile. Spencer acknowledged him with a curt nod. *For the time being at least we are honoured guests, it would appear.*

Spencer glanced at Savannah, who shrugged. It was obvious Francisco was the boss and the Señor wanted no harm to come to them.

Savannah and Spencer were perched precariously in the back of the Jeep, their weapons taken from them and thrown carelessly into the trunk of the Plymouth. Francisco had hefted Savannah's magnum in his hand. 'You know how to use this, *señorita?*'

'Oh yes…I know how to use it.' Savannah stared him down impassively.

'Will everything in our automobile be safe until we return?' Spencer had asked.

'These peasants, these *el paleto*, they wouldn't dare.' He smiled, drawing a hand across his throat. His sidekick giggled. 'This is our town, *compadre*. Here we take want we want. Do what we want.' Francisco smiled a mirthless smile

He leered at Savannah, licking his lips.

Francisco grabbed him by the throat, whispering in his ear, finally pushing him forcefully towards the Jeep. 'Fool, shut it. Drive.'

Francisco now looked worried, as he climbed into the Jeep. He managed a feeble smile. '*Señorita, señor* my friend has the manners of a pig.'

Spencer figured they were on safe ground, for the moment at least. 'Tell the son of a bitch the next time he steps out of line, it isn't his boss he'll have to worry about, but me, *comprende?*'

'Oh Cisco, my hero.' Spencer turned and winked at Savannah, who only just managed to stifle her mirth.

It was a two-hour drive on a narrow winding road, little more than a track high in the mountains. The basic ex-army Jeep's seats had no padding. They bobbed around like bronco riders in a rodeo. Savannah grimaced as the vehicle bounced in the air after hitting a pothole. Immediately lurching into another, its engine screamed as all four wheels were momentarily airborne.

The area wasn't heavily wooded, covered in grass and shrubs and the most spectacular wildflowers Spencer had ever seen. His thoughts once again returned to Australia and the long drives in the country and how Michiyo and Trilby had enjoyed the splendour of the outback with its harsh rugged beauty.

Savannah grabbed Spencer's arm. 'Just look, aren't they something?' There were vibrant reds, purple and yellows that somehow managed to look like someone had put on display just for their benefit.

As they turned around a bend, into a clearing, there in front of them was Señor Emilio Bustillos's *hacienda*.

'This guy has some serious money,' Savannah whispered to Spencer.

*This is some pile.*

Savannah nudged Spencer. 'Hey, I've read about this joint. It's famous. I think it was built in the 1500's, originally for the

Marque Del Valle De Oaxaco a really brutal Spanish nobleman. That bastard was just another Bustillos. He controlled the local peasants with all sorts of particularly inventive cruelty. Seriously you wouldn't believe what that sonofabitch used to do.'

It occurred to Spencer that over the centuries not a lot had changed *Where once there was vicious aristocratic tyrant, there is now a vicious commoner as a tyrant. Same dog, different fleas.*

The *hacienda* was surrounded by a solid brick and stone whitewashed wall at least eighteen feet high. Guard towers with unsmiling men armed with machine guns and rifles glowered menacingly at them.

Spencer nudged Savannah. 'Look over there.'

The gates were already opened as the Jeep clattered and banged over the rough cobbles. At the front of this vast mansion was a broad veranda. Reclining on a throne like chair was a solid block of a man, balding, wearing American jeans, a white short-sleeved shirt with bold red stripes and moccasins without socks. He was playing with a little boy no more than four, the child squealing with delight as the man threw him up into the air, then catching him with his huge ham-like hands.

On one side of the compound, men were erecting a dance floor and stage. There were trestle tables being set up, decorations everywhere. The red, white and green of the Mexican flag were stretched from post to post.

Spencer nudged Savannah. Sitting on a pad was a Sikorsky Choctaw helicopter.

Savannah whispered to Spencer, 'I feel like we've driven on to a Hollywood movie set, this guy must be a God damn local dictator or warlord. The LAPD have choppers like that, they cost a mint.' They turned their gaze to the veranda and the solid middle-aged man surveying the workers around him like a mediaeval emperor of old. His pugnacious features and stocky build reminded Spencer of photos of Il Duce, Benito Mussolini, the Italian war time ruler.

'There's something going to happen here. One hell of a celebration, that's for sure.' Spencer shook his head.

The man put the boy down, dismissing him with a pat on the behind.

He rose to his feet. '*Señor, señorita,* welcome to my humble *hacienda.* Sit, sit.' Pointing to the chairs placed around the polished oak table, as big as a flight deck.

'Enrique, *cerveza por favour.*' The waiter neatly attired in black trousers and white shirt scurried over to the bar in the corner, returning with three icy cold Budweisers, he deftly removed the caps, bowing as he handed them the drinks.

'Your health. I hope you don't mind, but I prefer American beer, rather than our local drop…now.' He rubbed his hands together. 'My name is Emilio Bustillos. What can I do for you?'

Before they could answer the little boy came running up to him, grabbing his hand. 'Papa Papa, come play with me.'

'Not now El Chapo, you go tell Enrique, I said to take you to the swings to play. Now off you go.' The little boy was clearly the apple of his father's eye.

'What a boy, eh, *señor?* He's my only son. El Chapo's his nickname, because he's very short for his age. But I tell you he's full of energy.' He laughed. 'His mother calls him El Rapido, the speedy one.'

Spencer smiled and waved at the child bouncing around the room with limitless energy. Spencer glanced sideways at

Savannah. This wasn't what they expected, a ruthless drug baron, uncouth and brutal? This man gave every impression of being a kind and doting father, a successful businessman. The wealth was obvious, but not overly flashy or ostentatious.

There were no gold-plated machine guns in sight, or enemies' heads cut off and pickled in jars for all the world to see. There was a stunning Rolls Royce Silver Cloud in the courtyard. A gold Rolex Daytona on Bustillo's wrist glinted in the sunlight, briefly reminding Spencer of the Rolex, given to him by his late father. But no, there was just the usual trappings of success. Could Savannah be wrong about this genial and pleasant Mexican gentleman?

Emilio Bustillos was indeed a gracious host. Insisting on inviting them to join him for lunch.

'My friends, I'm sure you're hungry after your journey. Come join me. My chefs have been instructed to outdo themselves. I'm sure you'll be pleased with what they have achieved. Come, come. Please be seated.'

Dish after mouth-watering dish was placed before them. The fragrant green garnish of the fresh cilantro and the deep herbal bitter notes of lemon enhanced the roast peppers. It blended perfectly with the aroma of the shredded pork. Smartly clad staff brought platter after platter, guacamole, thyme and potato quesadillas, burritos and tacos.

'*Señor* Marlowe, you must sample this Mexican red wine, it's called *Tempranillo*. And for the *señorita*?'

'The *señorita* would be very happy with a cold Budweiser.' Savannah smiled coquettishly.

Finally, the luncheon was over. Emilio burped, wiping his face on a serviette. One of the waiters immediately sprung forward with a light as Bustillos selected a Cohiba from a carved cedar humidor. He closed his eyes, drawing on the cigar. Appearing to be lost in thought, he exhaled a plume of fragrant smoke.

Spencer nervously glanced sideways at Savannah. The silence was prolonged. Spencer wasn't sure what to do, to speak or not to speak. Savannah shrugged. Eventually Bustillos smiled, removing the cigar from his mouth. 'Ah, *magnifico*,' he murmured, to nobody in particular. He smiled again, tapping the ash into what Spencer thought appeared to be a solid gold ashtray.

'Tell me, how can we do business?' the question was directed at Spencer. There was a tacit understanding between Spencer and Savannah, it might be a bit of a stretch for the good *señor* to be expected to do business with a woman.

'Señor Bustillos, first on behalf of me and my assistant here.' Spencer gave Savannah a cursory nod, thinking, *Right about now she would probably be happy to give me swift kick in the balls.* 'We'd both like to thank you for your hospitality. I can see you're obviously busy with planned celebrations—'

Bustillos interrupted. 'Yes, my daughter is getting married. This will be the biggest event that's ever been seen in these parts. I'm buying every scrap of produce in the surrounding area. Everyone is coming. The chief of police, even the Governor of Sinaloa will be here.'

'*Señor* Bustillos, I don't believe in beating around the bush.'

'I don't understand, bush…what bush?'

'Sorry *señor*, it's an American expression. It means I'll get straight to the point.'

'Excellent, I like a man who gets to the point, please…proceed.'

'*Señor* Bustillos, I want to buy all the girls you can provide. They must be young and pretty. And,' Spencer paused. 'Also, cocaine. And if you can get it…heroin.'

'Heroin and cocaine are not a problem…but sadly *Señor* Marlowe, I'm already supplying girls to a man in the US. He buys all I can supply and his turnover…well let's say, he certainly seems to get through the product quite quickly.'

Spencer felt cold fingers running up his spine. He forced himself to quell the bile he felt rising. 'Would that be…a man named Tex, in Shoshone Springs?'

'It could be…and you know…Tex?' Bustillos eyes narrowed.

'Ah…*Señor* Bustillos…that would be the late Tex.'

Bustillos drew back on his cigar, fixing Spencer with a hard unblinking stare, then abruptly he burst into laughter, he pointed his cigar at Spencer. 'And…Let me guess, you're the new proprietor?'

'Everything will be the same. We want the product delivered to Shoshone Springs, just as before.' Spencer nodded. Spencer felt squeamish referring to the girls as product.

Bustillos drew on his cigar, at the same time once again staring hard at Spencer. This, Spencer decided was a make-or-break moment. If Bustillos didn't swallow their story they were dead.

The ensuing silence was scary as Bustillos continued to stare; the silence broken like a gunshot as a waiter dropped a stack of plates. Shards of porcelain and the remnants of tacos and burritos scattered across the floor. Bustillos's head swivelled as he swore at the terrified man.

'*Imbecil!*' he yelled. Turning to Spencer and Savannah, he suddenly smiled. 'Señor Marlowe. I praise myself that I'm a good judge of character. I believe you are a man of honour, but…because I don't know you, I'd like a cash deposit, before we ship the next…shall we say…crop.' Bustillos laughed at his description.

Spencer breathed a sigh of relief. 'How much?'

Bustillos rubbed his hands together. 'Ok Señor, a kilo of heroin, a kilo of coke and five new girls all pretty and relatively,' and he chuckled, 'relatively untouched, the total price is the usual $50,000 US and I want deposit of $10,000. Which…I don't need to remind you I'm sure, if the goods are intercepted by the US authorities, the deposit is non-refundable. Is that satisfactory?'

'We'll need to go to Badiraguato to get the funds. That'll take a day or a little more, if that's ok?'

'Very good, and now…' Bustillos smiled, the same sort of smile as before, warm and welcoming just what one would expect from a genial family man. 'I'll take you and the *señorita* to see the latest crop.' Spencer wondered whether he was referring to the drugs or the girls.

'Enrique, take us to the girls.' Bustillos snapped a finger.

They sauntered across the courtyard. It was still a hive of frenetic activity. Men and women were setting up chairs and tables. Four burly men cursed, as they laboured to erect a giant wooden cross, adjoining an impressive altar on a separate raised dais, standing proud, telling the world, this was a catholic wedding, a wedding blessed by God.

'How do you like the cross, Señor?' It stood at least twenty foot tall, with an elaborate carved figure of Christ nailed to the crossbeams.

'Very impressive.'

Bustillos paused for a minute feasting his eyes on the spectacle. 'Yes, Señor Marlowe, we're all good Catholics here…and…the bishop himself is honouring us with his presence. He will be officiating. This truly, will be a wedding blessed by all that's holy.'

The smiling Enrique opened the doors of the car. Spencer and Savannah reclined on the Connolly leather seats as Enrique smoothly accelerated. The whisper quiet Rolls Royce glided as if floating on air.

'Nice automobile, *Señor* Bustillos.'

'Yes, and as you have probably noticed, air conditioning.'

'What'll they think of next?' Spencer glanced sideways at Savannah who just rolled her eyes, saying nothing.

They could see a large barn like structure only a few hundred yards from the *hacienda*.

'This's it.'

Once again Enrique sprung out, flinging the doors open with a flourish.

Enrique sprinted ahead to the double doors, jerking them open.

Spencer cast a surreptitious glance at Savannah, who stared fixedly ahead.

It took a few seconds for their eyes to adjust to the gloom. Spencer steeled himself for what he knew he was going to see. *Please Savannah, say nothing.*

The barn was just that, your average everyday working farm style barn, but there were no sheep, cattle or horses, just a steel cage similar to the one in Shoshone Springs. Inside were a dozen young girls. It reminded Spencer of photos he'd seen of WW2 concentration camps. Rough wooden bunks, stacked high. Buckets for human waste and trestle tables with jugs of water. The heat and the smell that hit them like a tsunami was gut wrenching. Spencer gasped as he struggled to keep the recently consumed tacos and burritos in place.

It was all Spencer could do not to scream. He felt the pain of these captives. Some were crying, some lay on bunks, others gazed imploringly at the tall *gringo* and the woman. *Surely a woman would help us.*

'*Señorita ayudanos por favor, por favor,*' One young girl cried out.

*Señor* Bustillos laughed. 'They never shut up, honestly.' He shook his head. 'As you can see, *señor*, all good stock. Not virgins, of course.' He laughed again. 'I think most were, when they arrived but, well my men like to have a good time.' He nudged Enrique. 'My God man, I think you've stuck your dick into every one of them.'

Spencer was surprised that Bustillos would make these comments in front of Savannah, who'd fortunately managed to stay silent.

Spencer managed a weak grin and tried to think of a humorous response and failed.

'Sadly, I can't have any fun. My damn wife watches me like a hawk. What do you Americans say? "You can't live with them and you can't live without them," eh. She'd cut my cock off with a rusty blade if she caught me at it.'

# CHAPTER TWENTY-EIGHT

# THE AVENGING ANGEL

Savannah was silent as the Jeep rattled and bounced its way back to La Tuna and the waiting Plymouth. The driver and his offsider had become their new best friends, realising Spencer and Savannah were now business partners of their boss.

'*Señor*, we have cold Coca Cola for you and the *señorita*.' This came from Francisco's companion, now very much regretting his earlier disrespectful comments to the *señorita*. His name was Juan, he was aware this American *señorita* possibly had the power of life and death over him. He was the very picture of a fawning lackey.

Savannah who certainly didn't forgive or forget, fixed him with a hard stare and in Spanish she sneered, '*Chupapollas.*' Juan blushed and looked away.

'That seemed to upset the little bastard. What'd you say?' Spencer whispered to Savannah.

'Cocksucker.'

With a crunch of gears, the Jeep lurched to a halt in the dusty La Tuna Street.

Without a word Spencer and Savannah jumped out and made their way to the Plymouth.

'All I could think about while that creep Juan was prattling on, was how nice it would've felt to put a bullet into the back of his head.'

'You haven't shot anyone for a while. You must be having withdrawal symptoms.'

'You're not getting a rise out of me, Pancho. Don't tell me you didn't feel the same, you smarmy bastard. I'm sorry but I'm finding it a bit difficult to find any God damn humour in any of this. I don't know about you, but I've never felt so helpless. All I could think of was putting a bullet into Bustillos. What I'd want is for him to know he was going to die. I want to be up close and personal. I want him to know Savannah Steele was going to…Hey, any way…I've just realised.'

'What, oh merciless one?'

'Yeah, I've just realised, God damn, do you realise in all the time we've known each other, you self-righteous bastard, you've never actually shot anyone? Sure, you've despatched a few guys to mobster heaven with your fancy ballet display, but actually…grabbing a gun…and pulling the damn trigger? So help me God, you're a God damn virgin, that's what you are.'

'What an interesting slant you have on things. So, when I killed the yakuza who'd whacked you on the jaw, back there in Tokyo, that doesn't count for anything, because I didn't shoot him. Interesting.'

'Well, I guess it's early days, any way you'd probably miss. Remember the Southern Belle. You didn't hit the target, not once. Doesn't that just beat all you ever stepped in?'

'I was just getting the hang of it. As it happens, I'm more than happy for you to do the shooting, just let me finish 'em off my way, Ok?'

'Sure Pancho, sure.'

La Tuna was still busy with drays, trucks, horse and mule wagons and carts loaded with produce for the big wedding.

The Plymouth as promised, slept untouched, standing alone, looking very much out of place in the Mexican backwater.

'Seeing as we're out the front of a cantina, let's have a drink, figure out what our next move is.'

The rough and ready, weather-beaten, tumbledown cantina seemed to beckon them. Emblazoned with a faded sign with what looked suspiciously like bullet holes. El Palacio, untidy and scruffy, had no competition.

'It sure doesn't look like a God damn palace.' Savannah sneered.

They dusted themselves off. The narrow road from the *hacienda* had been unsealed and rutted. The dust had swirled around them and over them. They felt dirty. Most of all dispirited. The plight of the girls weighed heavily on both of them.

Spencer slapped his hands on his trousers, grimacing as the dust swirled around him.

'Let's see if we can find somewhere to stay the night. I don't feel like a long drive back to Badiraguato. We can try and figure out just what we do next. We're certainly not going to go and rustle up Ten G's for El Thuggo, are we?'

They plonked down heavily on a rough pine trestle seat in the dimly lit Cantina.

'Time for a beer?'

Savannah nodded. 'Right at the moment I feel like grabbing a bottle of tequila and throwing away the cork. Anything to blot out the image of the girls.'

Spencer stepped up to the bar where an eager young barman, wearing a worn black cowboy shirt and blue jeans smiled and in broken English. 'Yes, it's a nice afternoon. Isn't it? And what I get?'

Spencer leaned on the bar glancing at the bottles of tequila, Bacanora and Kahlua. At the moment he too would welcome the numbing effect of copious amounts of hard liquor. *Probably not a good idea.*

'*Dos cervezas, por favor.*'

Spencer nodded at a wizened face peering out from a battered *sombrero*. Slouched at a battered table. One lonely customer, an old man nursing a beer. '*Saludo.*' The old man grinned, exposing a toothless smile. His rheumy eyes as faded as his worn calico trousers and his *camisa de Yucatan* shirt. Skinny feet with prominent hammer toes protruded from the worn cuffs of his pants, his old worn leather scuffs sat waiting beside him.

'*Saludo Señor,*' Savannah replied, trying to muster the semblance of a smile. Then in Spanish, she asked if there was any accommodation in town.

'*Si si señorita, señor.*' He nodded at Spencer. 'My daughter has a guest house. Nice rooms. Very cheap. No *cucaracha.*' He cackled with laughter at the word *cucaracha.*

'*Donde esta la casa? De huespedes, por favor.*'

The old man pointed through the window to house at the end of the street.

Spencer smiled at the old man. '*Gracias señor.*'

'I don't know about you killer, but a cold shower and a soft bed would certainly be welcome.'

Savannah nodded in agreement. 'And no *cucaracha.*'

The Pension Oliva was a handsome narrow two-story property with white stuccoed walls and double fronted carved oak doors, set back with a sturdy iron grill, bolted in front, probably designed to keep thieves and bandits at bay. The second story rooms had small balconies with pots of colourful blooms, attached to their wrought iron railings.

Spencer rapped his knuckles firmly on the heavy oak. In thirty seconds, the door creaked open. Grinning from ear to ear, as if she was party to a secret, the big chested lady, her lustrous long black hair greying at the temples, quickly scanned the street, ushering them inside she slammed the door.

'We need two rooms, please *señora.*' Spencer opened his wallet.

'Welcome. *Americanos* always welcome.' The smiling hostess accepted the US five dollar that disappeared quickly into her cleavage. Winking at Spencer, she yelled, 'Pedro, *vena qui.*' Placing a hand on Spencer's forearm, she winked again. 'If you need anything, *señor*, I'll be in the kitchen. My name is Elena.'

'Great, I think we're pretty much ok.' Spencer caught a glimpse of Savannah's scowl.

Spencer and Savannah plodded up the narrow-bleached wooden staircase.

'The Mexican momma was a bit forward,' Savannah growled. 'I think you won a heart. For God's sake she could see you were with me.'

'Hang on, just a minute. We have separate rooms. Anyhow, she was just being friendly.'

'Honestly Spencer, sometimes I think you don't have both oars in the water. Just being friendly…sheesh.'

Two surprisingly charming rooms greeted them upstairs. The flooring was an old-fashioned parquet with a blend of deep homely browns. A double bed in each room both with hand stitched magnificent quilts. The symbols of Catholicism were evident with a garish painting of Christ that also involved some lambs and a collection of rapt followers. On the bedside table rested a framed picture of another religious figure, a ferryman about to take a child across a raging torrent of water. Spencer peered at the inscription which he was able to translate as Saint Christopher taking Christ across a river.

'The patron saint of travellers no less. Well Chris please keep an eye open for us.

The houseboy, grunted as he struggled up the stairs with Savannah's suitcases.

Spencer handed the sweating lad a twenty peso note equating to about fifty cents, it was enough to have made a friend for life.

'*Gracias señor, Gracias*, if there is anything else you and the *señorita* need, just call for Pedro, anything *señor*, anything.' The boy exited, clattering down the stairs, exulting in his newfound wealth.

'Well.' Spencer grinned. 'I'm sure glad you brought so many clothes. Two suitcases, really? We should dress carefully for a night out in magnificent downtown La Tuna…now…where shall we dine tonight? Will it be the cantina? Or, let me see…I know, let's dine at the cantina.'

'Yep, the cantina will be fine. And as for my luggage, I told you everything I've brought had a God damn purpose, didn't I?'

'It's simply well-known fact women always bring too many clothes on holidays. Clearly, you're no exception. That's of. You'll notice I, of course have managed with one small case.'

'Spencer…*dear!* As you should be well aware, I'm not most women.' Savannah opened one of her suitcases. 'Now, smart ass. Just cast your peepers over this little lot.'

Spencer winced at the collection of guns and ammunition on display.

Spencer reclined on a chair in Savannah's room while she sat on the bed. She had an assortment of handguns before her. She paused, then selected a long-barrelled semi automatic. 'I think this little beauty may do the trick.'

'What's wrong with the tried-and-true cannon you normally use?'

'You really don't know a lot about guns, do you?'

Spencer shook his head.

'I can think of nothing better than blasting these creeps with the Magnum. But you can't effectively silence it and if we're going to stand any chance, the shooting has to be whisper quiet. This Hi-Power 0.22 doesn't have the punch of the Magnum but I'm using a special charge full metal jacket slug that's pretty darn good. Do you want me to explain about the load?'

'I'll take your word for it.'

Spencer watched as Savannah selected a bulbous silencer and screwed it onto the pistol.

'The silencer is as long as the pistol.' Spencer observed.

'I don't wish to be pedantic, but actually it's called a suppressor. This one's the best. It's the quietest available, you wouldn't even hear this in the next room.' Savannah's eyes shone. It was as if she was envisioning what damage she was going to wreak on the Mexicans.

'Just out of curiosity. Did you play with dolls when you were a little girl?'

'Yes,' she said coldly, 'and all my cute little girl dollies had God damn guns.'

'What's that old nursery rhyme? What are little girls made from? Sugar and spice and all things nice.'

For a brief moment there was a flash of anger. Savannah's jaw jutted and the corner of her mouth pointed downwards. Spencer waited for the outburst. All of a sudden, the laughter cascaded out of her. 'Spencer you bastard. Sometimes you razz my berries. You're damn well baiting me. Hell, I don't mind. The fact is we make a damn good team. You're the best God damn street fighter I've ever seen. And…' she said softly. 'I'm the best shot that you've ever seen. Right?'

*She sure as hell isn't going to change her ways, watch out bad guys, Savannah is coming.*

'God damn it.' Savannah jumped up from the bed. She began pacing the cosy balcony, looking troubled.

'What are you God damning about exactly?'

'We have the weapons. We know our target. We have everything but…' Savannah threw her hands in the air.

'But what?'

'Spencer, damnit. We don't have a plan. Ok we've got the weapons. We have a reason to see Bustillos again. But we need cash we don't have. We can't just turn up without the dinero and say, "Oh is it ok if we wire you the money *señor*?" Spencer we…are…screwed. Damnit, damnit, damnit.'

Spencer leant on the balcony, giving him a view of La Tuna and the mountains behind. Just at that moment he observed a horse and cart, laden with bulging crates of ripe tomatoes. 'I may have an idea.'

Savannah gazed listlessly at Spencer. 'Well, I'm plumb out of ideas. All I can seem to think about is those poor girls. Frankly I feel like going in with a suicide charge all guns blazing and dying in the attempt. So alright, my Australian time travelling man of mystery, hit me. What have you got?'

'I think this may work. Admittedly there are a couple of flaws, but listen and don't bloody well laugh.'

'I promise I won't laugh.'

'You see all those wagons and drays loaded with produce? Well…how about we buy one of them already loaded with tucker? I've no idea what we would have to pay, but one thing's for sure, it would be one hell of a lot less than the ten grand Bustillos is expecting.'

'What in the God damn hell is "tucker?"'

'Sorry, that's Australian. It means food, ok?'

'Go on.'

'So, we buy one of those carts complete with donkey or horse, take it up to the hacienda. We'll drop by the barn. The guard will think we simply got lost and he'd direct us to the hacienda. Initially I'm sure he wouldn't be suspicious. He'd just think some stupid peasants had lost their way.'

Savannah's face twitched. 'What about the perimeter guard? I kill him, or we just say we're here to drop food off for the wedding? It doesn't matter, I guess.'

Spencer nodded. 'Better if we only start killing when we have to. If they raise the alarm too early, we're buggered. Once we get to the barn and meet the guard, if you didn't mind awfully, you could perhaps shoot him, or them with the silenced pistol.'

'So far this is actually sounding like a plan. And yes, I think I could probably be tempted to shoot the guard. Mind you, I'd probably be more likely to shoot the bastard in the crotch. But then he'd scream and carry on, so I guess the good old double tap one to the head and one to the chest.'

Savannah hugged her knees. 'Christ almighty. This could work. We let the girls out. They'll have to find their own way home unfortunately… unless…'

'Unless what?'

'Look, Spencer. If the girls just scatter into the wilderness, they won't stand a chance. There are no farms out there and it's a hell of a long way to walk. Damnit, I reckon the then hopefully late *señor's* men will be searching high and low for their "product."'

'Well…' Spencer thought for a minute. 'If the girls can make their way to the road. And if we get out of the joint unscathed. We could pick them up in the cart and take them back into town.'

'That's a lot of ifs.'

They would also be making the drive back in a cart pulled by a donkey, so if his men had cars, they were in serious trouble. 'Sure, it's a lot of ifs. But I think you and I are agreed that we couldn't live with ourselves if we didn't give it our best shot.'

'Well, they say, God loves the righteous.'

'Since when exactly did you decide to become all holy?'

'Well, I'm not particularly. But right at the moment I'm prepared to accept all the help I can get.' She said with a grin.

'There's more.' Spencer held up a finger.

'Really, go on, please. This sounds great.'

'We then go to the hacienda. While I'm unloading the fruit and veg, you see if by any chance at all, that Bustillos is in the house alone, you go in and finish him off.'

'If I could kill that son of a bitch, I'd be a happy girl.' Savannah's eyes gleamed.

'Don't get to carried away. He may be downstairs as he was before, in which case all we can do is unload the produce and high tail it. He would need to be inside away from the others. It would mean you would have to slip into the hacienda unnoticed. Find him. Shoot him and get out. So, all of the stars need to be aligned.'

Savannah nodded, 'I reckon we're in with a chance. I've noticed although there's plenty of armed men there didn't seem to be anybody watching over him in the *hacienda*. I think they believe any danger would come from outside. And I don't think it would occur to him the farmers who are dropping their produce off could possibly be a threat.'

'You mentioned other possible flaws.'

'Flaw number one is we would have to look like native Mexicans and that could be difficult. Ah…unless?'

'And flaw number two?'

'When we leave, we'll be leaving in the same slow horse and cart, or whatever it is. And given the time it takes to get back to La Tuna they could well come after us in automobiles and that could get messy.'

'Why don't we see if we can slash some tyres? The Rolls Royce for a start.' Savannah asked. 'Not only do I have things that go bang. I have, da da!' Savannah reached into her bag. 'You might need this.'

'You do come prepared.' Spencer grinned as he accepted a Bowie knife in a scabbard.

'Just feel that blade.'

Spencer withdrew the vicious looking dagger. 'Hell, I could shave with that. But seriously…'

Spencer held up a finger to tell her what a terrible idea this was, but stopped. He felt guilty in advance for doing damage to that gorgeous Rolls Royce, but since a monster owned her, he stomped on his reservations. He slipped the knife and scabbard into his belt.

'We can also see about hijacking one of the *señor's* vehicles,' he added. 'It still doesn't help us get past the perimeter guard and in striking distance of the farm guard. Face it, Savannah, we'll never pass as locals.'

Savannah sprung up from the bed. 'Ahhh…an idea, whoa…I got it, I got it…just listen to this…first of all smarty pants let me show you what I have in my case and then you are going to worship the ground I walk on because of my undoubted brilliance.'

'Oh, don't worry, I do, I do,' Spencer murmured.

'Yeah, yeah funny. Now let me show you.' With that Savannah opened up her case with a flourish.

'What on earth is all that?' Spencer gazed at what looked like jars of paint, brushes and what looked suspiciously like makeup.

'This, you Australian yokel, is a makeup set…and I also have…' She delved deeper into the case. 'Wigs for every occasion…voila.' she held up a collection wigs, blonde, black and some colours in between.'

'So, we are going to masquerade as Mexican peasants?'

'The boy is bright.'

'Brighter than you think. I've had an idea also.'

'Ok boy wonder. I'm all ears.'

'Pedro.'

'Pedro…what about Pedro?'

'I would have thought it was obvious. I give the ever-so-obliging Pedro some *dinero*, that's Spanish for money.'

'I damn well know what *dinero* means. Get on with it.'

'I send Pedro out to beg borrow or steal peasant clothes for us. Brilliant huh?'

Savannah and Spencer were up before the dawn. Streaks of red slashed the sky. A cool breeze stirred up eddies of dust. Horses and mules stood hitched to a variety of wagons and carts, gathered in the town square. Snorting and whinnying horses blended with the *hee haw* of donkeys.

Everywhere there was every possible variety of fruit and vegetable Mexico produced. There was an excited chatter from merchants, drivers and their helpers. Wives and children had been recruited.

This was obviously a very big day of trading. This was *Señor* Bustillos's daughter's wedding. The *señor* who spent more money in La Tuna than anyone in living memory.

Spencer couldn't understand that these people must have been aware Bustillos was a drug dealer and was involved in questionable activities with local girls, and yet they appeared to simply accept this as a matter of fact. They surely must have questions about young girls who went to the US to work and never returned. Did they just sit back and think, "Well, there was bound to be a reasonable answer?"

There was one particular small farmer who was a very happy man. His name was Miguel Espina. Miguel at that moment was counting and recounting the biggest wad of *pesos* in the world, well possibly not in the world, but certainly the biggest stack of *pesos* in Miguel's world.

Miguel had sold his black gelding complete with his ramshackle dray, loaded high with melons, for the strange *señorita* and her *idiota* partner. Clearly, they were Mexican with ragged peasant clothes, swarthy complexions and matted black hair. The *señorita* spoke Spanish but with an unusual accent. The tall *idiota* said nothing.

'Do you know how to drive this thing?' Savannah whispered.

'How hard can it be?' muttered a nervous Spencer. It occurred to him in planning for every contingency he had sort of overlooked that he'd never actually driven a horse and cart.

'I mean seriously. How hard can it be?'

He had given the black gelding a reassuring pat on the head and given him a carrot. The horse eyed him suspiciously as he greedily gulped down the treat. *That seemed to go well.*

'Ok cowboy, show us your stuff. We have to get back to the Plymouth and pick up the things that go bang.'

Spencer pulled nervously on a rein. 'Giddyap, Diablo,' he begged. Diablo stood resolutely.

'Diablo?' Savannah queried. 'Is that his name?'

'How the hell would I know?' Spencer replied testily. 'I just made it up.'

Savannah burst out laughing, causing the assembled crowd to stare.

'What's so bloody funny?'

'Who the hell do you reckon had a horse called Diablo? Honestly sometimes you razz my berries, Spencer. That was the Cisco Kid's horse. Don't you remember we discussed how much I loved the Cisco Kid when I was young? The name obviously stuck in your subconscious.'

'Giddyap, giddyap…go.' Diablo stood motionless, his blinkered eyes affording him a limited view of the crowded market. Spencer gazed helplessly at the spectacle of this placid animal that seemed to have no ambition in life, and presumably would be happy to spend eternity just hanging out with his fellow beasts of burden. Spencer could see this whole bold plan falling apart just because Diablo had decided today would be a holiday. *Maybe it's his rostered day off.*

'Aha, I may have the answer.'

'Really.' Savannah rolled her eyes.

'What, oh sceptical one, is Spanish for giddyap?'

'Oh um…let me think…yes of course, *arre!*'

That was indeed the magic word. This was the starter button. The light switch. Diablo set off with a rhythmic plod. Unfortunately, not in the required direction.

'Bloody hell, now what do I do?'

'The reins, *idiota,* pull them to one side.'

Spencer pulled on one of the reins and Diablo obligingly headed off on the correct route. Spencer and Savannah and the phlegmatic Diablo were well on the way to the hacienda along with a cavalcade of farmers and merchants. In front of them was a *mariachi* band happily playing Mexican favourites while reclining on the back of a horse drawn flat top dray. Their songs became bawdier the more the tequila bottle was passed around.

'Just have a listen to the lyrics. These guys should be on TV.' Spencer grinned.

Spencer spoke reasonable Italian and the languages were similar. Savannah translated the bits he didn't understand.

'Well, there are some words that are very similar. I think he's suggesting the trumpet player's, uh…appendage um resembles a horse's…' Spencer laughed.

'Yeah. I get the picture. Change the subject. Please. I've just about had enough of God damn *mariachi*. A bit of Sinatra would be nice. Hell, I'm tired.' Savannah stretched and yawned. There was something mesmerising about this mode of travel.

As the cavalcade rounded a bend Savannah woke with a start. 'What. What in tarnation?'

'Wow, Savannah, aren't they gorgeous?' Spencer pointed at the flock of green parakeets as they hurtled off in a delightful chatter of chirping bird talk. The countryside seemed to be comprised of tree and birdsong together in one sensory palette.

The gentle *clip clop* of Diablo's hooves had them intermittently dozing.

'Hell. What now?' The dray had rolled into a dip in the road, Diablo snorted loudly as he laboured to pull it up the other side. Spencer woke with a start feeling like he had gone to sleep at the wheel.

He laughed to himself when he realised Diablo didn't require any input from him.

This, Spencer decided, was actually a delightful way to travel. If it hadn't been a dangerous mission, it would have been the perfect way to see the mountains of Mexico. The hypnotic clunk of the hooves, the gentle clink of the harness and the creaking of the old oak boards of their wagon was strangely soothing.

Diablo was an obliging, if uncommunicative companion, they would have been free to stop wherever they chose and no worries about fuel as that seemed to grow in abundance by the roadside. Spencer could appreciate the simplicity of the peasant lifestyle and understand the Mexican's use of the word *mañana*, meaning tomorrow. In other words, no hurry. *Whatever it is it can wait until tomorrow.*

Initially the other Mexicans had cast surreptitious glances at these two foreigners, who obviously weren't *gringos*. But who were they? And what were they doing here? Why had they commandeered Miguel Espina's horse and cart? Were they distant relatives perhaps?

Collectively the local Mexicans didn't appear to be particularly curious. Spencer figured they knew better than to ask too many questions. They remarked amongst each other. *'Agua Que no has de beber dejala corer,'* which means literally, 'If you're not going to drink the water, let it flow.'

Or in practical terms, "Don't get involved."

It was as if time stood still the procession of carts and wagons made its painstakingly slow progress,

'I don't think I'll ever criticise traffic jams again.' Spencer peered into the distance.

The warmth of the mid-morning sun as it danced through the trees had induced a collective torpor on the caravan of endless provisions. Horses and mules plodded. The clack of hooves on stone and the occasional whinnying now the only sounds. The hours rolled by.

'Hang on…I think we're getting close.'

Savannah reached into her case grabbing hold of her semi-automatic. 'I think the silencer may be a good idea.' She screwed the silencer into place, dropping the weapon into the pocket of her full, well-worn peasant skirt.

'Well, there it is. The *hacienda*.' Spencer glared at the sprawling, bloated Bustillos mansion, home to a small army of tooled up brigands.

Spencer slipped a hand into his trouser pocket and squeezed the cornicello. Feeling the outline of the ancient filigreed silver as it pressed into his flesh. *How the hell did I get myself into this?* He felt a moment of yearning for his wife and daughter. *I just hope I get out alive, and see them again.*

Savannah too was silent, at that moment they both realised just how audacious their plan was.

'Hey…what could go wrong?' Savannah attempted a smile that didn't quite cut it.

Diablo had started to speed up as if he recognised this sprawling mansion probably meant food, drink, rest and maybe a chance to chinwag with the other donkeys, mules and horses.

'Savannah, do you see what I see?' Spencer pointed to the right.

The cavalcade was travelling straight ahead to the main gates but there was another rough cobbled track off to the side.

'I reckon that track would have to lead to the barn at the back of the main building.'

Savannah glanced at Spencer. 'What's the bet that when they bring the girls in and out they use this road so as not to be seen by Bustillos's wife or children? I can't tell you how angry that makes me. His God damn wife would surely know what's going on. They just want to be spared any unpleasantness. I could shoot the lot of them. Bastards.'

'Try not to shoot any more than you absolutely have to, ok?' Spencer was worried far less about her motives or ability to kill all of them than he was about her getting killed by overwhelming numbers…meaning they'd shoot him just seconds after they put an end to her. It'd be less Cisco and Pancho, and more Butch Cassidy and Sundance. 'There's no saving the girls if we're six feet underground, okay?'

With reluctance Diablo responded to Spencer pulling on the reins. There were a few curious glances from the other Mexicans as they left the procession.

They *clip-clopped* on the stony track, the sound of the hooves echoing off the high stone wall that shielded them from prying eyes. They came to the end. In front was a small grove of olive trees and…the barn.

The gabled wood structure fashioned out of long perpendicular aged oaken boards that had at some time been painted red. The paint now cracked and faded. The timber doors had handles fashioned from cattle horns. They could see into the hayloft above the main double doors. It looked exactly as it had the day before.

All was quiet.

'No hay in the hay loft,' Spencer whispered to Savannah.

'Yeah, well they're hardly your regular farmers, are they?'

They anxiously surveyed the scene, on the lookout for any other armed men.

As Diablo plodded into the clearing, they could see the Jeep's driver, Francisco, reclining on a scarred bentwood chair, on an angle leaning against the barn. His *sombrero* pulled in front of his face. Next to him also leaning against the wall, a twelve-gauge pump action shotgun.

'I think the bastard's asleep,' Savannah whispered.

Spencer nodded, not wanting to wake him.

Savannah pointed to one of the melons. Spencer reached over, grabbing one, handing it to her…Diablo obligingly stopped outside the front door and then whinnied. Francisco awoke with a start. Immediately yelling in Spanish, 'Morons, you take your produce to the main courtyard!'

Savannah climbed down from the cart holding a melon. '*Si si, señor*, but while we are here, you might like one of our melons. Very juicy, very sweet.' Francisco hesitated. Savannah's Spanish was perfect but clearly not local.

Francisco frowned. 'You're not from around here…I know you…and you…' His gaze switched to Spencer who'd climbed down from the cart.

'*Maricon y puta.*' Francisco leaned over frantically scrambling for the shotgun, cursing.

He'd just pumped a cartridge into the chamber when Savannah's long barrelled Hi-Power 0.22 suppressed semi auto belched a gentle refrain. Once, twice, *phut phut*. The rounds tore through Francisco's head and chest. The classic double tap. Blood spewed out in a torrent and then stopped. His heart had ceased pumping.

Savannah grinned at her handiwork 'Amazing. A God damn 0.22. How about that?' Her melon lay on the ground, red flesh and black seeds blending with Francisco's blood.

Francisco's face no longer looked human. It was a ghastly mess of pulpy residue. Spencer couldn't help thinking, *the undertaker is going to have his work cut out making him look presentable.*

Spencer shuddered as he knelt down, unclasping a metal ring of keys tied to Francisco's belt. The keys were wet and slimy with blood and some sort of unidentified bodily goo. He was reminded of when he had to remove keys from the Texan in similar circumstances. 'I'll go and release the girls. How about you stay here and keep a lookout. You've got the gun.'

'Sure, Pancho.' Savannah grinned.

'Hey I'm Cisco, you're Pancho.'

'Yeah, whatever.'

Spencer wrenched open the door. The barn was poorly lit. He could see the girls sitting and lying listlessly on bunks and mats.

Spencer ran to the cage, the girls gazed at him with a mixture of hope and fear. He smiled and whispered, *Te est aban liberando'*

As Spencer opened the cage one of the girls, surely no more than thirteen he thought, grabbed him by the sleeve. *'Señor señor, por favor ayuda…Carmalita.'*

She pointed to a room next to the cage. Spencer remembered Bustillos saying how the girls were there for his men's pleasure. Until their departure.

Spencer smiled at the girl, saying, 'Don't worry,' in Italian, which was close enough that she understood.

There was a heart wrenching look of gratitude on the girls face as she whispered, *'Gracias, señor.'* Any doubts or misgivings he had about the operation were immediately dispelled. As he strode towards Carmelita, he felt himself being consumed with a cold rage. Just as he was about to open the door, it was jerked open. There before him was Juan, whose jaw dropped when he saw Spencer. The late Francisco's partner hastily yanked up his trousers. With an animal growl he launched himself at Spencer.

Spencer had never attacked with such relish. He felt like an avenging angel as he administered a vicious head kick. It was unlikely the Mexican saw it coming. Spencer put more force into this classic strike than he had ever done before. The snap of the Mexican's neck being broken and the solid thud as his head hit the doorframe resonated across the barn.

Spencer strode into the room. Carmelita was sitting on a single bed, holding up a dirty sheet to hide her nakedness. *'Por favor, señor.'* She whimpered.

*'Sei libero,'* Spencer comforted in Italian, which was close enough for her to understand. Spencer smiled reassuringly at her as he went to where the girls were now milling around free from the cage, but unsure of what to do next. He held up a finger.

'*Espere*.' Which he hoped meant "wait," in Spanish, he then jogged to the front door, opening it to see Savannah nervously pacing up and down.

'You took your God damn time.'

'Yeah, well, there was a patriot.'

'You didn't have a gun.' Savannah held a hand to her mouth.

She stepped into the barn and saw the Mexican with his neck at a very unnatural angle.

'Oh good, another one of the bastards dead.' She raised a fist and punched Spencer lightly on the shoulder, then gave him a thumbs up. As she glanced again at the body she mused, 'Actually, it's probably a good thing you didn't have a gun.'

'And why do you say that?'

'Well,' she chortled, 'apart from the noise; you would probably have missed.'

# CHAPTER TWENTY-NINE

# THE GIRLS

The girls huddled together, whispering amongst themselves, eyes wide, mouths open. Some crying, some looking hopeful. Spencer and Savannah could hear the questions as the girls whispered to each other.

Were these two strangers friends? Or were they being rescued only to taken to some other hellhole? The man seemed nice but wasn't speaking Spanish. Was he a *gringo*? And the lady, she looked like a field worker but spoke very upmarket Spanish.

Savannah edged up to a girl, who was still huddled fearfully in the cell, the girl drew back, her large eyes focused unwaveringly on this strange peasant *señora*.

'What is your name?'

'*Maria, por favor, señora.*' The girl cringed.

Savannah wrapped her arms around her. 'Maria. We have come to save you. You're not out of danger yet. You and the other girls will have to be very brave and do just as we tell you…ok?'

'Yes, *señora.*'

'Come now and join the others…Ok girls, pay attention. We don't have a lot of time. I want you to leave quickly. Follow the road that runs alongside the *hacienda*. Keep close to the wall so that nobody can see you, *comprende?*

The girls nodded vigorously.

'Now please pay attention. This is really important. You must walk along the road to La Tuna. You must walk just as quickly as you can. If you hear any automobiles, get off the road and hide.'

One girl, a little taller, a little older, stepped forward. '*Señora*, my name is Alexandra. I will make sure the girls do as you say.'

'Thank you, Alexandra. My name is Savannah. And this tall handsome *gringo* is Spencer.'

'*Hola!*' Spencer gave the girls a wave.

Savannah winked at Spencer.

'Alright girls, you must go quickly, Spencer and I have some last-minute business at the *hacienda*. And then we're heading back to La Tuna with our horse and cart. When you see us come and climb aboard? Now get going. Vamoose.'

The last to leave was Maria who waved, a hesitant smile forming on her childlike face.

CHAPTER THIRTY
# SAVANNAH HAS A PLAN

Diablo plodded happily towards the hacienda. Savannah glanced at Spencer. 'Keep your fingers crossed.'

'They're crossed already. But just run it past me again. What's the plan?'

'Simple. You start unloading the melons. I'm going hunting for that bastard Bustillos. It can't be much simpler than that.'

Spencer pushed the *sombrero*—liberated from the late Francisco—further back on his head. 'If he's downstairs on the veranda chin-wagging with his cronies you can't just go up and shoot him. It would be suicide for the both of us.'

'Look I'll confess if he's in plain view we're pretty well screwed. Let's just hope the Gods are smiling upon us.'

Spencer was filled with foreboding as Diablo continued to *clip clop* towards the *hacienda*. The big house loomed large ahead. He knew there were countless well-armed thugs who would shoot first and ask questions later. Spencer glanced sideways at Savannah. All he could see was implacable hatred and resolve. He was not entirely convinced Savannah wouldn't just grab her semi-automatic and empty it into Bustillos and to hell with the consequences. Spencer held the reins with one hand and with the he groped in his pocket for the reassuring outline of the cornicello. *Dear Bert, if you could possibly have known the circuitous journey this talisman would travel.*

'I do actually have something else up my sleeve.' Savannah smiled.

'Well thanks heaps for putting my mind at rest. Why do you choose now to tell me?'

'You seemed to get upset when I told you about the extra firepower, I brought along…so…I thought you might get a little grumpy if I told you what else I just happen to have with me.'

Spencer released the reins and threw his hands in the air. 'Hell's bells, Savannah. You risked us both being thrown into a Mexican jail with the artillery you sneaked past customs…go on, surprise me…let me guess you've brought along a miniature atom bomb to blow Bustillos and his *hacienda* to kingdom come?'

Savannah laughed heartily. 'Well, boy wonder, I will say you have a vivid imagination. I must say that's not such a bad idea. I believe they're making them smaller and smaller these days.'

'No…I've brought something Bustillos would be interested in buying.'

Spencer gazed at Savannah incredulously. 'What on earth do you imagine he could possibly want to buy, apart from these bloody melons?'

'Think about it,' she teased.

Spencer shook his head. 'I give up.'

'Quitter. Promise you won't get annoyed?'

Spencer glared. 'No. I damn well won't promise.'

'Ok.'

'Ok…what do you mean ok? Are you going to tell me?'

Savannah sighed and screwed up her face. 'Coke.'

'What do you mean…coke?'

'Well, I ah…brought along a kilo.'

'Just so as I get this right…As well as smuggling enough artillery to start a small war. You thought perhaps a kilo of cocaine might come in handy?'

'I admit, it was a bit risky.'

'A bit bloody risky…I don't know what the penalties are for all of this stuff you decided to cart across the border, but I reckon we would have both been good for ten years.'

Savannah was quiet for a few minutes. 'Listen to what I have to say. First of all, I apologise for not confiding in you. But I really did have a backup plan and here it is. If Bustillos is not hobnobbing with people on the veranda I'm going to approach one of the underlings. Show him the coke and ask to see his boss, saying that we have a lot of coke to sell. And then ask him to escort me to where dear old Emilio is, in the house. I'm betting he will probably be in his study. An empire like he has, must take a lot of organising.'

'What if said underling recognises you from the when we were here, last?'

Savannah shrugged. '*C'est la vie*. That's the chance I'll have to take.'

'Excuse me. That's the chance *we'll* be taking.'

'Yeah, ok we. Anyway, there you have it.'

'Just one minute…'

'Yep.'

'I have a feeling this is rather a silly question and I think I know the answer anyway…but exactly where did you get the cocaine from?'

'Well, yes I would have thought it was obvious. I was on an operation, and in a nutshell, I caught this guy with the kilo, plus evidence he was a member of a major Chicago crime syndicate; in fact, we knew he was a member. Which is why I was tailing him in the first place. I didn't realise he had the coke until I made the arrest. Nasty piece of work let me tell you, he'd been involved in a number of contract killings.'

'Allegedly.'

'Yeah sure, "allegedly," but the evidence was overwhelming.'

'Didn't you worry he would tell others in the FBI or whoever was interrogating him, about the coke which of course had gone mysteriously missing?'

'Look, we're about to enter through the main gate.' Savannah appeared a little uncomfortable.

'Savannah?'

'I know you won't believe me. But when I asked him to open his briefcase where the coke was, the bastard went for a gun concealed inside. Actually, the very same gun I gave to you a few days ago,' she said brightly.

'So, what you're saying is?'

'*Yeah*, Spencer I shot the creep.'

Their wagon laden with melons—and the tools of death and destruction—rolled into the *hacienda*.

'This looks like a movie set in the making,' Spencer whispered to Savannah.

There were gun-toting men barking orders. Carpenters and tradesman of all descriptions continuing with the erection of the stage. The *mariachi* band members gave Spencer and Savannah a good-natured wave. '*Buenos dios.*'

'All of this for some Mexican princess's wedding. Unbelievable.' Savannah shook her head.

'This guy really has it all.' Spencer pointed at the helicopter squatting benignly on its pad.

'Let's start unloading these melons. Can you see if Bustillos is on the veranda?'

Spencer climbed down from the wagon at the same time unlatching its crude wooden gate.

A thug swaggered over waving his machine gun, his Zapata moustache, *sombrero*, riding boots and flared trousers making him look like an extra in a spaghetti western. 'Hey *necio*, put those God damn melons over there.' He indicated a wooden holding pen.

Spencer wasn't sure what *'necio'* meant, but he was sure it wasn't a compliment.

*'Gracias Señor muchas gracias, ha ha ha, si gracias muchas gracias si si.'* He bowed and at the same time smiling a foolish toothy grin.

The Mexican gazed contemptuously at Spencer, then turning to Savannah, who twirled finger around her ear, the universal sign indicating that someone was mentally deficient. She smiled at the guard pointing at Spencer. *'Idiota.'* She winked at the sentry who laughed and sauntered off.

'I heard that,' Spencer whispered to Savannah.

'Look look, I can see Bustillos. I think he's just finished lunch. He's picked up that little boy. What'd he call him?' Savannah's voice was edged with excitement.

'I think he said El Chapo, because they thought he was going to be short.'

'Whatever. He's putting the little boy down and he's heading into the house. There's a woman at the table. She's now holding the little boy. I'll bet she's the mother.'

'I'll have these melons unloaded in a few minutes. Are you going ahead with this suicide plan of yours?'

'Piece of cake.'

Savannah grabbed the cocaine and made her way to the veranda. A group of guards was yelling at a bunch of townsfolk leading similar carts full of supplies, waving guns in the terrified faces of farmers and laborers. Waiters scurried with plates of mouth-watering BBQ. The lady was still at the table nursing the little boy, sitting opposite her was an older man, well presented, wearing a business suit. *He's got to be an accountant or lawyer.* Spencer noticed a noisy group of gun wielding brigands noisily wolfing their lunch accompanied by bottles of Budweisers and earthenware pitchers filled with what Spencer thought was red wine. *Obviously they don't imagine there's a lot worry about.*

Spencer watched as Savannah edged her way to the table, looking every inch a poor peasant woman in her shapeless black shirt and skirt, a large multi-coloured fabric bag in her hand. *'Perdoneme Señor, Señora.'*

'Yes, what is it?' the *señora* snapped.

Although he couldn't hear what she was saying to the woman, he was sure Savannah was trying to get her attention with the drugs. Savannah nodded vigorously and gestured to the bag. The *señora* gazed contemptuously at Savannah and asked her a question.

Savannah delved into her bag, grabbing the drugs, and this time Spencer could plainly make out the word on her lips: cocaine.

Savannah was no actor. He hoped she was able to convey just the right balance of subservience and respect.

The *señora* cast a cursory glance at the plastic bag, fixing Savannah with a hard stare. She spoke, something short and terse. She clearly didn't have time to deal with Savannah and wanted to make sure the party was ready as planned She turned and yelled at the table of guards.

'Jose, stop feeding your face. Come here.'

One of the seemingly endless supplies of armed gangsters sprang forward, abandoning his lunch. Jose was a clone of all the other armed men, only this one was massive.

Spencer was surreptitiously watching, his heart in his mouth, just waiting for someone to recognise Savannah. He whispered to himself. 'Christ almighty. Just look at King Kong.'

*This guy has to be at least six foot seven. He could bench press a Cadillac. And just cop that facial scar. He would have to be Bustillos's personal bodyguard. I'll just bet.*

Jose's face seemed to be set into a permanent villainous sneer. The scar just added to his air of malice. He wore the same tan leather flared trousers that seemed to be a uniform, they featured bold silver studs running down the lower side of each leg. He wore a ruffled white silk shirt with flared sleeves and a short tan leather vest with the same matching silver studs as his trousers. His sombrero hung at the back of his neck.

Spencer figured that Jose was the biggest and baddest of the thugs and his attire was probably akin to a badge of office.

Jose also had a shoulder holster with a snub-nosed matt black 0.38 displayed a little ostentatiously, Spencer thought.

***

'Jose, take this…woman,' the *señora* said, giving Savannah a disparaging stare, 'to see the *señor.*'

Savannah and Jose threaded their way through the sprawling hacienda. The meaty smell of the feast made her mouth water, but she did her best to ignore it. *This has to be bigger than the White House.*

She cast a glance back at the *señora. God willing, you're about to become a widow, you ugly pompous cow.*

They hurried through the *cocaína* where at least twenty chefs and workers toiled in the steamy heat.

'Need an extra set of hands at the grill. That *risotto* is ready to plate.' The yells of the white-hatted head chef penetrated the air

Jose and Savannah then passed through a vast gilded ballroom that wouldn't have been out of place in the mansions of European royalty. They started down a long-tiled passageway; its walls adorned with what Savannah suspected were priceless works of art.

Jose was obviously proud of his boss's residence, regaling Savannah with anecdotes of Bustillos's successes in the world of narcotics and other criminal acts.

'We are almost there, *señorita.* That last door on the right is the *señor's* study. It is truly magnificent. Perhaps ah…perhaps after you have finished your business, we might have drink?'

Savannah had the impression that her lowly status had been elevated in Jose's eyes as a drug dealer not just a humble melon farmer.

'What do you say, *señorita*? A little drink afterwards?'

Jose turned, facing Savannah, his leer turning to fear and confusion. His face drained of colour, 'No, *señorita*. No. Please…'

'Did you enjoy yourself with the girls, Jose?'

*Phut,* the small calibre full metal jacket round tore through Jose's chest, leaving a trail of mangled wreckage. His death was instantaneous; the slug exploded through his heart, bursting through his back and lodging in a renaissance painting on the wall.

Jose's body crashed to the floor, the sound carrying to the office.

*God damn. That's pretty impressive for a 0.22.* Savannah smiled.

'What was that racket? Is that you, El Chapo, playing a silly game? Be off with you.'

Savannah strolled into the office, the semi- automatic held at waist height. '*Señor* Bustillos,' she purred, 'how nice to see you.'

Bustillos was sprawled behind his magnificent seventeenth century desk, a look of confusion painted on his swarthy face. 'Who are you, what do you want? Hey wait a minute, you're the Americano who wants to buy some girls.' Bustillos laughed. 'You stupid bitch, just what the fuck do you want? It's a holdup, right?' He laughed again. 'You have no fucking way of getting out of here alive.' His eyes flicked momentarily to a loaded Colt 0.45 semi-automatic pistol sitting tantalisingly close to his right hand. Savannah stepped forward brushing the pistol off the desk. It clattered onto the tiled floor, sliding into the corner.

'I suppose that tall *gringo* is part of this also.' he sneered. 'Well let me tell you, you're both dead. Do you hear me?' His voice rose to a shrill crescendo, the veins on his neck stood out. He was Emilio Bustillos. He was the man. He was the kingpin. The controller of judges. Police chiefs and politicians. When he was angry men trembled in fear. Savannah could read his body language like a book.

She smiled. She felt good. All was right in her world. 'Emilio Bustillos. You have lived too long.'

Once again, the suppressed Hi-Power 0.22 spat. Once. Twice. The double tap. One to the chest and one to the head.

# CHAPTER THIRTY-ONE

# EL CHAPO

'El Chapo,' his mother scolded, stop annoying the cat. Go away and play.'

The placid Persian flicked its tail in annoyance at the little boy who kept prodding it and giggling.

The mother sat with friends on the broad veranda, watching with satisfaction at the frenetic activity as the workman toiled making sure all was ready for the upcoming wedding. She smiled; this was the pinnacle of her life's ambition. Her daughter would be wed in a ceremony blessed by God. Officiated by the bishop himself no less. The list of the rich and powerful coming to pay homage were, not only from of Sinaloa but from Mexico City itself.

A pig and a sheep were being roasted on a spit. This, a special treat for the workers, who'd been labouring day and night.

*Ignorant peasants, my God it's not as if we're not paying them a small fortune.*

She turned to address one of her friends and confidantes, Patricia Alvere. Her husband was a wealthy drug dealer. 'Patricia, I tell you Emilio is far too generous these…these.' And she waved a hand at the workers below. 'They take advantage of my husband's generosity.'

Patricia nodded wisely. 'Yes,' she agreed sadly. 'It's the same with Estevan. He discovered one of his dealers had cheated him, out of a small sum of money, but there's a principle at stake.'

'What did Estevan do?'

Patricia snorted. 'Just because the fool had just become a father, Estevan let him off with the mildest of punishments. He had his chief enforcer cut off one of the thief's fingers. In front of his wife. And then apparently, he said next time I'll cut your cock off.'

'She wouldn't have liked that, all they do is *chingar* all the time, they're like rabbits.'

'Frankly I wouldn't mind a bit of *chingar* myself, but Estevan always seems to be too tired.'

'Patricia, would you care for another coffee and perhaps one of those delightful churros?'

A click of an imperious finger, the maid sprung forth bowing.

'Veronica, two coffees and churros.'

The maid brought a tray laden with coffee and a plate of the *churros*, the delicious flour-based batter, rolled in cinnamon.

El Chapo had been standing by his mother's knee, quick as a flash he grabbed a cup of the steaming coffee, and tipped it over the sleeping cat.

The cat screamed in agony, bounding out of the chair. It then commenced running in circles trying to lick the vicious burns, searing its back from its tail to its neck. El Chapo giggled, pointing at the cat.

'El Chapo,' his mother scolded. 'That was a silly thing to do. Now Veronica is going to have to fetch another cup of coffee. Now, away with you. Go and annoy Papa.'

*Boys will be boys.* She gazed fondly at her son.

The little boy ran off at breakneck speed into the bowels of the hacienda. A trip to his father's study was still a journey into wonderland. As he passed through the great hall and down the long hallway dotted with suits of armour from the conquistadors. The armour stood like silent warriors, swords at the ready, as if waiting for an imaginary enemy.

The little boy was in awe of these brooding figures. He could imagine them springing to life, chasing him screaming and yelling.

As he came to the end of the hallway, he could see Jose lying full length on the floor.

El Chapo prodded the body, gazing into the sightless eyes, he paused briefly. 'Wake up, Jose.' He prodded the body again. Satisfied that Jose wasn't about to awake, he trotted the few steps to his father's study.

Papa was asleep at his desk. Papa must have spilt his wine, as his head appeared to be resting in a pool of it. 'Papa Papa wake up, please Papa wake up.'

The boy pulled at his father's arm to no avail. he glanced around the room. His eyes focussed on the gleaming Colt 0.45 semi-automatic pistol resting in the corner of the room. El Chapo glanced quickly around. He knew he wasn't allowed to play with Papa's special toy.

He sat down in the corner, gingerly picking up the forbidden fruit, marvelling at how heavy it was, its shiny silver surface. He studied the weapon, he stuck his tongue in the barrel withdrawing it quickly, his lips puckered in distaste at the bitter unpleasant residue.

El Chapo sat, his back against the wall, holding the barrel of the gun pointed at his chest. He gently squeezed the trigger.

# CHAPTER THIRTY-TWO
# THE ESCAPE

*What do I do now?* Spencer had finally unloaded the melons. The weapons were concealed under a worn canvas tarpaulin; Spencer hoped the conspicuous bulge would go unchallenged.

Nobody seemed to be paying attention to him. A few other vendors endeavoured to engage him in conversation, he'd grinned stupidly, babbling some words in Spanish. The message had finally sunk in, the tall good-looking *campesino* was not exactly working with a full deck. A few beans short of a taco.

Spencer yawned, stretched and ambled over to the red brick paved parking area. Pride of place was the Rolls Royce gleaming in the sunlight. A few yards away were a mixed collection of sedans, a soft top Jeep and an old British Bedford Truck.

Spencer made a show of peering into the Rolls, then strolling around the vehicle. A surreptitious glance showed a guard sprawled in a steamer chair gobbling a taco, a shotgun on the ground beside him. Spencer knelt and rammed the Bowie knife hard into the white wall. This hiss of the escaping air startled him. He felt his heart hammering, but the guard went on eating. Slipping the blade back into his belt, he made

"

his way to the other vehicles and managed to slice the tyres of the Jeep, the truck and three of the sedans.

'*Eh, tu. Idiota!*' The guard yelled angrily.

Spencer pointed at the Rolls. '*Muy bonito,*' he gabbled. '*Muy bonito,*' he yelled again, with a silly grin on his face. He was reasonably sure it meant very pretty.

Spencer's legs turned to jelly when the guard threw down his plate, grabbed the shotgun and strode angrily towards him. The Rolls Royce had a definite lean at the front where the front wheel rested on its rim.

The guard grabbed him roughly by the collar, spun him around, kicking his ass, sending him headlong into the Jeep. Spencer fell onto the bricks, his head hitting the slashed tire. The guard screamed abuse in rapid Spanish and kicked him in the ribs. Without a second glance the man stormed off, oblivious to the Jeep's flattened black rubber.

Spencer watched the retreating guard as he clambered painfully to his feet and staggered back to the wagon. His ribs were sore but he still felt like laughing.

*Idiota. Who's the idiota, now?*

Finally, Spencer saw Savannah crossing the veranda, striding to their wagon. She surreptitiously gave a thumbs up. She jumped up on to the springboard seat. 'Ok Pancho. Time to go.'

Spencer smiled, whispering, 'Hang on, I'm Cisco. You're Pancho.'

'After what I've just done. I'm definitely Cisco,' she whispered.

'Dead?'

'Did I ever enjoy putting those bastards down. When I think of those girls…' Savannah's eyes gleamed.

'Those bastards?'

'Spencer, let's get going. They're going to find some bodies shortly.'

'There you go again. I gather you've dispatched more than one.'

'Yeah, well I had to shoot his bodyguard as well. Don't tell you're going to go all holier than thou again.'

'No, I've decided on an amnesty.'

'What do you mean?' Savannah hissed.

'I really don't mind how many of these people you kill. But how about you slow down on the executions when and if we make it back to the USA.'

Savannah laughed, nudging him in the ribs. 'I tell you, shooting Bustillos was as good as it gets. Now for the love of Mike, get moving. Can't this animal go any faster?' Diablo was marching steadfastly towards the entrance, when all of a sudden, a guard armed with a carbine held up a hand.

'*Detener.*'

'What does that mean?' Spencer whispered to Savannah.

'Damnit, it means halt. I'll have to shoot the bastard.'

'Hang on.'

'*Dinero, dinero.*' The guard held up a brown paper bag.

'Would you believe it? I forgot we actually get paid for this.'

Spencer leaned over, grabbing the bag at the same time gabbling foolishly, a big silly grin on his face. '*Muchas gracias, señor, muchas gracias.*'

The guard winked at Savannah. She smiled, rolling her eyes and making the hand twirling around the ear motion again.

There was a joint sigh of sigh of relief as Diablo hauled the wagon away from the *hacienda*.

'I wish this damn horse could understand the concept of hurry up.'

'Our problems aren't his problems,' Spencer whispered.

Savannah's eyes darted from side to side, her head constantly swivelling as she scanned the road behind them. 'Damnit,' she muttered. 'If you're going to come, then come. Get it over with.'

'Calm down Savannah, the longer it takes for them to start chasing us, the better chance we have. Anyway, think positive. As it happens I don't think they'll be coming after us any time soon.'

'What are you talking about? That Rolls would be pretty darn quick.' Savannah snapped.

Spencer then told Savannah an abridged version of the tire sabotage.

'No kidding? Good work. But I'm still Cisco. And the sad truth is it's not going to take them that long to change some God damn tires.'

'For God's sake how about a bit of, you know "Smile, be happy eh". Bustillos and some of his goons are dead. I've slowed down the pursuit. We never thought we'd get this far. So, please, be a bit positive.'

'Positive?' Savannah snarled. 'The God damn positives are, sure you're right, Bustillos and the Mexican gorilla are dead. Apart from that I can't see a lot to be to happy about.'

'Really? Aren't you forgetting something?'

'What exactly? Hang on a minute. Let me guess, it's your birthday?'

'What you're forgetting is the girls. That's what this's all about, isn't it?'

'Thanks Pancho, you're right. That is the biggest thing. Do you know, I reckon that's just about as good as it gets. Let's just hope we find them and get them home safely.'

Spencer flicked the reins. '*Rapido, rapido,*' he urged Diablo, who snorted and maintained the same speed.

Savannah clapped her hands. 'Yep, that'll work. I don't know whether Diablo is a stickler for punctuation, but you should've said "*Ir mas rapido,*" Pancho.'

Spencer scowled at Diablo's rear end. 'I'm sure that's make a difference. He doesn't seem to understand I'm the boss. Anyway, changing the subject, there's always the possibility they won't find the stiffs for some time. Heck, we might actually get all the way to La Tuna. You never know.'

'No, damnit.' Savannah scanned the road again. 'We're fooling ourselves. The reality is they're bound to find the body of El Supremo and his bodyguard long before we get back to La Tuna. Plus, I'm sure we'll come across the girls before too much longer which will be extra weight for poor Diablo to pull.' Savannah gazed again at the slowly receding hacienda. 'Without a doubt they'll send a car or cars in search of us and here we are travelling at little more than a walking pace.'

'Just keep your fingers crossed. It may never happen.'

'Well, I'm preparing for the worst.' Savannah said as she reached into the wagon and pulled off the hessian bags covering her cases with the guns and grenades.

'Y'know, we have a tactical advantage.' Spencer looked thoughtful.

'Well, it's certainly not a surprise anymore,' Savannah mumbled.

Spencer glanced sideways at Savannah. 'Just listen…here we are travelling down this narrow mountain track. Sure, they have fast vehicles….and…and…in spite of what you just said, I think we still have an element of surprise.'

'What exactly are you prattling on about?'

'Calm down.'

'Sorry Spencer. I guess I'm a little tense. Please continue.'

'Atta girl…Alright, they've absolutely no idea of the weaponry at your disposal and, all though military history isn't exactly my forte, I have read enough to know that with the right ordnance and the right attitude miracles do happen. Think about it, step by step. They find Bustillos. They discover the flat tires. They repair them. They head off at full speed to capture and kill us, right?'

'Your point is?'

'My point is as I have already said, they couldn't possibly have any idea of what we have waiting for them. They'll have hand guns, shotguns, submachine guns, but they're behind us and it's a narrow road. They can only have one vehicle directly at our rear. So, what do they need that they almost certainly won't have?'

Savannah shrugged 'I give up. What?'

'What they would need is something like a bazooka or a, I don't know, a bloody armoured vehicle with a heavy machine gun. They could speed up behind us, open up with that and it would be game over. But, what would the chances of them having that sort of firepower?'

'Jesus, you're right.'

'And there is one other thing…'

'What's that?'

'You my girl…you. One of the best shots in the good old US of A. And probably the world. If that isn't a secret weapon, I don't know what is. And don't forget in any battle it's all about the morale of your troops. These guys have just lost their fearless leader, and as we say in Australia 'they'll be running around like headless chooks.'

'What in hell is a chook?'

'It's a chicken.'

'Thanks for sharing.' Savannah managed an eye roll.

With their nerves on edge Diablo inexorably pulled further away from the hacienda. Spencer glanced at Savannah. 'I hadn't checked but it's been some time now. What do you reckon, a half an hour?'

Savannah again turned her head, nervously scanning the road behind them. 'Yeah, I reckon, all of that, a little more perhaps. And so far, no sight of the girls. I reckon they'd be flat out running all the way to get as far away from the hacienda as possible.'

'Y'know, we might, we just might get all the way back to La Tuna before they find those two dead sons of bitches. What do you reckon, Pancho?'

'Nice thought, Savannah.'

'Umm that's Cisco to you.'

'I don't suppose I can argue, you've certainly gone to the top of the hit parade.'

'Hit parade,' she chortled, 'I like that. You certainly razz my berries, Pancho.'

'Do you hear that?' Spencer turned his head.

In the distance they could hear the roar of engines. Vehicles in a hurry. Savannah grabbed binoculars from her weapons case. 'I can see a Jeep with two men in it. Damnit, that's not all, behind that a, yes, a sedan. An old pre-war Dodge I think.'

'Great.' Groaned Spencer. 'I really needed to know what make and model it is.'

'Ugh and behind that, an open truck filled with armed men. Shit, I can see them all sitting in the back. Christ every God damn one of them holding a rifle. That's a serious lot of firepower. Hellfire and damnation, that Jeep's coming up real fast.'

Spencer flicked the reins willing Diablo to pick up the pace. 'I don't care what you come up with. But whatever it is make it quick.'

'Oh boy, I've got just the thing.'

The open topped Jeep was now only fifty feet behind. The man in the passenger seat had a pistol in his hand and a shotgun on a rack behind him. Lifting up a megaphone he yelled. 'Pull over, *gringos*. You can't escape. It'll only be worse for you if you don't do as you're told.'

Savannah pulled a grenade from its box, winking at Spencer. 'Just you watch this.' Pulling the pin and growling as she hurled it with all her might. 'Swallow this, bastards.'

Spencer watched in dismay as the grenade fell short, exploding harmlessly in a small ravine.

Flashing through Spencer's mind were his days as a youthful fast bowler in the Perth Cricket Club. 'How about, you shoot and I throw.'

Grabbing two grenades, he pulled the pins, throwing them in quick succession.

The Jeep driver's eyes were as big as saucers, as he tried swerving to avoid the grenades hurtling relentlessly towards him. His passenger stood up screaming in fear, as if by yelling he could change the trajectory of the two green orbs as they gracefully sailed through the air.

Spencer turned and watched as the twin emissaries of death rose into the sky, then beginning their descent. Harmless looking in their olive-green casing, the M26 fragmentation grenade. Nicknamed the 'lemon grenade' by soldiers, because of their shape.

*They look like a child's plaything. Spencer thought.* But he knew these weren't toys. They were death and destruction. Vicious pieces of shrapnel that can leave a man shredded.

The first grenade hit the flat bonnet of the Jeep and bounced onto the road. The second fell right into the driver's lap. Both driver and passenger scrambled to retrieve the grenade. Spencer could see the panic and fear written on their faces.

The first grenade exploded as it bounced down the mountain doing no damage apart from sending a flock of brightly coloured parakeets screeching in their hundreds as they flapped their way to safety. The second went up, exploding in a roar, engulfing the Jeep in a ball of fire. The Jeep accelerated, careering down the mountain side, finally running headlong into an ancient Cyprus tree and exploding. Spencer grimaced as he saw the men's bodies engulfed in flames. 'I think that's a six,' he murmured with satisfaction.

Spencer gave Savannah a high five.

The Dodge sedan immediately slammed to a stop. The truck behind almost rear ending it.

'Very good Cisco, now what?' Savannah was tense as she viewed the scene behind them.

Spencer raised an eyebrow. 'I'm Cisco again? Anyway, that's all well and good, but we've stirred a hornet's nest of angry Mexican bandits looking for revenge. They're going to stay out of range of the grenades, that's for sure and certain. The odds aren't exactly in our favour. Any ideas?'

'If you remember Spencer, the Kid always had something up his sleeve.'

'Don't tell me. I'm Pancho again?'

Savannah laughed, flashing him a quick smile as she peered through the binoculars. 'It looks like they're still coming. Yep, the trucks on the move, but keeping its distance. Whoa, hang on…someone's leaning out of the window. What a moron. He's got a handgun, and he reckons he can do some damage. I don't think so.'

'Well Cisco, what's next in your bag of tricks?'

'Pancho dear. I have the very thing right here.'

Savannah reached into the case, grabbing the Heckler and Koch. 'Oh boy, they're gunna just love this.'

Savannah jumped to her feet, screaming at the Mexicans as she sprayed the Dodge with rounds from the submachine gun. 'Hey you sons of bitches. I reckon your raping days are over.'

*Tok tok tok tok tok.* The air reeked of cordite. Spent casings clattered on to the floor of the wagon. The Dodge was peppered with holes. Men shrieked as they leapt off the rear of the truck, scrambling to find shelter behind any solid object. Others could be heard screaming in pain. There were howls of fury from two survivors who levelled their rifles, firing indiscriminately, the rounds flying harmlessly overhead.

'Isn't that something? What *idiota* brings a pistol to a machine gun fight?'

The man with the pistol slumped hanging half out of the window of the Dodge, his body riddled with holes. Steam and hot water gushed from the radiator; the two front tyres flapped impotently as the vehicle ground to a halt.

The mission to apprehend the two *gringos* appeared to have come to an ignominious end.

'What about good old Diablo? He didn't miss a beat. I wonder if he's deaf,' Spencer quipped.

'Well, Pancho, what's going to happen from here, I wonder? They're sure as hell not going to give up.'

The jubilation quickly dissipated.

'I'll tell you what's going to happen. Since we went around the last bend, we can't see them. But they'll push the sedan off the road and follow us at a safe distance in the truck. All they have to do is wait until we get to La Tuna. Once we're on flat ground they can cut us off. They can pin us down. They can get reinforcements…I can't see how we can escape.'

'If we can get to La Tuna before they do, and if the Plymouth is there and intact we may be able to get away. Once we're out of Sinaloa; I think we'd be ok.'

For the next twenty minutes, silence reigned; both Spencer and Savannah felt the peace and tranquillity of the mountain wash over them, for an all too brief moment in time there was no Mexican gangsters it was just the beauty of nature.

Spencer couldn't help reflecting on Savannah's ability to take violence and mayhem in her stride. One minute there's guns blazing, then it's a case of. *Oh well that's over, let's move on.*

'Spencer look, over there.' Savannah pointed to a couple of wild dogs.

'They don't look exactly like your pet pooch do they.'

'No, in fact they're the Mexican wolves known as *lobo*. I think there practically extinct. Beautiful, aren't they?' The wolves eyed them fearlessly as they loped along momentarily keeping pace with their wagon. Diablo who had taken the gunfight at the OK Corral completely in his stride now broke into a brisk trot; clearly, he didn't see *el lobo* as a thing of beauty.

Spencer shook his head. 'What is it with this horse? Bullets fly, grenades explode, he doesn't bat an eye, yet two overgrown doggies send him into a tizz.'

For that all too brief moment they were tourists enjoying the scenery, the fragrant odour of the pines and some identified native flowers, their lustrous blooms splashing colour haphazardly across the hills and tussocks.

Both Spencer and Savannah knew this peaceful and idyllic country scene was going to explode into a mini war zone when the Mexicans regrouped and descended upon them wanting to wreak bloody vengeance for the death of their leader.

Spencer turned scanning the road behind, he groaned. 'They got rid of that damned Dodge pretty quick.'

Travelling at what the Mexicans obviously believed was a safe distance, they could see the truck.

'There's a surprise.'

'Tell me.' Savannah hissed.

'I don't actually know a lot about trucks, but that one is an old British Bedford. Right hand drive as well. That's the one I disabled. They had a spare, I guess. They're making damn sure there're staying out of range. I knew it, the bastards are just going to wait until we get to La Tuna, then we'll be at their mercy.' Spencer continued to focus on the truck

'I don't think they're going to get to La Tuna any time soon.' Savannah smiled.

'You think you can sort things out?'

'You better believe it, Pancho.'

Savannah reached into the case, grabbing the Garand. 'I don't think the truck will be operational for much longer.'

Savannah lay stretched out on the floor of the dray, propping the rifle against the wooden rail. Unhurriedly she adjusted the sights, mumbling as she did so. 'Savannah's penalty for rape, you sons of bitches, is death. Now just see how you like this.'

She unleashed five rounds in quick succession. The telescopic sight made the unfortunate truck an easy target.

Savannah was in her element, gleefully fired round after round. 'Just cop this you bastards. Show your God damn faces!' She yelled in exhilaration. 'I've got enough slugs for every one of you. C'mon losers, show your faces.'

The truck's two front tyres exploded. One of the headlights, smashed and the windscreen shattered. Spencer could see the driver slumped over the wheel and the passenger with his head back, blood pouring from a chest wound.

'Y'know Pancho, I reckon that's the last of them, at least for the moment.'

'I don't want to be a killjoy, but listen.' Spencer cocked an ear.

*Whomp whomp whomp whomp.* They could now both hear the definitive sound of chopper rotors.

At first just an angry speck in the sky, within minutes the outline of a helicopter could be clearly seen.

'It's that bloody whirlybird. They don't give up easily that's for sure.'

'C'mon Diablo, how about a bit of hurry up for Uncle Spencer?' Spencer flicked the reins.

Diablo continued on, clearly unmoved by the predicament of his passengers.

'There it is…my God, it's coming in fast!' Savannah yelled.

The helicopter tore past them, the rotors screaming, the wind felt like a tornado. Spencer estimated it must have been doing about one hundred and fifty miles an hour. It was loud and scary. The draught from the blades rushed against their faces. A tsunami of wind and noise. The clatter of the rotors was deafening. They could clearly see the pilot with his red baseball cap and aviator sunglasses and ominously a passenger next to him carrying some sort of firearm.

Twice the pilot hurtled past them turning quickly and zooming in for a closer look.

Spencer turned to Savannah. 'I think he's wary. He's obviously got the message that we have some serious firepower, I wonder, should I give him a wave.'

'Yeah, Spencer you do that. Why don't you blow him a kiss as well? I want to see what his passenger's carrying,'

Just then the chopper did a tight turn and the passenger who was now facing them leaned out, opening fire. A spray of bullets from an automatic weapon chattered harmlessly above their heads.

'I don't believe it,' Savannah gasped. 'The fool's using a Thompson.'

'What's so dumb about that? I always thought a Tommy gun was fairly deadly.'

'Yeah.' Savannah chuckled. 'They're great when your fifty feet or less away. They're strictly close combat.'

'Ok, so he comes in at fifty feet and we're dead.'

Savannah chuckled again. 'The fool doesn't realise I have the world's best sniper rifle. This is embarrassing.'

'Embarrassing?'

'Yeah.' Savannah snorted. 'Either they're a pair of God damn amateurs or they've got no idea that I have the Garand. Just watch, the idiota is going to pay a high price trying to be a gangster. This's like shooting fish in a barrel.' She laughed. 'Almost too easy, like I said…embarrassing… heck even you couldn't miss.'

Savannah had the rifle in her hands as she lay on her back, bracing her feet against the wooden railing.

The helicopter shot up high then turning quickly as it descended on the wagon, they could easily make out the features of a Mexican, grinning, holding the Thompson machine gun.

Savannah raised the rifle, sighted it, drew a bead, firing twice. The deep boom of the massive cartridges exploding into life echoed against the side of the mountain. The first shot hit the fuselage doing no particular damage. The second hit the tail rotor. Spencer watched spellbound as the rotor shattered in a burst of sparks, little fragments of metal flew in all directions.

The pilot, who seconds ago had been smiling, now looked terrified as the chopper started spinning. Slowly at first, almost gracefully. The spinning accelerated. It reminded Spencer of a fairground ride. The helicopter plummeted to the ground hitting the side of the mountain with an almighty thump. Then immediately, the explosion. The pungent smell of the av gas hung in the air.

Savannah and Spencer sat; their heads swivelled staring in disbelief at the carnage that had unfolded before their eyes.

'I can't believe what I've just done,' Savannah gasped. 'It was so…final…so…I really can't find the words. Those two men…Their last moments. They must have been petrified.'

'Don't tell me I'm seeing, remorse or dare I say it…compassion?'

'No, you damn well don't,' Savannah snapped. 'Those bastards would have killed us in a God damn heartbeat. 'I know you think that I'm soulless and sudden death doesn't affect me, it does. It's just in this case just for a moment. These two men that I didn't know died horribly. Savannah held a hand to her face, then abruptly she burst out laughing.

'Gotcha…didn't I? Do I care? Not for one cotton pickin minute. As far as I'm concerned, I just hope that in the last seconds of their life they suffered pain before the flames consumed them…bastards.'

Spencer smiled at his companion. He felt like giving her a hug and then thought better of it.

'It's just the first time I've seen you show a flicker of emotion. Although it seems I got it wrong and I seriously thought you felt some compassion for those two villains.'

Savannah fixed him with steely eyes. 'Spencer, I know that my methods don't exactly meet with your approval. And I understand that. Believe it or not I respect you and your views, even though you came up with that bullshit time travel story.' She shook her head and muttered to herself. 'Time travel…seriously?'

A sombre silence had descended, the buzzing of Cicadas now sounded like a deafening shriek. Once again it was just the beauty of nature unspoiled by violence.

Savannah laughed, punching Spencer playfully on the shoulder. 'Hang on Mr Self-Righteous, how about you? Just about kicking that God damn Mexican prick's head clean off? We felt some remorse there did we?'

'Do you know? I've never been so consumed with so much…hate…rage, and I don't know what you'd call it. I guess simply vengeance. You're right. I hate to admit it but, the feeling of knowing he was dead…and then when I saw poor Carmelita who the bastard had just been defiling. Probably time to change the subject.'

'*Señor, señor, por favor.*'

'Look, that's Maria and Alexandra.' Savannah grabbed Spencer's sleeve.

One by one the girls arose from behind an ancient rock formation. Savannah yelled in Spanish. 'Hop on board girls. No time to waste.'

Spencer and Savannah were pleasantly surprised to see the change in the girls. The fear, desperation and anguish that had been written over their faces, now replaced with a *joie de vivre*. It was obvious they believed these two strange gringos would save them from the bad guys.

The girls chattered like the schoolgirls they were. Spencer was sure the horror of the previous weeks would haunt them forever, but right now they were free and looking forward to be reunited with family.

When the finally all clambered aboard, the last was the diminutive Carmelita, who needed a hand from Alexandra. Savannah addressed the girls. 'We'll be in La Tuna before much longer, can you all find your way home from there?'

'Yes, *Señora*,' they chorused.

CHAPTER THIRTY-THREE
# TIME TO GO HOME

The small down-at-heels village of La Tuna was a welcome sight. The little township that had struck them as being a Mexican shantytown was now viewed as their oasis, their springboard to a hasty exit from Sinaloa.

Savannah sighed with relief. 'Thank God the Plymouth is there, safe and sound by the look of things.' They nervously scanned the street looking for obvious *banditos*.

'Ok girls, head for home.'

'*Gracias señor, señora.*'

Savannah had climbed down from the wagon. Carmelita threw her arms around her. '*Señora* you've saved our lives. *Vaya con dios.*'

'Go back to your mama, little one.' Savannah was in tears as she hugged her back.

'Yes, oh yes *señora*. She'll be so happy to see me.'

'I don't want to be a killjoy, but we gotta go. We really don't know if the unGodly aren't going to appear.' Spencer climbed down from the wagon.

The Plymouth was parked at the front of their pensione just where they had left it.

Spencer had one quick glance, up and down the street. 'Let's grab our stuff and beat it.'

'What about the *caballo*, and the *el carro*?' Savannah patted Diablo's rump.

'Good ole Diablo and the cart?' Spencer asked.

'*Sí.*'

'Welllll, I guess we're about to make one Mexican *chico* a very happy chappie.' Spencer grinned.

Pedro was transformed from a humble porter to a man of means when Spencer presented him with the gift of Diablo and the wagon.

'*Señor, Señora gracias gracias.*' He gazed in awe at his newfound wealth.

Pedro prattled away enthusiastically in Spanish and broken English as he tore around, helping them get packed.

'*Señor, señora*, come back to La Tuna. We'll always have a room for you. Mi casa, su casa.

He was still trance like, not believing his good fortune.

Spencer and Savannah gave a final wave, slamming the car doors. '*Vaya con dios* Pedro,' Savannah yelled. 'Now Pancho, put your foot down hard on the go-fast pedal. Vamoose.'

The Plymouth accelerated in a cloud of dust throwing up stone and gravel. Spencer had his foot to the floor as the big V8 spun its wheels. The rear end momentarily fishtailing.

'Hell's bells Fangio, slow down!' Savannah yelled.

'Hey…we damn well did it. Didn't we?' Spencer took his foot off the accelerator and looked askance at Savannah.

Savannah threw back her head and laughed. 'We did, Pancho. We surely did. But meanwhile, let's not wind up wrapped around a God damn cactus.'

They quickly put some distance away from La Tuna. The V8 roared as it ripped along the potholed highway.

'Spencer, up ahead, a side track.' Savannah peered out of the rear window. 'So far so good, no God damn choppers or automobiles with Mexican bandits. I'm going to be a lot happier when we change out of these duds.'

The Plymouth jerked to a halt; Spencer stumbled out of the car hastily tearing off his peasant outfit. Savannah stayed in the car hurriedly pulling on trousers and a loose button-down shirt.

'Hit the road, Pancho…floor it.'

Spencer figured they now looked like regular Americans, albeit with traces of makeup.

'I know it's a long drive, but I opt for driving straight through to Hermosillo. At least then we'll be out of Sinaloa and I reckon a lot safer.'

Savannah nodded. 'The more distance we can put between the baddies and us the better I'll like it. I don't think they've given up, but they'll have a job finding us. Mexico's a big place. I'm not going to feel safe until I'm home and having a celebratory margarita with Inez. My God I've missed her. What about you and Maggio?'

'I think we've had this discussion before. Michiyo isn't a ball player and now I have a daughter as well.' He was silent for a minute. 'I'm not sure when I'll be seeing them.'

Savannah looked at him curiously. 'Here we go with this God damn man of mystery stuff again. Honestly Spencer I think I could strangle you. I give up.' She gazed into the distance and laughed, punching him playfully on the shoulder. 'We God damn did it, didn't we Pancho? That son of a bitch Bustillos is dead. We rescued the girls. God damn,' she muttered. 'We really did it.'

'Yeah, but don't go counting your tacos yet. We aren't out of Sinaloa and we sure as hell aren't out of Mexico.'

***

'Hey Carillo, you going to preen in front of the God damn mirror all day? Hit the road, show pony. Do something!' Sergeant Ronaldo bellowed.

Alejandro peered into the small mirror on his cluttered desk, running a comb carefully through his immaculate jet-black hair. He'd been daydreaming again, imagining himself reclining on a cane sun lounger by the pool in his Beverley Hills mansion, a cold beer in hand.

The Policia Federal Estacion Hermosillo was an ugly modern building, its high glass front and oddly flat concrete roof at odds with local architecture.

Alejandro shared a squad room with fifteen other officers, underpaid and looking for ways to graft a dollar, or *peso* from any villain, real or imagined who could be induced to pay a bribe. Each officer was expected to contribute on a weekly basis to his superior officer.

Pickings had been slim of late. The paltry sums screwed from local pickpockets and thugs had been miniscule. The phone rang.

'Hey, Carillo. It's for you.'

Alejandro grabbed his phone. 'Yes?' Alejandro sprang to attention. '*Señora* Bustillos, this is indeed an honour,' he stammered. 'What, Oh no. It cannot be. Yes, *señora*. Of course, *señora*. I have a pencil. Americanos, Si. A grey Plymouth. Si. Si, *señora*. Leave it me, *señora*.'

After frantically scribbling some more details. Alejandro hung up the phone.

# CHAPTER THIRTY-FOUR
# A PLEASANT DRIVE
# THROUGH MEXICO

'What's the speed limit in Mexico?' Spencer queried.

Savannah peered out of the window. 'I don't want to draw the attention of the Federales, but I don't think there is one.'

Spencer chuckled. 'Well, I guess it's pedal to the metal then.' The Plymouth with its 273 cubic inch motor tore up the highways and byways at an impressive rate.

Spencer remembered a book by Ralph Nader entitled 'Unsafe at Any Speed.' I think Mr Nader might have had this vehicle in mind when he wrote about the American car industry.

There was no doubt the big Plymouth went like a bat out of hell. But the steering felt as if it had a mind of its own and the brakes, *my God*. Spencer had tried one hard stop when a geriatric mule wandered in front of the Detroit rocket.

The mule gazed nonchalantly at Spencer as the Plymouth reluctantly slammed to a stop, smoke billowing from its brakes and tyres. It felt to Spencer as if an invisible hand had stopped the car just as the animal was about to be propelled into mule heaven.

Savannah shrieked at the top of her voice, stamping her feet on an imaginary brake pedal. 'Oh, that poor God damn mule, you nearly killed him.'

'Him? What about us, woman? We would've been sitting here in a pile of U.S metal just waiting for the *banditos* to come and finish us off.'

Spencer cursed the mule as it happily wandered off, oblivious to how close it came to a grisly death.

'Go back to your wife and children, you *idiota!* Savannah yelled.

'He doesn't have any children, dear.' Spencer smiled.

'Oh, really smart arse. How could you know whether or not he has offspring? He's probably got a wife, several mistresses and a whole lot of little mules that call him daddy.'

'I'll bet you the next round of burritos he has no little mules that call him daddy.'.

'Ok I give up. What do you know that I don't?'

'Oh, probably many things.'

'Alright you smug son of a bitch, tell me. I know you're dying to.'

'Well dear, you're about to learn something.'

'Spencer' she snarled 'Can you spell point?'

'Of course, I can.'

'Yeah, well how about getting to it.'

'Mules are the offspring of a horse mating with a donkey, but they themselves can't procreate.' Spencer smiled a beatific smile.

'Is that right?'

'You betcha, that's a genuine solid gold fact.'

'Well, you learn something every day.'

Spencer's face screwed up in dismay. 'Here's something you didn't want to know, there's an automobile coming up behind us and it's travelling very fast.'

# CHAPTER THIRTY-FIVE

# THE RISE OF ALEJANDRO CARILLO

Alejandro was the ninth son of Luisa and Jesus Carillo. Luisa was a proud and determined woman, from the moment she laid eyes on her youngest son Alejandro and as he sucked greedily on her breast, she knew he was bound for greatness.

*Señor* Carillo was a mid-level clerk in the sprawling corruption riddled Mexican civil service. Sadly, in his department overseeing motor vehicle transfers there was little scope for bribery and the Mexican *pesos* that were deposited in his bank account never seemed to stretch quite far enough.

*Señor* Carillo would sigh and mentally beseech his namesake to try and curb his wife's spending. Money was lavished on Alejandro, the only one of their sons to get a good education. The priests who taught him marvelled at the boy's capacity to absorb facts, figures and especially language. By the time Alejandro left school he had two particular attributes: he spoke perfect English and he was determined to not be poor like his parents.

Opportunities in Mexico were limited, but Alejandro had noticed the *Federales* in their smart uniforms as they swaggered though his neighbourhood. It didn't take the observant Alejandro long to work out that the bulk of their income was from bribes. This he figured could well be a short cut to wealth and the luxuries he craved. He watched American movies and marvelled at the easy lifestyle that was portrayed, everyone appeared to drive big-finned convertibles, and no one appeared to work too hard.

Alejandro applied for and became a *Federale*. Resplendent in his new uniform, he would pose before the mirror in his tiny cubicle of a bedroom, smiling as he brandished his shiny new Colt revolver.

Sadly, for Alejandro he didn't find the wealth he sought. In Mexico few people had any real money, those that did were generally unbribable as they were far too well connected.

All of this changed when Alejandro met Emilio Bustillos.

Alejandro cruised the bleak minor roads in outer Hermosillo, annoyed his superiors had assigned him a desolate area to patrol, with little traffic. Cursing, he fiddled with the unreliable police radio in the well-worn Ford Twin Spinner v8 cruiser. It'd spent the first years of its life patrolling the suburbs of Bel Air and Hollywood, in his dream town, LA. The impoverished Mexican Police Department bought most of its vehicles second hand from the US.

As he raised his eyes from the malfunctioning radio, he saw an automobile by the side of the road. Not just any automobile but a Rolls Royce Silver Cloud.

If Alejandro's eyes had stalks, they would well and truly be extended. A plump middle-aged man dragging a body out of the driver's seat?

Alejandro was in a quandary. You didn't have to be a genius to figure out this was a major crime scene, but a Rolls Royce? This smelt like opportunity.

His Ford drew slowly to a stop, scanning the immediate area he saw nothing amiss. Neglecting to switch on his police lights as was the usual custom. Normally he revelled in the sight and sound of the flashing red light. He did take the precaution of unbuttoning the flap on the holster of his Police Positive 0.38 revolver.

Carefully placing his police cap on his head and snapping on his aviator glasses, he padded cautiously to the Rolls.

The chubby middle-aged man didn't seem at all perturbed by the sight of a police officer, 'Don't just stand there. How about a hand.' This wasn't posed as a question.

Alejandro was stunned, as he got closer, he could see that, yes indeed there was a corpse. The deceased was a young man with a very big gunshot wound to the head.

'You grab the shoulders and I'll grab his feet,' the man instructed. 'We'll throw him into the ditch.'

Alejandro was like a robot. He grunted under the weight of the corpse.

'Heavy son of a bitch.' The chubby man grinned, kicking the body down the slope into the drainage ditch. As the corpse slid into a muddy pool of water the man held out a hand. 'Emilio Bustillos. I discovered that piece of shit was an informer. Feel like a beer?'

Alejandro nodded dumbly as Bustillos went to the back of the Rolls. Opening a refrigerated walnut cocktail bar, he grabbed two Budweisers.

From that day Alejandro was on the payroll.

## CHAPTER THIRTY-SIX
# THE FEDERALE

Savannah peered through the rear window. 'Whoever it is, they're in one hell of a hurry.'

'Police…do you think?' Spencer glanced sideways at her.

'*Federales,* Spencer, *Federales.*'

'Whatever, but why do I feel like some guy who's just robbed a bank and about to be taken down by the long arm of the law?'

'Well,' Savannah sniggered 'our little sojourn in Mexico has left a trail of corpses. Of which, I might add you've contributed.'

'I can't see that we could have a problem with law enforcement. Our problem surely is with the late Emilio Bustillos and his crew?'

Savannah continued to peer at the rapidly approaching V8 Ford decked out in its police livery. 'You may be right. But this is Mexico, not the good old U S of A.'

Savannah reached into the glove compartment, grabbing the snub nosed 0.38 revolver. 'Just to be on the safe side, tuck this into your belt and pull your shirt over it.'

'Is this really necessary?'

Before Savannah could answer, lights flashed and the siren wailed a mournful sound that never meant good news in any language.

Spencer eased the Plymouth onto the shoulder of the road. A quick glance at the surrounding area showed they were in a heavily wooded area, no local peasants or farm workers to observe any unfolding drama.

'Probably just a licence check. Or to make sure our papers are in order,' Spencer said unconvincingly.

The blue and white police cruiser pulled up behind them. The *Federale*, tall and lean with an uncharacteristically spotless uniform, nonchalantly climbed out of his vehicle. Pausing to admire his image in his side mirror he slid a pair of aviator glasses from his belt and pushed them into place, simultaneously adjusting his snowy white peaked cap.

'Just check this guy out; he's got to be the Errol Flynn of Mexican law enforcement.' Spencer chuckled at the swaggering figure. A Zapata moustache and glistening black knee-high boots with jodhpurs and a uniform looking like it had just come from the uniform shop and unwrapped that morning.

'Yeah, but the Colt isn't just for show,' Savannah whispered.

The officer sauntered up to the passenger door. Placing his hands on the door sill, and in perfect English. 'My name is officer Carillo. Identification please.'

'Certainly officer.' Savannah reached into her handbag, retrieving her papers and handing them over.

Spencer noticed the high Aztec cheekbones and the underlying dull redness of marijuana eyes as the officer removed his sunglasses.

Spencer winked at Savannah, who stared fixedly ahead.

*This guy looks like a Hollywood version of a cop. He's not going to be a problem.*

The officer examined the documents closely. 'Would you mind stepping out of the car, ma'am?'

Savannah shot Spencer a worried glance. Opening her door, she stood facing the cop.

'Turn around. Place your hands behind your back.'

'Officer, what seems to be the problem?' Spencer called out.

'No problem, sir,' he said breezily, snapping handcuffs onto Savannah's wrists.

Spencer climbed out of the driver's seat, his muscles stiff from lack of activity. He turned to see Savannah being thrust into the back of the cruiser.

Spencer stood motionless. The *Federale* slammed the passenger door, at the same time grabbing his revolver and aiming it at Spencer. 'Move away from the driver's door, sir. I'm going to do a quick search of your vehicle.'

'Officer, if this is about drugs or anything we're not supposed to have, I can assure you, there's nothing.'

'Step away from the driver's door, *gringo*.'

The officer did a superficial search of the car, at the same time keeping Spencer covered.

'Officer, I can assure you we're just tourists.'

Spencer's plea fell on deaf ears. 'Do you intend taking us to police headquarters in Hermosillo?' Spencer had noticed the side of the cruiser emblazoned with the sign attesting that the cruiser was from that particular town.

The officer smiled, staring hard at Spencer. 'No *gringo*. We'll be going back to La Tuna. *Señor* Bustillos's family have plans.' He laughed. 'Oh yes do they have plans!'

Spencer turned and nodded at Savannah who tried hard to smile.

'So, we're going back to La Tuna, huh?'

'Well *gringo*. Here's the thing. For whatever reason, the late *señor's* family mainly want the *señorita* for the games they have in mind.'

'So, what about me?'

'Well, *señor*. As I said, they mainly want the *señorita*…and as for you it was $10,000 but it was "dead or alive". Sadly, I only have one pair of handcuffs so…'

Spencer noticed the gun was held rock steady. The *Federale* stood relaxed, gun in one hand, the other resting on the open car door.

At that moment Spencer knew he had only minutes, perhaps seconds to live. He weighed up a frontal attack. Although he knew there were few with his ability and reflexes, all the *Federale* had to do was squeeze the trigger.

'First things first, *Señor.* Reach slowly into your back pocket, remove your wallet and throw it on the ground.' The *Federale* fingered his impressive moustache as if it were a new arrival he wasn't yet quite used to.

Spencer put his hand behind his back, feeling the outline of the 0.38. Grabbing it, and without taking aim, he fired a shot. The round went wide, hitting the door frame with a metallic clang. In a flash, it ricocheted into the *Federale's* neck. Blood gushed onto his pristine white shirt. In a momentary flash of horror Alejandro, the apple of his mother's eye, knew his day had come. He futilely placed a hand on the gaping hole. Blood poured like a dam broken after winter rain.

Alejandro Carillo, the straight A student, the *Federale* destined for great wealth, was dead. Spencer saw a steel ring laden with keys hanging from the dead officer's belt. He hurriedly unclasped them. Rushing to the police cruiser, he almost slipped in the pool of blood, leaching into the fertile earth of Mexico.

Spencer threw open the rear door. 'One of these keys has to be for the handcuffs.' Savannah's practised eyes glanced at the collection. 'That little chrome one on the end.'

Spencer undid the cuffs, giving Savannah a reassuring smile, silently grateful the shot had only hit Carillo.

Savannah leapt out of the car, casting a disapproving eye over the dead cop. 'Jesus H Christ,' she yelled. 'I knew you were a rotten shot. But you missed him at what…about six feet? I don't believe it.'

'Whoa, hang on a minute, a bit of gratitude wouldn't go astray. He's dead and you're free.'

'Yeah, thanks, Cisco.'

'Oh, so it's my turn to be Cisco?'

'Yeah, Spencer, I think you deserve it…but seriously your shooting kills…'

'Well as it happened. I planned it.'

'Planned what?'

'I mean anybody could have shot him at that range. But I decided to impress you and go for my celebrated trick ricochet shot.'

'Honestly Spencer, sometimes you razz my berries. Trick shot!' Savannah snorted.

'Well girl, trick shot or not, here we other with another corpse that needs disposing of.'

Savannah stood, hands on hips and wearing a scowl. 'Do you know, I think my love affair with Mexico might be coming to an end.'

Spencer surveyed the scene. 'That area over there is heavily wooded. I can spot a track leading in. How about we put his body back in the car? I'll drive it in as far as I can and hopefully no one will find it in a hurry. We're in the middle of nowhere.'

Spencer drove the police cruiser deep into the heavily wooded forest. Upon the forest floor lay trees of yesteryear, fallen in storms long forgotten. Low slung branches scraped the duco. The track, rutted with wheel marks from countless horse drawn wagons. It felt as if they were in another time and place. The overhead foliage blotted out the sun. The atmosphere now dark and mysterious. Savannah shivered. The ancient trees with their sprawling limbs stared like silent sentries guarding the darkness.

'This looks exactly like a place where you'd expect to find a body. This's creepy.' Savannah shuddered.

Spencer too felt the weight of the oppressive humidity; it was if they had been transported to another planet. 'Just look at that.' Spencer pointed at a massive tree almost as wide as the car. 'Isn't that something? I've never seen a tree like that.'

Savannah peered through the heavy foliage at the massive specimen. 'If we leave the car behind that, it could be undisturbed for some time.'

They set off at a brisk trot back to the Plymouth. Spencer stamped on the gas and the car shot forward.

'Well, Cisco.' Savannah smiled at Spencer. 'Let's get out of Mexico and don't spare the horses.'

# CHAPTER THIRTY-SEVEN

# GOODBYE MEXICO

'Thank God, Tijuana.' Spencer glanced sideways at Savannah, the border officials sleepily waved some cars through and stopped others. They'd waited for an hour behind a sluggish, tired array of automobiles and trucks all waiting to exit Mexico.

The oppressive heat and the exhaust fumes began to take their toll. Spencer nervously gazed behind him, half expecting a wail of sirens and armed *Federales* to come running waving pistols. Border guards checked some vehicles closely, but most vehicles were being waved through. There didn't seem to be a system, appearing to be purely random.

'I'd bloody well go and bribe the bastards, if I thought that'd work.'

'God damn,' Savannah muttered, 'I sure hope they don't check the trunk.'

Spencer couldn't help himself; he was overcome with a fit of the giggles. 'Yeah, well. you could always tell them you had just been to a firearms convention and your topic of conversation was…what's needed if you want to start a small war.'

'For Chrissake shut up. They're staring at us.'

Spencer gazed listlessly at the Tijuana Street scene. He stretched out on the broad grey rear vinyl seat of the

Plymouth, all windows wound down. Sweat turned their clothes into damp rags. The long line of cars in front, barely moving. Four sombrero wearing Mexican men were noisily playing poker on a flatbed truck in front of them. A burrito stall had hurriedly set up, taking advantage of the traffic stoppage.

'*Burritos, cerveza helada.*'

The heat, the flies, the incessant din from car radios got on Spencer's nerves. He started to see Mexican hitmen, or *sicarios* as they were known, lurking behind every building. He imagined loitering groups of men were staring at them. Sinister men with sinister motives. A young boy no more than ten banged on his door, and in a loud voice yelled. '*La naranja por favor, Señor. La naranja.*'

The beaming gap-toothed lad held up a bowl of oranges.

This smiling young boys offering of ripe fruit was just what Spencer needed to dispel the dark bout of paranoia that had descended on him. '*Cuanto cuesta el naranjo?*'

The boy grinned, holding his hand to his forehead to protect himself from the sun, he spoke to Savannah. '*No entiendo, no entiendo.*'

Savannah laughed, once again she made the twirling motion with her finger. '*Idiota.*' She pointed at Spencer.

'What the hell's going on? I simply asked him how much the oranges cost.'

'Ah…no, dear. You asked him how much the whole God damn tree cost.'

The Plymouth passed through the border with no questions. Spencer climbed into the front and took the wheel.

Holding up a hand Savannah acknowledged with a high five. Relief rolled over them in waves.

'My God girl, we did it. We really did it.' Spencer threw his head back and roared with laughter.

'Hey Cisco, watch the damn road. I want to be in one piece when I see Inez.'

Spencer gunned the car. 'One more toll booth, the Playas De Tijuana, then it's a straight run.'

'How about stopping at La Jolla? I'll need a coffee by then.'

It finally sunk in as Spencer parked the car at Harry's Coffee Shop in Gerard Avenue at La Jolla by the Sea, that they had nothing more to fear. They grabbed a seat at the front of the building under the protective shade of a big red canvas umbrella.

Savannah ordered cinnamon rolls and coffee from a very chipper, young waiter wearing white cotton trousers white shirt a dinky little red bowtie and a red side cap with the Harry's logo. She laughed as she placed the order, the waiter looked puzzled as he quickly scurried inside.

'Did I miss something?' Spencer asked. 'That poor kid thought you were laughing at him.'

'I didn't mean to laugh. It was just that he was so American. And I guess he was just such a welcome sight.'

The brewed coffee came in big stoneware mugs. It was fresh hot and strong. The cinnamon rolls came piled high on a plate.

They drained the last of the coffee and polished off the last roll. Spencer grabbed the check and placed a five-dollar bill on the table.

The rest of the drive to LA was largely in silence. Both Savannah and Spencer were lost in thought, both mulling over the events that had transpired since they had met in LA at the coffee shop a year ago.

Spencer hadn't thought about Michiyo and his baby daughter for weeks he thought guiltily. *What if this time it's different? What if this time I don't go back?*

Spencer sneaked a glance at Savannah and thought how glad he was to have met up with her again. And although her utter disregard for due process and the inconvenience of things like juries, judges, and trials was still disturbing, he had to admit those that had been exterminated were in no way a loss to society. He mulled the word 'exterminate' for a minute. *Exterminated… that's the perfect word, these abominations, those people that prey on the vulnerable for their own twisted and evil reasons simply need to be exterminated just like household pests, cockroaches, lice, fleas.*

Spencer shuddered at the memory of Zachariah Colchester saying those dreadful words. "Yes, and they're so expendable." Spencer remembered a phrase he'd heard, "The banality of evil." *That's the reality,* he decided. *The devil doesn't prance into the room breathing fire and brimstone, his horns jutting into the air, a vicious gleam in his eye. No, he wears expensive suits, lives in gilded mansions, spreads death, destruction and misery, and at the same time living a life of respectability.* Sadly, these destroyers were protected by other rich and powerful people, who turned blind eyes to the occasional rumours of dark deeds carried out by equally depraved underlings.

Spencer felt in his pocket for the comforting outline of the cornicello.

# CHAPTER THIRTY-EIGHT
## SANTA MONICA PIER

'Hey *muchacho*, have another beer. You're being very quiet over there!' Savannah yelled at Spencer across the table.

Spencer raised his glass, a fragile smile on his lips. 'Any more of the amber fluid and I'll be elephants.'

'Savannah, can you translate for me please? What's the boy talking about, elephants?'

Savannah grinned 'Aussie slang, Priss. Elephant's trunk. Drunk'.

Californian weather at its best. Spencer gazed at his companions; it was a party atmosphere. The tensions of the Mexican trip were already starting to fade, but dark clouds were beginning to roll through Spencer's subconscious, starting with images now popping up like an unwelcome guest. Images of his daughter. With a jolt he realised he was having trouble visualising her. Michiyo, beautiful Michiyo, her face would flash before him, always painted in worry. 'Where are you Spencer, we need you.'

The unbidden images were tinged by guilt. *Are you enjoying your life too much to return to us?*

*How long has it been?* Slowly he began counting off the days, the months. *It's been a year.* Hurriedly Spencer pushed the unwanted images to the back of his mind. *It's out of your control, you can only play the cards you've been dealt.* He forced himself to focus on now. *This is real, this is your life.* What was he going to do, look into time travel technology?

'Waal, big boy, what now? You're going to be a G man forever?' Priscilla grinned.

Spencer was dragged out of his maudlin thoughts. 'Why not Priss? Savannah and I make a good team. Her boss Dale Fletcher is happy to keep me on. He wants me to undertake a formal training course. So, who knows? As it happens, I think Savannah and I have a few loose ends to sort out.'

Spencer gazed out at the Pacific, the surfers, the swimmers. He squinted into the sunlight. Was that Catalina Island he could just make out?

The warm California sun was having the desired effect. Spencer started to focus on his plans. *I'm going to have to get an apartment, something near the beach. A car, yep, nothing fancy. Dennis could point me in the right direction. Definitely an automatic.*

Spencer's attention was suddenly focussed on an attractive Asian lady strolling towards him, long black hair, white bikini. 'It can't be.' He bolted upright. The name Michiyo beginning to form on his trembling lips.

The colour ran from his face, as the lady ran to a tall surfer, throwing her arms around him. No, he thought dully, an illusion. *A bit like my life. Is that an illusion?*

Once again Spencer felt the rustling of unease. *What is my purpose? Where do we go from here? Am I here to stay? Do I make plans for a future that may never be?* He forced himself to focus on the moment. *You can only play with the cards you've been dealt. C'mon focus on now, damn you. It's all you have.*

Priscilla, Savannah and Inez were chatting animatedly. Spencer leaned back, his hands behind his head, thinking what delightful company they were. They'd gathered on the pier The Beach Buddies were noisily setting up their equipment.

'A toast to Savannah.' Inez raised her glass of Coca Cola.

'Sure, what's the occasion?' Spencer raised his glass.

'Go on darling, you tell them.' Inez poked Savannah gently in the ribs.

'I didn't want a fuss. It's my birthday, ok?'

Prissy leaned over and kissed Savannah. 'Waal honey, I wished I'd a known. I'd have baked a cake, but I'm sure you got a nice present anyways.'

'Inez bought me a lovely watch.'

'You're still wearing your FBI special,' Spencer said.

'I bought a lovely gold watch from Harry Winston in Beverley Hills. And Savannah still wears that awful FBI monstrosity. It looks like what a...how do you say...lumberjack, that's it. It is what a lumberjack would wear. *Estoy molesto.* I do not understand, really I don't.' Inez shook her head.

'It's a great day. It's my birthday so let's have fun. I'm sorry Inez, I really love the watch, honestly I do. But it's so nice, I feel it should be worn only on special occasions,' Savannah said unconvincingly.

The Beach Buddies blasted out their latest composition. Prissy jumped up. 'Waal who's goin to dance with this country gal? You, big boy?' she pointed at Spencer.

'Actually, I need to run over a few operational matters with Savannah.'

Inez spoke, 'I'll dance with you. Have your business meeting with Spencer. We'll keep out of your way for a while.'

Inez stood, following Priscilla to the dance floor where they performed a very creditable jive.

Spencer couldn't help noticing just how good the Beach Buddies had become, they seemed more professional in every way, they had well and truly embraced the surf culture turning their original compositions into songs about surfing and everything related to the craze, the cars they drove, the blonde girl surfers and the new surf speak, describing waves and wipe outs. The crowd just lapped it up.

The lead guitarist's fingers danced over the fretboard of his Fender Stratocaster; the twelve-bar break had feet a-tapping. He was letting rip on one of their compositions, *Surfin USA*. Spencer wasn't an expert, but he was sure that the melody line was a rehash of a Chuck Berry song, but what the heck it worked. Of course, they sung about the cars. *Little Deuce Coupe,* all about a teenager's love affair with his hot-rod.

## CHAPTER THIRTY-NINE
# UNFINISHED BUSINESS

Sprawled untidily in her chair, Savannah's face looked like a smiley emoji. 'Well, Pancho, what would you like to know?'

'Hey wait a minute, I thought I was Cisco.'

'Only till we got back to the US of A, partner.'

Spencer grinned. 'Yeah ok. Now just fill me in, has there been any fallout from what happened in Mexico?'

'Like what?'

'Well, I thought perhaps seeing there was a trail of dead bodies. A deceased *Federale* officer, there might just have been some diplomatic squawks from the Mexican government.'

Savannah took a long pull on her Coke. 'People get killed all the time in Mexico. Hell, they don't know our identity. I never went through the normal channels. Dale Fletcher doesn't even know we went there…so…mission successful. The girls were rescued. The prime bad guys are dead and well, all's right with the world.'

Spencer studied Savannah's smiling visage for a moment. 'Not everything's right with the world, is it?' Spencer prodded.

'There's always going to be some unfinished business.' Savannah shrugged.

Spencer glanced at the dance floor, Inez and Priscilla were now doing the "stroll" laughing and waving at Dennis who waved drumsticks back at them. The Beach Buddies really had the crowd rocking.

'I can't believe that you're prepared to let Colchester and Charlie off the hook.'

'Spencer, the reality is Zachariah Colchester is so well connected and has so much money, that his legal team would stall the judicial process for years. His powerful friends would throw up every conceivable obstacle and could very easily destroy me and my career in the process.'

Spencer chewed on his lower lip his eyes boring into Savannah's.

'What…what's that look for, you son of a bitch?'

Spencer sighed. 'Why do I get the impression you're not being entirely honest with me?' He stabbed a finger at her. 'Ok, what about Charlie?'

'What about Charlie?' Savannah snapped.

'He doesn't have the money or the political clout that Colchester has. Why can't we go after him?'

'God damnit Spencer. 'Don't you think I might have explored all the options where Charlie is concerned? After all, that's my damn job.' She spat the words out.

'Ok…ok…I'm not questioning your professionalism but…that guy's just plain evil.'

'Yes, that may be,' she said tartly, 'but the last time I looked there isn't a specific law against being evil.'

Spencer scratched his head, once again he stared at the happy throng on the dance floor.

'Savannah, we can't just let these bastards get away. They're going to keep doing the same stuff. More drugs, more vulnerable girls.'

Savannah looked like she was going to say something, then thought better of it, eventually leaning forward. 'Spencer, we've nothing of substance on Charlie. Tex is dead. Charlie and Colchester can deny ever knowing him.'

There was a break in the music, Priscilla and Inez flopped into the wicker chairs.

Inez swallowed the last of her Coca Cola with relish. 'That dancing is thirsty work.'

Priscilla chuckled. 'And I'm ready for a beer, waiter.' The young college boy waiter scurried over casting a lustful eye over Priscilla. 'Hey handsome, how's about you fetch us four cold Buds?'

# CHAPTER FORTY

# HOLIDAY SNAPS

Priscilla raised her glass of Budweiser. 'Cheers!' She grinned, licking her lips in appreciation. 'Alcohol has its critics.' She laughed. 'But it's still the greatest aphrodisiac there ever was.' She winked at the young waiter, who couldn't seem to take his eyes off her. 'Damnit all, I gotta remember I'm on R and R. No doubt about it, there's nothing like a beer or two to turn a girl's fancy too…and as some wise fella once said, candy's dandy but liquor's quicker. Now Spencer, tell us all about the trip Savannah and you did to Mexico,' Inez said. She was under the impression it was a speaking tour, discussing law enforcement techniques with the Mexican Government.'

Spencer almost choked on his beer. He turned his gaze on to Savannah who sat with a hint of a smile.

Inez chimed in. 'Speak, Spencer. Savannah said very little, I understand she was the guest speaker at some police seminars in a city called…what was it? Hermosillo?'

Savannah spoke. 'Yes, Spencer, tell us all about Hermosillo. What was that guy's name? let me see now…was it Emilio Bust…Bustillos? Yes that was his name. I got the impression that he wasn't very well. I do hope he's ok. He was such an obliging gentleman, wasn't he?'

Spencer looked daggers at Savannah. 'Ah yes, Hermosillo. Lovely town, friendly people, I do remember one of the organisers was a giant pain in the ass.'

'Really,' Savannah replied. 'What was…his name?'

'Don't you remember Savannah? His name was Cisco?'

Priscilla momentarily took her eyes off the waiter. 'You mean like the Cisco Kid, on television?'

'Yeah, that's the one, only this Cisco was rude and overbearing and quite frankly I suspected as a law enforcement officer he would have been a vicious brute.'

Savannah scowled. 'Personally, I thought Cisco was terrific. I suspect he would have been firm but fair when dealing with criminals. Actually, I thought the junior officer Pancho was the problem.'

Inez looked puzzled. 'Seriously, do you mean there were two police officers, like the Cisco Kid and Pancho?'

Spencer at this point had difficulty controlling his mirth. 'No Inez…I think the junior officer's name was not Pancho, I believe it was just a nickname, or *apodo* as you would say in Spanish.'

'So, Spencer, tell us about Pancho.' Inez nodded.

Spencer smirked at Savannah. 'Ah yes…let me see now. Pancho was truly delightful, charming, educated, very handsome guy, loved by everyone he met, I would suspect. But I think his boss Cisco was…secretly jealous of him. Awful to see when the boss uses his power and influence to keep his talented subordinates from rising to their full potential.'

Savannah by now couldn't control her mirth and burst into a paroxysm of laughter. She pointed a finger at Spencer and still laughing. 'This doesn't end here.'

'I don't understand.' Inez glanced first at Spencer then at Savannah.

Spencer turned to Inez. 'Sorry Inez, Savannah and I just had a different opinion of the two organisers. It's not important.'

The music had stopped. Dennis bounded up to their table. 'Do you mind if I join you?'

Dennis fell into a chair still clutching his drumsticks, sweat running in rivulets and breathing heavily from the exertion. He laughed as he wiped his brow. 'I tell you man, beating those skins is hard work.' He paused to guzzle a beer Spencer handed to him. 'Thanks Spencer, you gotta know we're so grateful for your suggestions. This surf stuff is a real blast. Everyone just loves it. Did you hear the last number we did?'

Spencer smiled and nodded, pleased to see Dennis so happy with his newfound success. 'Isn't that a song you did before?'

'Spot on, we reworked it…at your suggestion I might add, it used to be called *Summer Safari*, we changed it to *Surfin Safari* and guess what?'

Spencer shook his head.

'We've been offered a record deal. We're recording that number next week. How about that? The only sticking point is the name of the band. They don't like Beach Buddies. They still want something that has something to do with the surf culture. They've thrown around a few ideas, like 'California Guys' but we didn't like that. And would you believe 'The Surfin Dudes' I mean really? Actually, the front runner for a name is your suggestion, 'The Beach Boys.'

Spencer clapped Dennis on the shoulder. 'I'm sure you'll get the name sorted out, anyway the band's sounding just great, your keyboard player's very good.'

'He's the creative one in the band, that's my brother Brian.'

'Dennis, I predict great things for your band. They sound like winners to me.'

Spencer leaned over, shaking Dennis's hand. 'Dennis, I think it's just great. I couldn't be happier for you and the boys. From here on I'm sure it's going to be fun, fun, fun.'

Dennis gazed quizzically at Spencer and slowly repeated the last three words. 'Fun fun fun. Do you know Spencer,' he said excitedly, 'I can hear a song in that. Yeah I can hear it now. I'm going to run that by the guys? Fun fun fun, we can do something with that.'

CHAPTER FORTY-ONE
# THE SUN SETS

Spencer reclined, relaxed and happy, being in the company of Priscilla, Savannah and Inez. He had that comfortable feeling of being with old friends or family. Even though Priscilla and Inez were relatively new acquaintances, he felt as if he'd known them for years.

Tucked away in the dark recesses of his mind, scratching and clawing to be heard was an insistent voice reminding him. *You won't be here forever. Don't get too comfortable. And remember you don't really belong.*

With a jolt he recollected his previous sojourns to the past, the friendships he'd made, only to have them obliterated in an instant when he awoke to find himself back in his century, back with his beautiful wife Michiyo. And now his baby daughter Trilby.

His pleasant afternoon was slowly evaporating as his reality sank home. *You're a stranger in a strange land. You can only play the cards you've been dealt. These people are transient in your life.*

His head was spinning. He was an outsider, looking in, an observer. It occurred to Spencer this may be what an LSD trip might feel like. On the one hand a disconnect, on the other, new truths being revealed.

In that moment he knew, he knew absolutely, he wasn't meant to stay. Laid out before him in full technicolour was the truth, his truth. Earlier he'd reflected with sadness the passing of his old comrades: Trilby, Irwin, perhaps Roxanne. He remembered the mesmerising Lee Kuan Yew and so many more. The realisation hit him a jolt, an electric current that doesn't kill but rewires the brain. He threw back his head, laughing out loud. Savannah peered nervously at him. Inez clutched Savannah's arm, murmuring something.

Spencer was smiling, giving him the appearance of someone deranged.

He now realised none of these people were gone forever. He was Spencer Marlowe. The forces that sent him here could at their will send him forwards, backwards, in and out of time. There was no such thing as death. There was always going to be a future. Still smiling, he waved at Savannah, who nervously waved back. Spencer realised he loved Savannah, absolutely, like the sister he'd never had. *I reckon I'll be back. I hope we meet again.*

Spencer rocked back and forth on his ancient wooden club chair; his eyes momentarily focussed on the whorled timber decking of the Santa Monica pier. *These timbers are as old as time, they've probably been around since before I was born and will be here after I've gone.*

These mundane ramblings in his mind only exacerbated his unease. *As old as time? How old is that? How old am I? Do I have a beginning? Is there an end?*

He turned his gaze once again to these delightful people; Dennis had engaged Priscilla in a conversation about hot rods and was explaining to her about high lift cams, extractors and four-barrel carburettors. To Spencer's surprise Priscilla was holding her own in the conversation.

'Yeah, Dennis, my wheels are a 60 Chevy, with the 348 cubic inch motor.'

'Wow baby, I'm impressed. I'll just bet it's a rocket.'

Spencer leaned back in his chair noticing the vivid hues around him. The sea was glistening and shiny, hurting his eyes, a man walked by wearing a Hawaiian shirt. *Oh my God, loud colours, there should be a law against it.*

The rosy glow that had enveloped Spencer just a short time ago had evaporated. All of a sudden, he was desperately lonely, he missed his wife, he wanted to pick up his baby daughter again, he wanted to hear her happy gurgling as he tickled her, making her laugh. *I want my century; I want my life back.*

He clambered to his feet feeling old and tired, he felt in his pocket for the comforting outline of the cornicello, for a brief moment a vision of Bert Weadley's face flashed before him.

'I want you to have this Spencer, It's a good luck charm.'

The memory of Bert, his only friend when he was incarcerated in the brig in the Northam camp the first time he had been thrust into another century, not knowing whether he was going to be shot as a spy, momentarily brought a smile to his face.

'Hey gang, I'm going for a stroll along the pier. I won't be long.'

Savannah turned to Inez. 'Spencer looks odd. I'm going to see if he's ok. Hey Cisco, do you want some company? You don't look great; I have to say?'

'I'll be alright. I think I've had a little too much sun, but I'm glad to hear I've won the title back again.'

'It's only temporary. I've got a few things planned and I'll be Cisco again, just wait and see.'

'Does this involve shooting someone?'

'I think you're ok. Go for your walk.'

Spencer wasn't ok. He wondered off down the pier, past the Playland Arcade, past the Hot Dog on a Stick stall. He paused for a moment to marvel at the Loof Hippodrome with its famous merry go round, the music tinkling like a cascade of happiness, intermingling with the joyful sounds of children's laughter. Hearing these happy sounds only increased his melancholy. All the time the bright hues around him were pummelling his senses his feeling of unease grew.

Spencer strolled to the end of the pier; some workmen were replacing some decking.

He braced himself against a railing, his hands gripping it as if to save himself from falling off the end of the world, there was movement. *Is the pier moving? Is it an earthquake? California's renowned for quakes.*

He shut his eyes, a welcome relief from the swirling colours, leaning against the old section of rail, his grip now like the clamp of a steel vice.

Then he heard a voice, a rough voice, angry, brusque. 'Hey Mac, step back from the rail, it aint safe.'

A lady screamed. The rail snapped, its ancient timbers weakened by years of salt spray and a harsh summer sun. He was falling, falling…

# CHAPTER FORTY-TWO

# DEATH IS THE FAIREST THING IN THE WORLD

Loma Vista Drive was an exclusive address; if you lived there, you'd made it. This wasn't a street for your average garden variety millionaire. This was a street for the super-rich, the real powers behind the metaphorical throne. Many of the residents of Loma Vista Drive could pick up the phone and speak directly to the Governor of California. Some could even speak to the President of the United States.

The old, shabbily dressed crone looked singularly out of place. She hobbled with the aid of an ivory handled walking stick; her body stooped. Tufts of hair poking from her unfashionable cloche hat were lank, grey. Holding a hand to her chest for a moment, she paused. The long walk up the steep gradient had taken a toll on her aged limbs. Her coat was dull grey wool. The torn cotton stockings were black, as were her scuffed oxford shoes. She carried a large bag fashioned from carpet. Adjusting her pince-nez, she peered myopically at the sign before her, proudly spelt out in polished carved timber on the high stone wall, 16 Loma Vista Drive.

She leaned momentarily against the pillar, catching her breath, she observed the quiet watchful façade. Then, making her way up the long drive, she paused again, this time to admire the statue. A scantily clad girl, cast in bronze, poised dramatically in a diving position above a fountain, water gushing from her mouth.

The gardens at the front of the mansion were a work of art in themselves, with so many colourful blooms. Californian poppies and bearded irises, their sweet scent wafting across the old lady's nostrils. A magnificent oak tree with weathered boughs and well anchored roots sat in brooding splendour, a fixture long before the Spanish had rampaged through the America's. There were eucalypts, introduced to California from Australia in the gold rush of 1848.

The lady hesitated before ringing the bell on the tall layered solid wooden doors that would easily have repelled any villains and thieves. They were testimony to the work of skilled artisans, long dead.

She could hear the sound of the doorbell resonating in the hallway. The door opened, a man, unsmiling, his height and build would certainly discourage devotees wanting to spread the good word from the book of Mormon.

He gazed disparagingly at the old lady, clearly not the usual type of visitor. With ill-disguised contempt, he barked. 'Yes?'

'Milo,' the old crone cackled, 'I have something for you.'

Milo frowned.

'Let me see…now where is it? Yes, here it is.'

Milo gasped in horror, he stumbled back, to slam the door.

*Phut, phut,* two rounds from a silenced 0.22 tore through his chest and his neck. Savannah had aimed for his head but Milo had enough time to jerk it back. Either bullet would have killed him instantly. The chest shot had blasted its way into his heart, before burying itself in the adjoining wall, the neck shot…well that was entirely superfluous, as Milo was already dead.

The now very spritely old lady leapt over the body, then bending over to grab him by the shoulders. She grasped the late Milo, pulling him clear so she could shut the door, while muttering to herself. 'God damnit, you're one heavy son of a bitch, Milo.'

She kicked the door shut, gazing around, emitting a low whistle of appreciation of a mansion that was both tasteful and opulent. *You may be a piece of shit, Zachariah, but you sure have good taste.*

Perched on a marble plinth was a priceless bronze bust of the founder of the Roman Republic Lucius Junius Brutus. Savannah had no idea who this worthy gentleman was, but she guessed it was a very valuable piece.

She paused to get her bearings, then heading off at a brisk walk along the lush carpeted passageway, where she hoped to find Zachariah Colchester. A voice rang out. 'Who the fuck was that at the door, Milo?'

Savannah smiled. *Perfect.* She followed the sound until she came to the door of the study. A light from a desk lamp threw its welcoming beam onto the bottle green carpet.

Savannah sauntered into the important man's office. He stared coldly at the old lady. Her dress was coarse, cheap and frumpy, but her smiling features radiated youth and vengeance.

He wasn't alarmed. Annoyed. Confused, certainly. His man Milo was very good at making sure unwelcome visitors never got past the threshold.

'Who the fuck are you?' he demanded. 'Hey wait a minute, you're that fucking FBI bitch I had checked out. You got a warrant you ugly cow? Eh, eh…no I thought not.'

'Milo, you dumb son of a bitch, come here. Throw this stupid slut out and be fucking quick about it.' His voice rose to a crescendo. 'For fuck's sake Milo, fucking answer me, you dumb Greek bastard!'

Savannah smiled at the sight of this powerful man yelling impotently for a response that would never come. Savannah was happy. All was right in her world. 'Milo won't be able to help you, Zach.' She purred in a voice as sweet and seductive as a $200 whore.

Zachariah screamed again, this time a scream edged with fear. 'Milo get here this instant. You dumb fuck.'

'Zach dear…you don't seem to get it…Milo's deceased.' The smile on Savannah's face chilled him to the bone.

Savannah had the long barrelled 0.22 behind her back. She pointed the weapon at Zachariah. The bulbous silencer added to the air of menace. She would have sworn that Colchester's lustrous head of salt a pepper hair suddenly had more salt and less pepper.

For the first and last time in his life Zachariah Colchester knew real fear. Gut wrenching fear, turning his vitals to jelly. 'What do you want?' he croaked, his eyes open wide, transfixed by the sight of the long barrelled Hi-Power with its evil looking suppressor, aimed unwaveringly at his chest.

Trying to smile, to muster the bonhomie he'd used so successfully to seduce women and politicians. 'Listen lady…I get it…I know a shakedown when I see it. 'He raised his hands in a "I give up, you got me' gesture." 'What's this going to cost me?'

'Zachariah Colchester, you have lived too long.'

# CHAPTER FORTY-THREE

# CHARLIE AND THE AVENGING ANGEL

The Bitter End was a folk club in the Chesterfield Square neighbourhood of Los Angeles. This was a less than salubrious area but for Charlie it was a gig, a paying gig of sorts, if you can call tips and free cappuccino payment.

It was a quiet night at the Bitter End but the charismatic Charlie with the piercing eyes had a coterie of young woman at his feet applauding every song.

The Bitter End was like a lot of folk music venues in the 60's. An old house in a low rent district. Lots of dim lighting, to hide the worn floor coverings. Candles jammed into old wicker wrapped chianti bottles. Cheap comfort food. Hamburgers, French fries and pizza. The walls featured posters advertising past and future music events. The Kingston Trio and Miles Davis were going to play the Lighthouse Cafe. Dion and the Belmont's had been at the Troubadour. It was if by having banners up advertising popular acts the Bitter End was part of show business big time, when in fact it was a seedy club in a rough area. struggling to attract paying customers and quality performers.

This was rough, tough LA. Drug addled hookers plied their trade on the mean streets, their ruthless masters, generally gun wielding hard eyed black men, never far away. They drove

Cadillac pimp mobiles. Jive talking, street wise hustlers, selling everything from stolen car radios to cartons of baked beans, anything that made a dollar could be bought and sold.

Charlie felt comfortable here in Chesterfield Square, these were his people, sharp eyed and vicious, the switchblade and the Saturday night special were as common as Saks Fifth Avenue outfits on Rodeo drive.

The motto of the denizens of Chesterfield Square was, "Never give a sucker an even break."

Charlie sat perched on a stool with his Gibson Jumbo six string, plugged into a Fender Twin Reverb Amplifier. He was singing through the house P.A, mostly self-penned songs about prisons, road gangs, unrequited love. Songs about pain and suffering seemed to always have an audience.

Charlie's life mirrored the songs he performed. In and out of jail most of his life he'd found a direction, he was destined for the big time, he'd offered his self-penned songs to the up-and-coming group, the Beach Buddies. He hoped they'd record one of them.

The Bitter End started life as a California Bungalow. It'd been many things, but it remained basically a bungalow with the inside gutted, creating space. The kitchen had been tacked on. The short order cooks clearly visible, smoking cigarettes, throwing down Budweisers, churning out greasy cholesterol-laden offerings to the not too discerning customers. The toilet facility, dirty stained and foul smelling, was a hastily erected clapboard structure in the back yard, shared by women and men.

Charlie noticed an attractive woman, slightly older than the nymphets gathered adoringly at his feet. The lady was a Mary

Travers look alike. Mary of Peter Paul and Mary fame had made fashionable the long straight blonde hair this mysterious lady also wore. Charlie had tried to smile at the lady hoping for some acknowledgement, so far there had been no response. This didn't particularly bother Charlie as he liked them young, very young.

'One more number girls, then I gotta go to the john.'

He finished the set off with Johnny Cash's Folsom Prison Blues.

'I hear the train a-comin.'

The bored barman stoically washed glasses pouring the occasional beer, nothing very exciting ever happened at the Bitter End.

*These folky types don't get drunk, they buy one God damn cappuccino and sit on it all night.*

The barman too, had noticed the Mary Travers clone.

*Not a bad looker, I'll just bet she's one of those university types. Probably here for a bit of rough before she heads back to Beverley Hills or Bel Air. If you said boo to the snotty nosed bitch she'd run for cover.*

'Ok girls, when you gotta go you gotta go. Back in ten.'

Charlie carefully placed his Gibson on its stand, winking at one of the young girls who giggled and nudged her equally young companion.

Charlie made his way to the rear of the Bitter End strolling through what had in its glory days been a well-kept yard, where children once played with families gathering for barbeques. He passed a couple embracing passionately in the shadows, he didn't notice the Mary Travers lookalike quietly padding behind him, her long blonde hair glinting in the moonlight. Charlie's thoughts were on the young girl he'd winked at.

At first glance, Charlie was an unprepossessing sight. Short with long black hair and beard, clad in denim jeans and shirt. Cuban heeled cowboy boots gave him a bit of height.

It was the eyes. Black as coal and hypnotic. Girls, young girls would fall under his spell, then find themselves subjected to violent sex. Some would be repulsed and scurry back to the safety of family, but there were others who seemed to tolerate being treated like an object. They would then do anything to glean the odd word of praise or perhaps even affection, to these girls Charlie was a drug, a dangerous addictive drug that'd drag them down to a life of decadence and evil.

The stench of the toilets assailed his nostrils before he entered.

At least in prison the John was always clean.

He jerked open the rough wooden panelled door, smiling at the sign emblazoned in bold letters: "Gentlemen your aim is cleanliness." He thought as he had before, *I don't think your God damn aim was too good.*

His hand groped for the light switch, 'Mother fucker light doesn't work.' He trod cautiously up to the once white vitreous china urinal, blocked as usual, with cigarette buts floating in the waste. He undid his fly. He felt, or sensed somebody behind him, 'beat it pal. I don't like company in the John. I ain't no faggot.'

'Did you enjoy the girls, Charlie?' A soft sweet feminine voice whispered.

Before he could turn, the piano wire that now encircled his neck bit through skin muscle and his carotid artery.

There was a brief effort to clutch at the vicious garrotte, but death was too quick.

The lady felt for a pulse knowing full well that there wasn't one, carefully unwrapping the wire embedded deeply in Charlie's neck, then pressing the winder on her watch, hearing the faint ratchet sound as the wire slithered back into the timepiece.

In the half-light she could see Charlie's face half immersed in the stale urine, sloshing in and out of his open mouth. His sightless eyes not noticing the sodden cigarette butts swirling, eddying over him. The lady smiled in satisfaction.

With a spring in her step, gathering her bulky handbag, she gazed cautiously around. The light had drained away, there was barely enough, even for shadows. The amorous couple still embraced. A cat yowled. In the distance a siren wailed. Soundlessly opening the side gate, she strode in the direction of the bus station, pausing only to remove the blonde wig, discarding it into one of the many bins scattered haphazardly along the darkened street. She glanced back at the blue neon sign on top of the old house, "The Bitter End." She smiled again.

# CHAPTER FORTY-FOUR
## HOMECOMING

'Spencer, wake up, you've been asleep for an hour. It's 7:04 in the evening.'

Spencer gazed at his beautiful wife, he felt tears starting to well up, 'You've no idea how good it is to see you.'

Michiyo frowned. She gently stroked his face, and asked, 'Have you been away?'

He nodded. 'Yes. But I'm back now.'

'Well Spencer chan, I know just how to celebrate your return.' She gazed seductively at him a twinkle in her eye. 'And…after…we can watch television. The hotel has cable TV. Baby Trilby's asleep. The new Sharon Tate movie 'The Avenging Angel' is on tonight. I just hope I look as good as her when I'm her age; she must be at least seventy.'

Spencer stared at Michiyo, momentarily uncomprehending; he threw back his head and laughed, 'Oh Cisco.'

THE END

# AUTHOR'S NOTE

Dear readers,

I do hope you have enjoyed *LA Confrontation*. The fourth in the Spencer Marlowe series.

I would be delighted to see some more reviews on Amazon and Goodreads as they would ensure more in The Spencer Marlowe and now Savannah Steele stories.

And yes, Savannah reappears in the next instalment *The Chicago Story,*

Read on for a sneak peek at Spencer and Savannah wreaking havoc on the bad guys.

# THE CHICAGO STORY

## CHAPTER ONE
## WELCOME TO YOUR NIGHTMARE

First it was the meld of odours; the sanitary tang of antiseptic, the slaughterhouse stench of blood and vomit, the incongruous scent of get-well carnations. Then slowly a dark veil began to lift. Through lidded eyes he saw a starched angel in white, a crisp cap perched primly on her head. The angel chatted, not to him. He noticed her elongated vowels. 'Would you like a carfee, arrfercer?' *Where in hell am I?* The veil dropped, the voices grew fainter, like he was being sucked into a tunnel. Then again, darkness.

The man jerked. An alarm beeped. An intercom crackled. Running feet thudded on linoleum floors. Somewhere in the background came the muffled sound of a TV. He turned his head. Dozing in a chair by his bed sprawled a police officer, his navy pea jacket slung casually over the back of the steel-framed hospital chair. On the cop's shirt sleeve, he saw an octagonal Chicago police logo.

*I'm in Chicago?* He tried to speak; his mouth was dry.

'Water, please, may I have some water?' He noticed a jug resting on a cabinet by his bed. He reached for it. His hand pulled up short, shackled to the steel rung of the bed. The cop folded his arms across his chest.

'So, sleeping beauty awakes. About fucking time. You want water, eh? When I fucking say so.'

'Where am I? What's happened?'

'I wasn't born yesterday. Save it for the judge. Shut up. When I'm good and ready you can have a drink.'

*Who am I? What have I done?*

The door swung open; a woman burst into the room. From her dark grey worsted suit to her thick black stockings, sensible court shoes and large unfashionable black leather bag, she looked corporate; an accountant? *Maybe she's a lawyer?* She held a hand to her mouth.

*Someone I know? A friend?*

'My God Spencer, what have they done to you?'

The lady's voice opened the floodgates. The man's body screamed as a jarring flash of lightening split his brain. His whole body felt like it'd been hit by a train.

'Who the fuck are you? Get out!' The cop sprung to his feet; his teeth bared as he gripped his holstered 0.38 revolver.

The lady was authoritative, brusque, imposing. She held up a badge, thrusting it like a clenched fist within an inch of the cop's nose. The cop flinched. He looked like a veteran, maybe early forties; the beginning of a paunch, red hair, Irish heritage the man thought. *This's a cop used to dealing with low life and crims.* He looked solid, dependable, nobody's fool, but he visibly quailed at the sight of this commanding female. He caught a glimpse of a shoulder holster. Her revolver was large, its worn, scarred walnut grip sending a clear message.

In a voice barely a whisper, the lady speared a finger at the cop. 'You listen to me, flatfoot. Undo those God damn handcuffs. You better believe I mean now. Right now!'

The cop whined, 'Lady I got orders. I can't just undo the cuffs. Be reasonable.'

'It's not "Lady". It's Special Agent Steele of the FBI. Listen up you sonofabitch, and listen carefully. Undo those cuffs now or I'll have you walking the beat on the Southside for the rest of your miserable career. Now do it.'

'Yes Ma'am.' The cop fumbled; he dropped the keys. 'Sorry Ma'am'. He hastily scooped them up, and in a practiced motion, unlocked the cuffs.

CHAPTER TWO

# SAVANNAH THE UNSTOPPABLE

'Do you mind?'

'Huh?'

The cop stared at Special Agent Savannah Steele.

'Do you mind?' she repeated.

The cop blushed.

'Sorry Ma'am.' He sprung to his feet, indicating the empty chair.

Savannah Steele sat down as if she were the Queen of England and the throne had just been vacated.

'Oh my God, what a day.' She smiled at the cop. 'My feet are killing me. Now, officer…?'

'Officer Doolan, Ma'am.'

'Officer Doolan, would you be so kind as to go to the canteen and fetch two cups of coffee? Black. Mine has two sugars and Mister Marlowe's does not.'

The cop hesitated. In his world women don't tell him what to do.

Savannah Steele's gaze was unblinking.

'Yes Ma'am. One with two and one without.'

THE END

If you enjoyed *LA Confrontation* a kind word on Amazon or Goodreads would not only be appreciated but would guarantee more Spencer and Savannah adventures.

# KELVIN WHITE AUTHOR

I'm a West Australian author, having been born in Perth and living in WA for most of my life.

As with so many authors, my background is awash with varied careers: taxi driver, musician, roof tiler, shoe salesman and a plethora of others.

Given I have always been an avid reader, it was inevitable I would eventually put pen to paper. My first publication was the time travel adventure, "The Singapore Saga", featuring central character Spencer Marlowe. I was delighted when positive reviews appeared on Amazon and Goodreads. I was hooked. The first *Spencer* novel was followed by the next instalment, *The Hawaiian Intervention*, and then *The Manhattan Sting*, introducing Special Agent Savannah Steele. And now, *LA Confrontation*, once again featuring Savannah Steele.

Amidst churning out the *Spencer* series, I have also published with co-author Allan Butler, our rock and roll memoir, "Oh How We Rocked". This memoir, complete with photos of the bands and musicians we worked with, is a fun look at the music scene in Perth in the 1960s '70s and '80s.

Having enjoyed writing the musical memoir, my next project was the crime novel, *Birthright*, written in collaboration with acclaimed Western Australian author Dr Bruce L Russell. Working with Bruce added a whole new dimension to my writing experience. Bruce and I are about to release our next crime novel, *The King of San Francisco*, set largely in the United States in the 1970's and published by Vivid Press.

I have found the collaborative writing experience very rewarding and an extraordinary learning platform. As a consequence, I entered into another collaboration, *Undercover Heat*, with American author Tali A. Sandbridge. Tali is the author of the *Love Throughout the Centuries* series. Her debut story, *The Ghost and Mrs. Smyth*, features characters Jake Webber and Angie Smyth and their discovery that they were lovers in past time periods, setting the stage for a series which I found to be quite enthralling. This story was followed by book two, *The Great War*, book three, *Peachtree Plantation*, and book four, *Mackenzie's Hope*.

The collaboration with Tali Sandbridge was a lot of fun, as the writing process inter-wove the differing Australian and American dialogues, attitudes and cultural perspectives. "The Russia Brief" is a crime story moving between New York, Perth, Sydney and Bali. It's gritty, fast-moving and sexy, and is available on Amazon in kindle and paperback.

The next Spencer Marlowe story, *The Chicago Affair*, will be published late 2024.

www.ingramcontent.com/pod-product-compliance
Lightning Source LLC
Chambersburg PA
CBHW030805210726
48290CB00002B/439